The Poorest Creature

The Sailing Master, Book Five

A Chronicle of the First Opium War

Rocket Science Press
SHIPWRECKT BOOKS PUBLISHING COMPANY
Winona, Minnesota

Other Books by Lee Henschel Jr.

Book One - Coming of Age, Rocket Science Press, 2014
Book Two - The Long Passage
Book Three - Letter of Marque
Book Four - Gods of Clay
Book Five - The Poorest Creature

The Beggar's Coin - Short Stories of Vietnam & the Epic Poem, *the 'Nam*
Short Stories of Vietnam

Also available:

To read more of the life and times of Sailing Master Owen Harriet go to:

https://www.amazon.com/stores/Lee-Henschel-Jr.ingPortalEnabled=trueAmazon

You can read excerpts from all five books in the Sailing Master series and purchase paperback and ebook versions.

The Sailing Master, Book Five

The Poorest Creature

A Chronicle of the First Opium War

Lee Henschel Jr.

Cover and interior design by Shipwreckt Books
Cover painting by Denise Brown
daydreamsbydb.com

Shipwreckt Books Publishing Company
357 W. Wabasha Street
Winona, Minnesota 55987

Library of Congress Control Number: 2026934085

ISBN: 979-8-9898405-9-5

for Johny

Contents

1. Tomorrow?

My orders arrive by currier.

London, 2nd May, 1839

Mister Harriet,

> You are herewith requested and required to report 8 May to the Isle of Dogs, 9 Ferry Street, at four bells in the middle watch. Sir James Wynyard, Rear Admiral of the Blue (retired)

… to participate in a sin against humanity; not stated as such, but the sin is implied. I sign the order just as my granddaughter, Sami, calls to me.

"Grampa! Come see the goldfish!"

I join her at the little pond in back of our home, in Portsmouth. Soon her mum joins us.

"Wash up! Time for dinner."

When Sami runs off, Rachael asks. "Orders?"

"After a fashion. Bound to have come by now. Been on my pension for six months."

"When do you leave?"

"Tomorrow."

After dinner, my son, Albert, sits with me in the front room.

"Your kit's all packed then?"

"Leaving on the morning coach."

"Something to do with the opium trade?"

"Very likely."

Albert finds the latest edition of The Galway Vindicator and reads aloud. "'We believe they will soon be engaged in a war unjust in its origin, a war more calculated in its progress to cover England with permanent disgrace.'" Albert puts down the paper and looks at me. "Permanent disgrace, father. Do you disagree?"

"I do not. But consider the very tea we're drinking, along with the porcelain pot it's served in, and that silk dress you bought Rachael for her last birthday. Are they not all products from

China? To be sure, the Crown would prefer to come by all of it through reciprocal trade, same as the agreements we have with other countries. Tuns of ale for puncheons of wine, bolts of wool for bales of cotton, and the like. But not so with the Chinese. They don't want or need our trade goods in exchange for theirs. They want our silver. And over the last two hundred years they've accumulated approximately sixteen million ounces in specie. Not to put too fine a point on it, Albert, we're running out of silver. And it's only in the last few years that we've begun to redress the imbalance. And when the Chinese banned opium late last century it only made it more expensive."

"Well, maybe you can ask to be assigned to The Nautical Almanac. Its editor owes you a favour, I think. So perhaps it's time to call it in. I forget. What's his name?"

"Horace Ludlow. And the favour he owes is because I've never asked for one."

"Then why not ask for a posting here in Portsmouth? England's at peace with her enemies. And you've said yourself that the duties of a sailing master will eventually be taken over by lieutenants. And steamships will join the fleet soon. Even less duties for a sailing master. Perhaps now's the time. I mean, for you stand down."

"I could stand down, but not yet. Besides, steamships or not, The Nautical Almanac's library of charts is kept up to date by sailing masters, not lieutenants. And as for England being at peace. Yes, for the time being. But it would appear the Daoguang Emperor is most displeased with England for reversing the flow of silver."

Rachael steps in. "By using opium transported from India to addict the Chinese, then demanding payment in silver to feed their habit. Forgive me for asking, but what would Becca have said about that?"

"That it's a crime. Though in the end she'd agree that I have no choice but to serve, even if it means escorting East Indiamen convoys laden with chests of opium bound for China. But since my good wife is dead five years, your point is moot."

Later that evening, I listen at my granddaughter's bedroom door while her mum tucks her in.

"But, mummy, I don't want Grampa to go away."

"I know, luv. No one wants him to go."

"And he doesn't wish it."

"Oh? Did he tell you that?"

"No. I just hear it. Can you hear it, mummy?"

"No, my curious child, I cannot. But I guess you're right. Grampa doesn't want to go. Except he must."

"Why?"

"Because he's in the Royal Navy and must do as they say."

"But I love Grampa."

"Yes. We all of us love him."

A brief silence before Sami asks. "When will he be back?"

A deep sigh from Rachael. "Soon. I hope soon."

"Tomorrow?"

2. The Lesser Portion

That night I lie awake thinking about what Sami said. For it's true, I don't wish to go. But how would she know that? On this last home leave I've enjoyed her active imagination more than ever before. But as of late, I suspect there's more at play than a child's creative power. More like a thing first visited upon me when I wasn't much older than her. Some small voice whispering in my ear, meant only for me to hear. But as I came of age that voice grew quiet, until receding into the depth of memory. Has this remnant of the past now returned to dwell in my granddaughter's subconscious mind?

Many years ago, when I first spoke to my sister Peg of this whispered voice, she believed it was Morgan y Dylwythen Deg. The Welch name for Fata Morgana, who could have once lived in a realm shared with our great grandmother, Sara Cedric, for Sara was Welsh to the marrow in her bones. But I dare not speak of Morgan y Dylwythen Deg to Sami's mum and dad, and I will never utter the name out loud. Such is so, because I've come to cherish my family more fully than I ever thought possible, and don't wish to put them at odds by awakening an old haunt. Albert's my only child, and a fine son. A steadfast and respected wheelwright in Portsmouth. He's not yet fully repaid the hundred pounds I lent him to set up his own shop, but he's honourable, and a sharp trader, same as his mother, and I know he's good for it. And I must admit I didn't like Rachael overmuch when she and Albert were courting. She's a firebrand who's never shy to speak her mind. But I've come to learn that much of what she says smacks of the truth, even if at times hard to digest. Unlike her cooking, which is always most toothsome. She reminds me of Peg, a woman who also speaks her mind. If Racheal and my sister were ever to align in some common cause, it would behoove Albert and me to stay far to windward. Besides, Rachael gave birth to Sami, the living image of my beloved wife, Becca, and the unending joy of Albert's life.

The truth is, I don't want to report for duty not just because I'll miss my family, but because the odds are in favour of me participating in the opium war. A war that, as Albert quoted from the Vindicator, "will cover England with permanent disgrace." Enough. It's nearly first light. I must seek the last vestige of sleep.

*

The London coach from Portsmouth always stops overnight in Guildford, and arrives at Waterloo Station the next day, midafternoon. From there I hire a hack to convey me to Dolan's, a humble inn where I first stayed with my mentor, Sailing Master Ignatius Comet Lau, many years before, and on occasion have used ever since. Not far from Dogs Island. Mrs. Dolan's long dead; may God rest her kind, if somewhat penurious soul, but the establishment has kept her name, just the same. I arrange for an evening meal and one night's lodging and inform the concierge that I'll be leaving early in the morning, so will "pay before," as Mrs. Dolan would have put it. It's only then do I notice the small satchel tucked away in my kit. Ten pieces of horehound candy, along with a note from Sami, scrawled in her endearing hand.

> Grampa I will mis you it is good candy
> Sami

After a mutton stew that evening,, I walk to Dogs Island for a glimps down Ferry Street. A narrow lane steeped in the squalor of an untold number of benighted souls. The address I have is for Dove's, which is no more than a run-down pub. I don't know why I've been ordered to report here, but when I return later tonight, I shall bring my brace of pistols, for this dark alley is not half seedy.

I walk back to Dolan's and rest until the lamplighter calls out. One of the morning. I rise and quietly depart for Ferry Street. At this hour I stand alone in the lane, with only a furtive cat appraising me before moving on. I approach the inn. Locked. I tap on the door, just as a voice calls from the gloom.

"Mr. Harriet."

I rest a hand on the butt of my best pistol. "Stand clear and say your name."

A man steps from the shadows. "My name is k." He points at Dove's. "Come. Let's go in and have a chat."

"It's locked."

"I have a key."

The place reeks of stale sweat and ale. A dim cave to be sure, though looking somewhat better in the dark than before k lights a taper. We sit at a small table that rocks unsteady on the uneven floorboards. I look close in the faint light to make out k's features. Most plain, with nothing to mark him from the next man.

"Why have I been ordered to report here?"

k pulls out a sealed envelope and sets it before me. "Open it."

One slip of parchment folded over. I draw the taper near and read.

> Harriet,
> k is my agent under orders to recruit you on a mission of utmost importance.
> Semyon

Semyon. The very name serves as far better confirmation than any stamp sealed in wax.

"Do you remember him?" k asks.

"A name from the past. He died on the Mekong. Thirty-seven years, four months, and nine days ago."

"So quick with numbers, Mr. Harriet." k gives me a hard look. "However, Semyon didn't die."

"Nonsense. Théophile Oignon confessed to killing him, then burying him in a grave marked with nothing but a crucifix made from a twig."

"The Onion? Who would believe anything that man might say?"

"No one. But Semyon was dying from gangrene when he ordered me to leave him behind. I regretted it, but I was very young and knew no way other than to do as ordered."

"But he survived his ordeal."

"How do you know?"

"Because he's my grandfather, and I've served him ever since he returned from the Indochine. His left leg was amputated just below the knee. Cut off by his own hand while still on the Mekong."

"God Almighty!"

"And now my grandfather wishes me to enlist you in a mission."

"Why didn't he ask himself?"

"Actually, he did. Semyon's true name is Admiral James Francis Wynyard, Rear Admiral of the Blue, retired."

"Then tell the Admiral he should find another man."

"But you're already another man. Your name was not at the top of the list, Mr. Harriet, but your comportment, along with your experience as a sailing master, has nevertheless placed you high. Besides, time's running short. His plan's been set in motion."

"A plan that now involves me."

k nods. "A plan that began in 1820, when the East India Company began enlisting the merchant fleet to transport even more opium to China. The increase in trade buried the Chinese in addiction."

"I still fail to see how this involves me."

"Because who would think a mere sailing master would be involved in what's to come? Besides, my grandfather says you're a resolute chap."

"He knew me in 1803. How does he know I'm still the same man?"

"He doesn't. But after he submitted your name, I observed you for a time."

"I didn't notice."

"Of course not. One of my talents is to go unseen. How a man behaves when he thinks he's unobserved is a fair measure of his worth." k shifts in his chair. "Last month you were here in London to clarify something for The Nautical Almanac. After your appointment, you stopped at a bakery and bought a baguette. Do you recall what happened next?"

"No."

"Then I'll remind you. You happened to walk past a beggar sitting in the gutter. When he saw that you had a loaf of bread, he reached out a filthy hand and made a piteous sound."

"Oh, now I recall."

"And without hesitation you broke the baguette in two and gave that starving wretch his next meal. Many would do the same. Common goodwill and all that. But here's the thing. You gave away the larger share and kept the lesser portion for yourself. A rare act of kindness, Harriet, and a quality the Admiral seeks for this mission. As it turns out, it was the final proof I needed to recommend you. Although after following you for a week I found you a dreadful bore. A fellow who goes unnoticed." k leans into the pool of light, grinning. "And to go unnoticed is just what the Admiral wants for this undertaking." He wrinkles his nose. "This place is odoriferous. We should leave."

"Not until you tell me where we're going, and for what I'm being considered."

"We're going to Greenwich. After that, you will no longer be my responsibility. Come, I've hired a boat."

"Why didn't we just meet at Greenwich at a civilized hour, rather than some wretched pub in the middle of the night?"

"Discretion, sir. On the grounds of the Royal Observatory all comings and goings are noted, even those of a sailing master. Be assured someone would ask why you were there. And the fewer questions, the better. However, you won't be there long. There's a frigate waiting for you at the quay."

*

In the zodiacal light of false dawn I recognize the silhouette of a Lively Class frigate moored alongside the Royal Observatory landing. How could I not recognize it? For this ship has been my home at sea for near forty years. Every long passage. The tedium of untold days. A churning sea of humanity. All of it rising now in a sigh of recollection as we pass beneath her dolphin striker and hook on at the entry port.

k observes my reaction. "Knew you'd recognize her. Even in the dark."

"Thought I'd never see her again. Six months ago The Gazette reported her as paid off and waiting to be struck from the books."

"False information, Harriet, published to deceive foreign agents who would keep count of Her Majesty's ships. Actually, for the last six months *Eleanor*'s been in dry dock at Falmouth undergoing a refit."

We make our way below decks to stand before the great cabin, where a marine sentry comes to attention and is about to slam the butt of his rifle on the deck to announce us, just as a lieutenant, tricked out smart, opens the cabin door and steps out.

The man looks me up and down. "You must be the Sailing Master. I'm Lieutenant Ramsey. First Officer."

"Yes, sir. I'm here to report."

"Captain de Clery's busy. You'll have to wait."

k steps forward. "The Sailing Master is ordered to report with no delay."

Ramsey only shrugs, then walks off.

"No matter, k. Gives me time to conduct an inspection, beginning right here."

"I know as a sailing master one of your duties is to inspect provisions, but I assure you all victuals are already onboard. And your logs and charts have been sent from The Nautical Almanac."

"What I wish to inspect has nothing to do with stores, or my logs and charts."

I stand beneath the carlins where, forty years ago, I slung my hammock as a cabin boy for my uncle, Captain James Cedric, the very first to command *Eleanor*. The carlins have been replaced many times over, but what I seek consists of nothing tangible, but rather a premonition, the feel of where I first heard the Sukiyama warning me of the ship's purser, Émile Coutts. Diminished, to be sure, but even now there remains a certain resonance as I rock and sway in the distant past.

"Are you quite done, Mr. Harriet?"

"Not quite. There's one more place I wish to visit. It's on the orlop. Stay here."

On my way below, I glance sidelong down the gun deck and stop abrupt. Four long guns have been removed. Two to port, two to starboard, all of them amidship. In their place is a great store of dry goods. Gunny sacks of dried peas and beans, bins of onions and potatoes. Cases of salt pork and bully beef. Cartons of sea biscuit stacked to the beams, and crates of dried apricots, raisons and pears. I've not seen a frigate's rations in such great quantity. Or as many rockets, along with tripods to launch them. Five full racks, with each rack stenciled in black:

Congreve Signal Rocket
twelve pound
blue star cluster - white star cluster
24 count

Most curious, to carry that many rockets. Yet I move on to the orlop, where again all is not as usual, for there are several additional racks of water casks installed on the deck.

As six bells of the middle watch ring out, three in the morning, I stop at the exact spot where Coutts and Pogue once discussed the fate of poor Tate, an orphaned stowaway not yet seven years old, who was discovered only after *Eleanor* was at sea. I recall their voices overheard from my hidey-hole, hiding there because of another warning from the Sukiyama. A sure sign to stay clear of these two.

On that night, Coutts would ask. "What did you do with him?"

And Pogue's reply. "Stuffed him in a gunny sack and heaved him over."

"Good God, man! You drowned the boy?"

"He was already dead, 'cause you killed him."

"Not my fault. You know I have a temper. Didn't mean to kill him, just knock him about to make him do what I want. Lucky he was a stowaway. Not on the books. Never be missed."

I stand silent in my reverie while a whisper calls forth the name of a place few Englishmen have known. The Forbidden City. But I doubt this is some sort of premonition. But rather my own misgivings about what will be without doubt a subversive mission. For if this operation involves the opium trafficked out of Bengal, then certain it will involve the Forbidden City. I dismiss the foreboding as premature, if not false. But just then comes a tug at my sleeve. A ship's boy on an errand.

"Beg pardon, sir. The captain, he sent me to fetch you."

I pat the lad on his scrawny shoulder. "Thank you, sonny. What's your name?"

"Gravy Walters, sir," he replies, and then pipes honour bright. "I'm ten!"

"Very well. Lead the way, if you will."

*

Captain Quinten de Clery sits at his desk. A man composed of spare bones and wiry flesh, and looking most young to be in command of any warship. Yet there's a cast to his eye that bespeaks the gravity of his office.

"Sailing Master Owen Harriet reporting, sir."

de Clery points to a chair alongside his desk. "Sit. I'm about to dine. To save time I'll brief you while I eat. Join me, if you wish. Cold roast beef."

"My honour, sir."

"Now then, on this voyage you will assume the normal responsibilities of a sailing master, plus several supernumerary duties." His steward brings two trenchers of sliced beef, a pot of horseradish, a pitcher of ginger beer and two glasses, both of which de Clery fills to the brim.

"From Jamaica Station. Enjoy it." He takes a long draw, smacks his lips and sets down his glass. "A question, Mr. Harriet. Do you not ask why a frigate whose keel was laid forty years ago would still be in service? And I answer you this. First: despite her age, *Eleanor*'s still one of the fastest frigates in the fleet. And a fast ship's always better than a slow one. Second: The East India Company, at times it's referred to as John Company. In the near future we'll be joining what is, in fact, an East Indiaman convoy, although for diverse reasons every ship in this venture operates under private charter. The convoy's designation is Chittagong Thirty-seven and will be departing from Calcutta. *Eleanor* will join them to sail as an escort. Always remaining to windward of a certain vessel, mind you, listed on the manifest as *Durness*, out of Liverpool. An older frigate such as *Eleanor* is likely to go unremarked, and passing unnoticed will serve our needs very well. I will tell you now, Mr. Harriet, this is an independent action, known only to a chosen few at Whitehall." He nods at my empty glass. "Like it?"

"Yes, sir. Very much."

"Pity I can't offer you another glass. Must ration the stuff." He calls for the steward to clear away, then waits for the man to depart.

On deck, the Eleanors begin to muster. de Clery turns a critical ear, then continues.

"Now then, Chittagong Thirty-seven will be bound for Canton, and as such will pass by Purba Island. Do you know this island?"

"I do, sir. It's situated just beyond the Hooghly River delta, which is the gateway to Calcutta. Coordinates are twenty-one degrees, sixty-five minutes north, by eighty-eight degrees, seven minutes east."

"Your reputation for retrieving information with no need of a chart is well deserved. However, we do not intend to raise Purba. Your duties on this voyage will include sailing us undetected . . ." He raises a brow, "I repeat, undetected, all the way from Land's End, making down the west coast of Africa, rounding the Cape, and then halfway through the Indian Ocean before bearing north for Purba Island. That's where we heave to and lay unseen below the horizon, well off the coast of Purba. It's there we shall await Chittagong Thirty-seven's arrival." He rocks back. "One more thing. In about 1833 the East India Company lost exclusive control over the opium trade. It created an opportunity for more traders to glut the market, and that influx is what roused the Admiral to act. Observations?"

"Yes, sir. Concerning the voyage you describe … it will require a resupply at some point along the way. Yet you say we must proceed undetected. So now I understand the need to carry less guns. The space allows for more rations so we can remain at sea for a longer period of time."

"You understand correctly, Mr. Harriet. Anything more?"

"There's a seamount rising off Purba Island, sir. Allow me to provide the details."

From the quarterdeck, one bell rings out. Four-thirty in the morning. The morning watch begins, and de Clery's attention is drawn to his duties.

"It will have to wait."

"Yes, sir. But if I might ask, where is k?"

"He left. Said his duties were fulfilled once he saw you onboard. Do you know what he said when I asked him what the k stands for? He told me the k is silent. How clever."

The thunder of bare feet on deck as the bosun calls for the watch to man the halyards. de Clery steps to his cheval glass, adjusts his bicorn and shoots his cuffs. He finds me in his mirror. "We shall be getting underway soon. See to your duties."

*

Once in the Strait of Dover and standing well into the Channel, I'm again summoned to the great cabin, along with *Eleanor*'s four officers.

Captain de Clery begins. "Stand at ease, gentlemen. Long overdue for introductions. My First Lieutenant, Ewald Ramsey. Proceed, Lieutenant, if you will."

Ramsey steps forward. He's the officer who brushed me off when I first came onboard. A stout man of middle age. Close-cropped nap of blue-black hair and looking most natty in his best rig. He begins introductions.

"Lieutenant Galen Dovecote, Gunnery Officer."

A small, tidy man with a ruddy complexion and wearing thick spectacles. New dress uniform, if a bit too large. Brass buttons polished.

Ramsey goes on. "Lieutenant Thomas Andrews, Third Officer."

A portly fellow with wheat straw hair and watery blue eyes. Uniform pressed, but of marginal quality.

Ramsey continues. "Lieutenant Enoch Slotter, Forth Officer."

Slotter's too old to be a lieutenant. And his sullen eyes express the discontent of being long since passed over. Uniform faded and worn.

Dovecote and Andrews are likely to advance up the ladder of promotion. But not Slotter. His ambition's gone stale.

Ramsey ends with me. "Mr. Harriet, Sailing Master."

A good thing I've made the time to put on my best day rig. Black suede bicorn, blue frock coat, white breeches. Not unlike the uniform worn by a lieutenant.

de Clery takes over. "We embark with just four officers, gentlemen." He pauses, waiting for that deficient number to sink in. "A frigate normally has at least two more, so you'll be stretched thin. No doubt you've also observed we're below ship's complement. One hundred seventy-nine ratings, to be exact. Generally a ship will have rations for sixty days at sea. However, for our mission we have doubled that amount, including the water ration. All meant to extend our range for what will prove to be a very long voyage. I tell you this now, at the onset, for now is none too soon to begin conserving what we have." He pauses to look at each one of us in turn. "You have your time pieces with you."

To a man.

He turns to me. "The Sailing Master will now synchronize your chronometers to Greenwich Meantime. Proceed, Mr. Harriet."

Perfect timing, for the minute hand of my watch reads but one minute of ten. "On my mark the time will be exactly ten." I observe as the hand jumps. "Mark."

Just as the ship's bell rings four times in the forenoon watch, de Clery dismisses his junior officers, but motions for Ramsey and me to stay on.

"Mr. Harriet, I should like to know where you got that chronometer."

I retrieve the watch from my waistcoat. A gleaming timepiece glowing yellow gold, and the diameter of a sovereign.

"A gift from my mentor, sir. Sailing Master Ignatius Lau. But it was first presented to Mr. Lau by its maker, and good friend."

I read aloud the inscription on the back.

Ignatius Comet Lau
My Esteemed Colleague
Upon his Promotion to Sailing Master
Plymouth, 19th day of June 1774 - Anno Domini
Thomas Mudge

"Mudge? The horologist?"

"Yes, sir."

"One of England's finest watchmakers. How is it your mentor would give you this watch made by Thomas Mudge?"

"Mr. Lau and I were close, sir. He was getting on in age and had no one to bequeath it to. He didn't want it to end up in some pawnshop, so he gave it to me upon traversing the equator for my very first time, in 1798."

"I see."

Lieutenant Ramsey coughs, and de Clery nods for him to speak.

Ramsey stands broad afoot to meet *Eleanor*'s pitch and roll. "You're aware, Mister Harriet, that in the Royal Navy the duties of a sailing master will eventually be assumed by lieutenants."

"I'm mindful of that." But my reply is addressed not to Ramsey, but to de Clery. "Do you wish to put me ashore, Captain?"

The steward steps in. "Beg pardon, sir, but the purser's here to make his report."

"Show him in." de Clery tugs at his frock coat. "Now then, gentlemen, we shall take up this up at a later date. Dismissed."

But for Ramsey, it seems that later is now. "Rest assured, Mr. Harriet, that if you were to be put ashore, I'm quite capable of performing your duties, along with my own responsibilities as First Lieutenant. In the future there won't be much need for sail. Steam's my future, not yours."

"I'm sure you're right, Lieutenant. But as for now let's pool our knowledge of the current conditions at Purba Island."

A brief hesitation before Ramsey responds. "I would need to refer to the Almanac before making comment."

"You won't find any reference in the Almanac regarding a change in the colour of the sea off Purba, sir."

Ramsey stiffens. "Then how are you in possession of this information?"

"It's in the marginalia of most sailing masters' personal logs, sir. These are the shared notes, the apocrypha, you might say, that are rarely transcribed into the published Almanac. For several years now sailing masters have noted a change at Purba. It would appear there's a seamount slowly rising near the island's windward coast, and it's now to within thirty feet of the surface."

The shallow depth startles Ramsey. "*Eleanor* could run aground."

"Yes, sir."

"Is the captain aware of this?"

"I was about to tell him yesterday but his duties called him away."

"Then I'll inform him."

"Very good, sir. And when we approach those coordinates, I shall ask the captain to send a leadsman to sound the bottom just off Purba. Unless you want to assume the responsibility."

*

After passing Land's End, *Eleanor* begins to rise on the Atlantic swell. As eight bells of the forenoon watch ring out, I shoot the noon line and return to the chartroom, which also serves as my quarters. A cramped cabin. Its single lantern swings in a gimbal above the chart table, set atop a stack of drawers containing *Eleanor*'s navigational maps. It leaves just enough space for my berth. Spartan to be sure, with barely enough room for a man to turn on his heels, and confined even more when de Clery steps in.

"My apologies, Mr. Harriet, but I wish to have a word with you in private."

"Of course, sir."

I close the door.

"After we cleared Ushant, I had Lieutenant Andrews alter course to take us across the Bay of Biscay. We're now under full sail and I hope to remain that way for several weeks, or at least until we reach the fortieth parallel and run due east along the Roaring Forties. A course charted to remain out of sight of land, but not necessarily so with passing ships. That's why I'm speaking privately with you now." A tug at his waistcoat. "As of today every officer will be reminded at the onset of his watch to stay hull down of any ship, if possible, and to avoid all communication. If for any reason some vessel tries to close on us, I've instructed the signals midshipman to have the Yellow Jack ready to hoist."

"An extreme measure, sir, to fly a quarantine flag."

"Which brings me to Chittagong Thirty-seven. Or more to the point, a certain East Indiaman vessel sailing in that convoy."

"*Durness*?"

de Clery nods. "Every ship in Chittagong Thirty-seven will be transporting chests of raw opium to Canton. That is, all but for *Durness*. My orders are to safeguard her arrival at a specific godown. They are the warehouses used for transshipping goods bound for Peking. Such as what's in *Durness*'s hold, for it contains the very reason of this venture, and if the wrong individuals in London suspects what she carries, it would compromise the mission. Not even *Durness*'s captain is aware of what he's transporting. Its secrecy is paramount, and the Admiral does not wish for the Royal Navy's involvement to be known. At least not until Purba Island. So as for now he expects us to go unseen until our rendezvous with Chittagong Thirty-seven, at Purba."

"Are you aware of the situation at Purba, sir?"

"Lieutenant Ramsey informed me of a seamount rising to within thirty feet of the surface. He told you, as well?"

A simple question, but I don't wish to undermine Ramsey's authority by telling de Clery that it was me who informed the lieutenant of the seamount, not the other way around. I hesitate, thinking of how to reply, when a rogue wave catches *Eleanor* amidship, followed by a great many shouts and laments.

de Clery and I hasten from the chart room, and once on the companionway we see that the watch is already backing sails. A sure sign someone's gone overboard. By the time we gain the spar deck a dozen men are casting lifelines. And on the quarterdeck, Stoner, the bosun, has already swayed out the captain's gig.

de Clery's voice booms overloud above the din. "Name the man who's gone over!"

"It's Sauce Walters, sir."

I can't help but react. "Sauce? Do you mean Gravy, the ship's boy?"

"No, sir. Sauce Walters. He fell from a topsail yard when that wave took us. Gravy's his little brother."

"There!" Someone calls out. "Hundred yards dead astern. Bloody hell. He's going under."

de Clery points to four men. "You. You. You and you. Man the oars." And to Stoner. "Man the tiller. Go you now."

The gig makes for where Sauce was last seen. Gravy darts from the waist and climbs onto the taffrail to search for his brother.

"I see him! It's me Saucy. Look there! I see him!"

He points to his brother coming to the surface and gasping for air, but soon he goes under again.

Gravy screams. "No! He mustn't become drowned. Not me Saucy!"

The oarsmen ship oars and Stoner throws a line. But no one grabs on. Sauce fails to resurface for one long minute. And then one more.

"May God rest him," someone moans.

Gravy's about to jump in after his brother, and I barely manage to grab his shirt and yank him from the taffrail. He fights me off and runs back, but a man holds him back and won't let go until I catch up.

"Give him to me. I'll take him below."

But take him where? A ship's boy has but a small hammock and a slim space between guns where he's permitted to sleep. But I won't leave Gravy alone. The boy's near blind with agony after watching his brother go under. Crying frantic now, panting for air and thrashing out. I pick him up, but he stiffens and tries to break free.

"Leave me be! He's me Saucy. He promised not never to die." He pounds on my chest. "I hate you!"

I let him flail away until I hear a tiny voice calling from within, and I speak low to Gravy.

"Tate. This time I'll take care of you."

Gravy stops fighting and stares at me, eyes wide, blinking and remote. I say no more but carry him to the chart room and lay him in my berth. Jesus Madrid follows after me and stands at the door holding a small measure of brandy. He gives it to Gravy and watches him drink it down, then leaves.

I sit with Gravy as the brandy takes effect, hearing the davits creak as they sway the captain's gig back onboard, the sails booming as they refill. We're getting underway, leaving Sauce

Walters behind. I open my journal, mark the date, the time, and our position:

23 May 1839
17:41 hours
50°N x 6°W
Lost at sea - Sauce Walters, Able Seaman

And in the marginalia:

Left behind, his young brother,
Gravy Walters, ship's boy
Who will care for him, if not me?

3. A Desperate Measure

One day south of the equator. One week since Sauce Walters went overboard.

At seven bells in the morning watch, nine o-clock, the bosun paces among his men, all on their knees to holystone the quarterdeck.

"Of a will, me beauties!" Stoner barks, "or you'll not be done 'til the horse latitudes!"

Midshipman Peter Zenith stands his watch at the binnacle but moves to the spar deck to stay out of their way. A good opportunity for me to engage the young man.

"Mr. Zenith, as junior midshipman you're in charge of the ship's boys."

"Yes, Mr. Harriet." His trepidation sounding more like a cautious question than a reply.

Zenith's skinny as a heron, with a bobbing Adam's apple and wearing an overlarge uniform flapping in the stiff breeze. He stands at strict attention; in mortal fear he's done something to cause my displeasure.

"As you were, Zenith. I only wish to know if you're seeing to their education."

Zenith stands more at ease. "A challenge, sir. They've all come aboard without numbers or letters."

"Not surprising. But are you making headway?"

"Well sir, it's like this. Back in Wrexham my father tutors the squire's children. He says you can lead a horse to water, but you can't make him read a book."

"A bit of horse sense in that."

"Yes, sir. Though father's sure never to say as much to the squire. But even so, sometimes he succeeds. My father has a way."

"I should like to hear it."

By now the men have worked their way to the spar deck, and we move forward to give them room.

"I'd be pleased to tell you, sir, because I've a mind to try it with the ship's boys. To teach them their letters first you must help them form their thoughts. Start with simple questions. What did you eat today? Where's the wind? Get them thinking about what they're bound to know. If you can engage their young minds, sir, it prepares them to start learning the alphabet, don't you see?"

"I do. Go on, if you will."

"Yes, sir. Then after a while you go on to spelling out actual words. Teach them how to write their names. It's a great thing, sir, when a lad learns how to write his own name. It inspires them." Zenith hesitates and then asks. "May I ask you something, sir?"

"Yes."

"Last Sunday, the Captain's bible reading was very good. It's just that . . ."

"Yes?"

"It's just that it lacked inspiration."

"And?"

"And I'm wondering, sir, if I'm to see to their education, does that mean I should also see to their religious education?"

"Do you aspire to be a cleric, Mr. Zenith?"

"Oh no, sir. I aspire to succeed in the Royal Navy. It's just that my father teaches Sunday school in Wrexam, and sometimes he'd let me teach a lesson. He says leaning your letters by reading the bible is the time-honoured way to learn how to read. And discussing chapter and verse keeps the idle mind busy, if only for one day in the week. It could help *Eleanor*'s ship's, boys, too. Besides, there's little else to read onboard *Eleanor*."

The bosun comes up to us. "Beg pardon, gentlemen." We move forward to the bow chaser.

"The lads might do well by your father's method. Did you know that Admiral Lord Nelson began his career as a ship's boy?"

"I do, sir. Sir Francis Drake, as well. I wish to be promoted someday, Mr. Harriet. But who'll follow in my place once I advance? Perhaps a young lad who started out as a ship's boy. Maybe even one of *Eleanor*'s. But whoever it is, he must be able to read and write."

"There's adequate time remaining on this voyage, Zenith. We only just crossed the equator last night."

"I know, sir. It was the first crossing for all four of us midshipmen. So to mark the occasion we had Cookie roast the capon we went together and bought for our mess."

"I have something for the ship's boys to mark the occasion, as well. Three of them. Right?"

"Yes, sir."

I reach in my pocket to bring out the satchel of horehound Sami gave me. "Take this. It's horehound candy. Dole out one piece each as a reward for their first time across the equator."

"I will, sir."

"Mind you, each one gets a piece. I was a ship's boy once, with nothing but a hammock and one plank of deck to my name, so I know how much a piece of horehound will mean to them."

*

Twenty miles due south of the Cape of Good Hope. Eight bells in the forenoon watch.

"Mr. Oliver, as senior midshipman, I call upon you to report the noon line."

Lark Oliver steps away from the quarterdeck rail. "Our current position is thirty-one degrees south, by eighteen degrees east, Mr. Harriet."

"You're accurate with your longitude, Mr. Oliver. However, the latitude you cite would place us in the middle of False Bay."

The young man pales. "There must be something wrong with my sextant."

"Give it to me." I examine the instrument. "There's nothing wrong with this sextant. Let me see your derivations." I go over them. "As I suspected, you've made a mistake. Next time, double check your figures. However, let us make use of your error by considering just where your calculations would have put us."

I turn to the next midshipman, Gaylord Abbot. "To begin, Mr. Abbot, why is it called False Bay?"

Abbot frowns in thought, then concedes. "I don't know, Mr. Harriet."

"It's named False Bay because it could give false hope to any ship bearing west and looking to round the Cape of Good Hope with the intention of proceeding up the Atlantic coast of Africa. False Bay's a sizable body of water, and under certain conditions might be mistaken for the ocean. The entrance of the bay is thirty miles wide, and at its widest point it's forty miles across, east to west, and fifty miles from north to south. For centuries, and even to this day, its eastern headland, Cape Hangklip can be mistaken for Cape Point, which is to the west."

Of a sudden *Eleanor*'s sails begin to luff. I look to the sky and study the low broken clouds racing easterly. I call to the duty officer. "Lieutenant Dovecote. I believe we've just entered the Roaring Forties. Please send word to the Captain that I recommend reducing sail."

I turn to another midshipman, Nigel Moon. "Now then, Mr. Moon, do you see why entering False Bay could present a problem?"

"I do, sir. My uncle was in the Royal Navy, sir. He said once his captain mistook Hangklip for Cape Point and they went sailing into False Bay quick as you please. Took weeks to get out."

"Your uncle was fortunate. The list of shipwrecks in False Bay is long. So let us be thankful for Mr. Oliver's miscalculations, for we are a good twenty miles south of False Bay, and about to enter the Indian Ocean."

The thunder of bare feet running on deck, the squeal of block and tackle, the creak and groan of *Eleanor*'s main yard, all of it bringing the lesson to a close as the midshipmen scurry to their stations.

*

One-hundred miles east of Cape Hope. Well into the Indian Ocean. *Eleanor* plunges on through a big sea. Captain de Clery, First Lieutenant Ramsey and I stand at the binnacle taking measure of the changing conditions.

"Mr. Harriet, how would you judge the wind?"

"At least thirty knots, sir, steady from the west."

The Captain turns to Ramsey. "Latest chip log?"

"Making fourteen knots, sir. Recorded at the start of the first dog watch."

de Clery nods. "Tell Lieutenant Andrews to reduce sail. Mizzen top gallant and reefed forestay sail only."

The carpenter comes to report. "One foot of water in the hold, sir."

"Very well." He calls to Gravy. "Fetch the bosun."

Gravy's off and running but returns over quick with terror in his eye.

"I seen it!"

"Saw what?" I ask.

"Fire!"

Ramsey shakes the boy. "Where? Say where!"

"On the orlop. Near them rockets."

The Captain wastes no time. "The Congreves! Ramsey, you have the helm. Harriet, come with me."

When we reach the orlop Lieutenant Slotter's already fighting the flames threatening the Congreves. But when he comes too near the flames his stockings catch fire. I douse him with a bucket of seawater and try to pull him away. But he fights on, just as the flames are about to set fire to the first bank of rockets. Another bucket of sea water, and then several more as men rush to extinguish the blaze. But another fire breaks out, edging its way toward the powder magazine. de Clery takes his coat and smothers the licking flames.

Slotter falls to the deck and the men gather around. The loblolly, Jesus Madrid, pushes his way through. "Stand clear. Give me room." He takes but one look. "Someone bring a hammock and take this man to the officers' mess."

As they bear him away everyone sags, relieved that the fire's just about out. Some mutter his name.

"It's Slotter wot saved us."

"Aye."

But de Clery cuts them short. "Stoner, take a detail to the hold and pump out the bilge. Harriet, stay on the orlop and make sure the fire doesn't reignite. Leave everything as it is. This fire didn't start on its own and I intend to find the cause. For now, I'll be with Madrid."

*

Midshipman Zenith stands with me to keep watch. As the smoke clears, I notice Gravy Walters sitting on the deck, head down, most dispirited.

"You did good, Gravy."

He looks up. "I wasn't afraid, sir."

"Of course you weren't. Tell me, did you see what started it?"

"It was ..." he looks away.

"Say it out, lad. It's your duty to report what you see."

He summons his courage. "It was a man who started it. He made a pile."

"A pile of what?"

"I don't know. Except the men, they use it when they stuff the seams."

"Oakum?"

Gravy nods. "He made a small pile next to the rockets. And then he lit it. On fire!"

"What did he use?"

"Flint and fire steel. And then put them back away. In his pocket."

"Did you recognize him?"

"No, sir. His back was at me."

"What was he wearing?"

"Clothes."

"What sort of clothes. Day slops?"

"No."

"Then what?"

"A coat. Breeches."

"An officer?"

"I don't know. It was dark. And then I ran to report it. But I wasn't afraid, sir."

"Of course you weren't."

I turn to Zenith. "Stay here, Zenith. You're in charge. Keep checking for hot spots. I'm going to tell the Captain what Gravy just said to me."

For his surgery, Madrid's made use of deck space on the officers' mess, just outside his own quarters. He's already stripped Slotter to the waist and cut away his hose and breeches. His long stringy hair is singed, eyebrows scorched bare. Great blisters swelling on both hands and rising vicious on his legs from ankle to knee. He lies on his back trying to bear the pain as Madrid peels away the seared skin. Lieutenant Ramsey stands with de Clery, both watching as Madrid works.

I join them. "A word with you, sir. The ship's boy, Gravy Walters, just told me he saw someone light that fire."

"Did he say who?"

"I asked him, but he said the man's back was turned to him."

"Then it could have been anyone," Ramsey observes.

"Maybe so," I reply. "But I think we can narrow it down. Has anyone checked to see what's in Lieutenant Slotter's pockets? Gravy said that whoever did it used flint and steel to set a pile of oakum on fire, then put them back in his pocket."

Ramsey interrupts. "Are you suggesting they might be found in one of Lieutenant Slotter's pockets?"

"I don't know, sir."

Madrid finds us. "The lieutenant's been badly smoked. I've coated his burns and dosed him with laudanum."

"How long before he's fit for duty?" de Clery asks.

"At least a week, sir."

"Very well. But for now I have business with Lieutenant Slotter that can't wait."

"But he's incoherent, sir."

"Can't be helped. I ask that you stand clear until we're finished. Mr. Harriet, it was you who asked what's in Lieutenant Slotter's pockets. So proceed."

The Captain and First Lieutenant observe as I extract the contents of Slotter's frock and waistcoat. Pocket watch. Plug tobacco. A pay chit. But no flint and steel. That leaves only his breeches to examine, which lie in a heap on the deck. I reach down. In a side pocket I feel a flint and stand aside. Ramsey steps in and removes a flint and fire striker, then gives me a dark look.

"Do you gloat, sir? Do you relish putting this officer in an unfavourable light? A man, I might add, who at this moment is incapable of speaking for himself."

"No, Lieutenant, I take no joy in it."

"Nor is it proof," Ramsey contends. "Anyone onboard has the means to start a fire."

When Slotter begins to groan, we look his way just as he opens his eyes. Blinking and unfocused, and with his brain likely addled and unable to comprehend his surroundings.

de Clery says his name. "Lieutenant Slotter, you're under the care of Mr. Madrid. You will survive your injuries."

Slotter blinks. His face transforms into the rictus of a grin as he utters his given name. "Enoch did well." Then, once more, he succumbs to the laudanum.

Madrid returns and asks us to leave.

*

When the men muster for the next watch, Captain de Clery addresses them.

"The fire on the orlop was intentional. Started with flint and steel. At the next grog ration I want everyone who's in possession of flint and steel to present it to Mr. Harriet. Be prepared to provide at least two witnesses to vouch for where you were when the fire started. Go you now and see to your duties."

At the next grog ration there's one midshipman, the carpenter's mate, Cookie, and four ratings who bring me their flint and steel, along with the name of the mates who can speak for them. However, the last man in line brings nothing.

"Name?"

"Cheeky Dravitts, sir. Able Seaman."

"I see no flint and steel, Dravitts, so why are you here?"

"I have both, sir, but when I looked for them, they was gone. I didn't light no fire, though. And me mess mates, they can say where I was at when it started."

I show him the flint and steel found in Lieutenant Slotter's pocket. "Are these yours?"

"Aye. Can I have 'em back?"

"Later. As for now, I'll see that the purser allots you an extra ration of grog."

"Oie! Thankee, sir!"

That evening I stand in the great cabin along with Ramsey, making my report to de Clery.

"All the men have accounted for their whereabouts. But one of them, Cheeky Dravitts, claims his flint and steel were missing. When I showed him the objects in question, he admitted they were his."

Ramsey has his doubts. "How do you know every man onboard has reported his flint and steel?"

de Clery speaks up. "Point well taken, Ramsey. But whether or not they were all reported, how is it that Dravitts's flint and steel ended up in Lieutenant Slotter's possession? Tell me, Ramsey, what do you know about Slotter?"

"Very little, sir. His last ship was *Port Erin*, a twenty-gun sloop on station in the North Channel. Served without distinction. Keeps to himself when not on duty. Lieutenant Dovecote has the berth next to him, and I've seen them in conversation. Perhaps he can tell us more about Slotter. Shall I send for him?"

Dovecote comes double quick, adjusting his glasses and attempting to button his coat, all while attempting to stand at attention.

"You sent for me, sir?"

Ramsey begins. "I want you to tell us what you know about Lieutenant Slotter."

"Oh yes, sir. Of course." Dovecote ponders, but not overlong. "Well, sir, he inspects the guns, sir. And discharges his duties well enough."

"We're more interested in the man's background."

"Oh. Right you are, sir."

"Now then, you're likely the only one onboard who's had dealings with Slotter. What does he talk about?"

"He doesn't talk much, sir. Mostly he's preoccupied with his name. Or his namesake, I should say. Enoch. Oh, and I might add that the Lieutenant's in the habit of referring to his own self by that name."

"How do you mean?"

"'Enoch will stand his watch. Enoch will be watchful.' That sort of thing."

"Unusual. But is it important, Lieutenant?"

"I don't know, sir. Except he claims that in the bible Enoch lived to be three hundred and sixty-five years old. And for some reason that's why the Lieutenant believes he's old enough to deserve better. His tone of voice always sounds resentful, sir. Blaming his lack of promotion on others. Or I should say, he resents others for having a patron to help them advance their careers, whereas he's never had anyone speak for him. Says he should have been promoted after his last ship, but the captain of Port Erin wouldn't put forth his name. Slotter says it's time for him to see to his own promotion. Should do something to stand out."

"Such as?"

"When I ask him that, sir, he goes quiet."

"We know where Lieutenant Slotter was during the fire. But do you know his whereabouts just prior to that?"

"No, sir."

A long pause. All goes quiet but for the hawser straining at the tiller, one deck below, and the muted cries of the top men calling from the rigging, one hundred feet above.

"That's all, Lieutenant. You're dismissed."

Late that evening I sit writing in my quarters when Madrid pays me a call.

"A word with you, Mr. Harriet?"

I set down my quill and strew a bit of fine sand across my last entry.

"Yes?"

"It's Lieutenant Slotter, sir. He's improving, but he needs better rest. There's too much activity in the officers' mess. I hope to move him to my quarters. Madrid hesitates, then goes on. "There's something more, sir. That's why I've come to see you. It's the men. They're divided about Lieutenant Slotter. Some say he saved the ship. Others say he's the one who started the fire. Below decks the talk's starting to turn ugly."

"You think the man's in danger?"

"I don't know sir. But to be safe, will you come with me when I ask Captain de Clery if I can move Slotter to my quarters? I can keep better watch on him there."

*

The next day the men stand in line for their noon ration of grog. Cheeky Dravitts's best mate, John Apple, comes around, hoping to trade sips in return for some small favour.

"Cheeky, for a sip I'll stand the last hour of your watch."

"No, mate. But if you stand the last two …"

"Agreed. But then a gulp, not a sip."

"Done. But only if you mend Jode Hector's Sunday shirt for 'im. He don't sew none too good, so he trades me sips to patch it some. You patch Hector's shirt, and I still take his sips."

de Clery, Ramsey and I stand on the quarterdeck listening to the give and take. Ramsey's amused.

"Good Christ, they need a barrister to keep it all straight."

But de Clery seems to have something more on his mind. "Ramsey, as my First Officer it's your duty to carry out my orders without question. However, it's incumbent upon me to hear your opinion. What's to be done with Lieutenant Slotter?"

Ramsey replies forthwith. "I think there's not enough evidence to charge him with arson, sir. If that's what you have in mind."

"And you, Mr. Harriet? You've experienced the apocalypse of a fire onboard."

"In the Mekong delta, sir. June of 1804. Captain Harrogate turned *Jupiter* into a fire ship."

"Then I value your thoughts. Proceed."

"Yes, sir. As of yet no one's been accused of starting that fire, and the men fear whoever lit it will start another one. And because of the extra rations stowed on the gun deck the men know we're on an extended voyage. That only adds to their unrest, sir. They'll grumble below decks until the man's caught."

"Do you think Slotter lit that fire?"

"I don't know, sir. But I do think you should question him further, and he should be kept under observation."

"Then we shall proceed to Madrid's quarters. Harriet, make note of Slotter's reactions while the First Officer and I sound him out." de Clery turns to Ramsey. "I want you to put him at ease. No intimidation, mind you, just name the facts and let his answers unfold as they may. When I think it's time, I'll step in. If possible, I intend to discover the truth directly from him."

Ramsey clears his throat. "What do you believe the truth is, sir?"

"I withhold judgement. But if Lieutenant Slotter can prove to me that he didn't light that fire, then the investigation will continue."

"And if he can't prove his innocence to your satisfaction?"

"Then once we rejoin the fleet a hearing must be convened. It will be up to the Admiralty Board to make a finding."

"There's always the chance he'll confess, sir. But not likely. Arson's a hanging offense."

"So it is. But if Slotter admits to the crime I'll recommend he be shot, rather than hanged."

*

In Madrid's quarters, Lieutenant Slotter sits upright in his berth when de Clery, Ramsey and I come to debrief him.

Ramsey begins. "Madrid says you're recovering, Lieutenant."

"Yes, sir."

"You were fighting the fire alone. Commendable."

"Enoch thanks you, sir."

A shared look between de Clery and Ramsey.

"Now then," Ramsey goes on, "how is it you happened to be there?"

"Enoch was on the gun deck inspecting the starboard battery, sir, and smelled smoke coming from the orlop."

"Who was with you on the gun deck?"

"Enoch was alone."

"Did you call for help?"

"Enoch called, but he didn't think anyone could hear him. He had to make a choice. Run for help and let the fire spread or fight it on his own. It was threatening the Congreve rockets, sir, so Enoch stayed to fight and hoped for the best outcome."

"Yes, of course. One must always hope for the best."

Ramsey looks at de Clery, and the Captain gives him a slight nod.

"Now then, it's been reported that a man wearing a coat and breeches was seen lighting that fire. Did you see anyone?"

Slotter's face drains of colour. "No one. Enoch saw no one."

"By now I'm sure you've heard how the fire started."

"No, sir."

"Flint and steel. They were used to ignite a pile of oakum."

"Enoch didn't know."

de Clery takes over. "Two days ago while you were incoherent, we examined the uniform you were wearing when you fought the fire. We found flint and steel in the pocket of your breeches."

Slotter shifts in his berth. "Is Enoch under investigation, sir?"

"The entire incident remains under investigation."

"But it was Enoch who risked his life trying to put out that fire. Now you accuse him of lighting it?"

Eleanor shudders as she tops a swell and races down the backside. The lantern casts oversized shadows that circle the cabin in a macabre dance. The moment has arrived for de Clery to accuse Slotter. But before he can, there comes the muted hail from a lookout.

"Deck there! Sail on the horizon! North by east."

de Clery motions for Ramsey and me to come with him onto the quarterdeck. By the time we arrive, Lieutenant Andrews has already sent Mr. Zenith aloft with a scope to keep an eye on the approaching vessel.

"Still hull down, sir. Two masted brig flying the Union Jack. On the same heading as us. Closing a bit."

Once more Zenith calls out. "Signal hoist from that vessel. Three-eight-two-nine."

The signal midshipman, Mr. Oliver, thumbs through his book trying to decode the hoist.

de Clery stands nearby, tapping his foot. "Come, Mr. Oliver. I don't have all day."

"Ah, here it is, sir. the-blue-camel … the-blue-camel-has … yellow . . . lips."

Oliver's absurd decipher amuses even the Captain, who hides his grin by turning to me. "Mr. Harriet, be so kind as to assist the midshipman."

"Of course. The hoist asks what ship we are. And states they have mail."

de Clery watches as the brig continues to close. "Very well. But there will be no mail for us, at least not on this day. Mister Oliver, hoist the yellow jack."

The brig sheers away instanter. The Eleanors all know what the yellow jack stands for, and they know the Captain's flying it false to keep all ships at bay. Still, the men don't like overmuch missing a chance for mail, and mutter as they go about their duties.

"Could 'a been news from home. Or letters."

"In a pig's ear, mate. When you ever get a letter?"

"Not never. But that ship … maybe it finally brung one from me wife. Or me dolly."

"Or both! Ja-Ja!"

No letters for anyone. No newspapers for the officers to share. Just two ships passing wide on the open sea. Soon falling below the horizon. Soon forgotten.

*

The watch changes. And changes many times over before the Captain once again questions Slotter. In the middle of the night, de Clery summons Ramsey and me to the great cabin.

"Gentlemen. It's been a week since that fire, and as of yet I've charged no one. However, there's no man other than Slotter who hasn't been accounted for. Time to press him. Come."

Ramsey and I accompany de Clery to the officers' mess. Madrid sits outside his quarters, reading a book by the light of a taper. Ramsey asks if Slotter's awake.

"I think so, sir. He doesn't sleep much."

"What's his condition?"

"The man is melancholic by nature."

"What's that mean?"

"It means he's in a perpetual state of anguish and doubt." Madrid taps the book in his lap. "Like this fellow, Hamlet."

"Belay that, Madrid. Just tell me if Slotter's regaining his strength."

"He is, sir. But slowly."

"Good enough. The Captain wishes to continue his interview."

Madrid leads us in. Slotter lies awake, looking at us through the dim light.

"Light a lantern," de Clery tells Madrid, "then leave us."

When Madrid departs, de Clery addresses Slotter. "Sit up, Lieutenant. The loblolly says you're in recovery."

Slotter answers reluctant. "If he says so, sir."

de Clery begins to pace, hands held at his back. When Slotter asks if Enoch's still under investigation, de Clery stops in mid-stride.

"Enough of your charade, Lieutenant Slotter. You will no longer refer to yourself as Enoch. And I ask without prevarication. Is it not true that you started that fire?"

Slotter stares into the middle distance. "I submit, sir …"

de Clery cuts him short and restates the question. "Is it not true that you started that fire?"

"I did what I thought best."

"Or did you only do what you thought best for you?"

"I did what needed to be done , sir."

"And in your mind what needed to be done was curry the favour of a promotion board. To have them reward you for your brave efforts to save this ship. But instead, you risked burning us all alive. Including yourself."

"I understood the danger, dared fight that fire on my own."

"Or at least fight the fire until it was discovered. Discovered along with you fighting it single-handedly, of course."

"It was a chance I was willing to take. I put my life at risk to put out that fire."

"A desperate measure. You believed this was your best chance, didn't you? You've been a junior lieutenant for seven years. Been passed over too many times. Time to take matters into your own hands." de Clery stoops to face Slotter eye to eye. "I ask you directly, Lieutenant Slotter. Did you light that fire? Before you answer, know you this. The penalty for arson is death by hanging. But if you confess to the crime I'll call for a summary judgement rather than a prolonged courts martial. And in that hearing I'll advocate for you to stand before a firing squad, rather than be hanged. Neither is the right way to die, but a firing squad is quicker, and less painful. Sometimes the hangman makes a mistake, and there you dangle."

Slotter buries his face in his hands, both still dressed in gauze. "I meant to do well."

"I will ask you just once more, Lieutenant. Did you light that fire?"

Slotter says nothing.

"I take your silence as an admission of guilt."

Slotter nods.

"Say it aloud, man."

"Yes, I did it. For Enoch's sake."

A restive air pervades the cabin, until de Clery breaks the spell.

"Ramsey."

"Sir."

"Strike Lieutenant Slotter's name from the watch bill. Confine him to quarters. Post a sentry at the door."

4. The English Play Chess While The Chinese Play Go

Eleanor continues her easterly plunge along the fortieth parallel. It's been a week since Slotter admitted his guilt. As a result, senior midshipman, Lark Oliver, has been promoted to Acting Lieutenant, with all duties and privileges commensurate with its rank. As Sailing Master, it's my responsibility to introduce the fledgling lieutenant to the study of ocean currents. Therefore, just after the noon line, I send Gravy Walters to fetch Oliver to my quarters.

"You wished to see me, Mr. Harriet?"

"Yes, sir."

"Sir?"

"Of course. You're an officer now, Lieutenant Oliver. You must expect and demand to be addressed as sir. I see you've brought a sheaf of foolscap and a pencil. Lay them out. You're about to have an introduction to ocean thermals."

I lean down to open a cabinet and withdraw a rectangular rosewood case, three feet by one. The interior is padded with green velvet to conform to the contours of the glass instrument that lies within.

Oliver gasps. "It's very splendid, sir. What is it?"

"A Galilean Thermoscope. A watertight glass cylinder filled with an aqueous solution, with a brass hook at the top." I remove it from its case, and with great care suspend it by its hook from a beam so that it swings free in *Eleanor*'s motion. "It measures thirty inches long, and about nine inches in circumference. Note the horizontal gradients along the length of the cylinder, with each mark assigned a number. And look here, inside the cylinder are five bulbs floating in the solution, all at different levels."

"They look like small onions."

"No. Each bulb is made of glass and filled with coloured water. Two red, two blue, and a purple one that serves as a reference.

From each bulb there hangs a brass ring, and from each ring depends a tiny weight."

"This is an instrument?"

"Yes. It's used to determine the temperature of the ocean at any given depth."

I pause for Oliver to catch up with his notes.

Soon he looks up. "Like the water in a lake? Warmer on the surface. Cooler at the bottom."

"Correct. Oceans are much the same. That's important to know because the difference in water temperature is what creates a current. Such as the Great Indian Gyer which we will be entering in about a week. And with the aid of this Galilean Thermoscope, you and I will determine just when there's a change in temperature."

Oliver scribbles away, then dots his pencil to a stop.

"Then what?"

"We're making about one hundred miles in a day. At this rate we'll reach ninety degrees of east longitude in about a week. At that point I'll ask Captain de Clery to haul our wind, but only for about ten minutes. And in those ten minutes you and I will set out in the cutter to measure and record the temperature of the water at three different depths. Ten feet, twenty, and thirty."

I watch him as his eyes glaze over in a fugue.

"Do you understand?" I ask.

"I'm not quite sure, sir."

"Just try to absorb what you can, Lieutenant. We'll go through this several more times. Now then, to go on, the glass bulbs are all sensitive to water temperature. After we note where each bulb floats on the gradient, that's when we submerge the thermoscope. After a few soundings, we'll check to see if the blue bulbs begin to rise, and the red ones begin to fall, all while the purple one remains constant. Taken altogether, those differences will indicate a current. And at this longitude it can only be the Indian Gyre. That's when I suggest to Captain de Clery that we alter course and bear north by east, better to make use of the counterclockwise flow of the gyre's current. It will take *Eleanor* farther east than Purba Island, but in the end, it will deliver us there much sooner."

He exhales in a deep sigh. "It's complicated, sir."

"Agreed. Finding a current is tedious work. But methodical. Not like what takes place on the quarterdeck."

"Sir?"

"The sea, Lieutenant. The only thing that never changes for the sea is its indifference. So you must learn to expect the unexpected. When things are going as planned, that's when you need to consider what might happen if . . ."

"If what, sir?"

"Best left to your imagination, Oliver. Just keep working the problem at all times."

"Yes, sir."

"Enough. Review your notes. After noon line tomorrow we'll go over this again."

*

At first light on the next Sunday morning, I stand on the maintop watching the spindrift scud across a slate grey sea when Jesus Madrid comes through the lubber hole. We both hold firm on the windward shrouds to brace against the buffeting wind.

"Mr. Harriet, I hoped I might find you here."

"You'll find me here at least once a day to smell what's on the wind. And today, after forty-seven days at sea, I smell the faint must of verdant land. We're still far from any coast, but close enough to know it's there."

Madrid sniffs the air. "You've a keen nose, sir. I smell nothing but the ocean."

"There's a small island out there. Île Amsterdam. Thirty-seven degrees South, by seventy-seven degrees East. The place is too far removed to be of any importance, although seal hunters use it for a seasonal camp. And last year a British barque, *Lady Munroe*, ran aground there. Only twenty-one survived, rescued after two weeks by an American schooner. I'm pleased to have caught a whiff of the island this morning. It helps confirm that we'll soon be approaching the Indian Gyre."

We watch a lone petrel hovering over *Eleanor*'s wake, in search of its next meal. No such luck. The bird soon dips a wing and carries off on the wind.

"Mr. Harriet? Some of the men think we're bound for Georgetown. But we're on our way to Canton."

His gaze holds me unflinching and bespeaks a man who knows the truth.

"Mind what you say, loblolly."

"Captain de Clery says it's time for me to tell you what I know."

"Which is?"

Though we stand far above the deck, and with no top man nearby, Madrid still takes care to speak low.

"Semyon. Sir James Wynyard, Rear Admiral of the Blue, retired."

When I say nothing, he goes on.

"His agent recruited me to partake in this mission. Same as you."

"k?"

"k's real name is Anthony Wells. We were roommates at Magdalen College. That's where I met his grandfather, Sir James Wynyard. The Admiral asked me once about my plans. I told him I wanted to become a doctor, but family problems forced me to quit my studies."

"So you ended up as a loblolly."

"For now. But Sir James took a liking to me. He offered to become my patron if I went on this voyage to serve as loblolly. Then, when I returned, he'd help pay my tuition."

"A generous offer. But mind you, we're bound for Canton and in the past Admiral Wynyard was known for his sub rosa activities. We could be mistaken for opium traders and held for ransom. though neither of us would bring much. If it comes to it, best try to escape."

"Where?"

"The Paracel Islands. Approximately sixteen degrees north, and one hundred eleven degrees east. It's been charted as a small archipelago. But hard to reach because at that longitude on the South China Sea there's no prevailing winds."

"Are they populated?"

"No There's no fresh water, little vegetation and none of the islands have more than five feet of elevation. Vulnerable to tidal waves. But despite the risk, some fishing fleets call there on occasion. So there's a fish camp on one of the islands, Money Island, in case they have to lay over. Always a ration of food and water stashed away. Left there by the last fleet to call."

"In the Jucar Basin of Spain we always leave a jug of water at the well for the next traveler to prime it."

"Same principle seems to apply on Money Island, so it could be a good place to run and hide. But I don't think that will be necessary because *Durness* won't be carrying any opium. Her hold will be filled with chandler goods."

A slight pause before Madrid gets to the point of his visit. "Along with one hundred chests of something else, but not the Wodenstoke Porcelain listed on the bill of lading."

"Porcelain?"

"Yes. The Emperor likes Wodenstoke and has lifted the trade restriction. The Admiral's made use of the easement, and in each chest there's a top layer of Wodenstoke, a gift ostensibly from Robert Jordain, but actually used to cover up contraband. Vedic soma."

"What do you know about soma?"

"Well, it's a paradox. But very real." Madrid sees my puzzled expression and goes on to explain. "I first read about it when I was at Magdalen and realized that soma and tea share a quality. They both act as a sedative when you're anxious, but when your lethargic, they act as a stimulant."

On deck the noon grog is rationed out, and the men begin their Sunday make-and-mend. Billy Hawke pipes a lively jig on his ocarina and *Eleanor*'s best dancer, Noah Jackwell, does a hornpipe. Madrid taps his foot as we watch from the maintop and goes on.

"But beyond the paradox, it's through the process of elimination that botanists believe soma's origins trace back to a plant known as Nelumbo nucifera. It's commonly referred to as the Indian sacred lotus. No one actually knows for sure, though. That's because some claim that five thousand years ago the Vedic hymns promised that soma was a sacred gift from the gods. I wouldn't know. But what I do know is that its fibrous stems are cut and pressed to extract a white latex that's mixed with milk and consumed in a ritual. Admiral Wynyard claims is was soma that saved his life in the Indochine."

I nod. "A monk administered it. I remember him. A boy monk named Quay."

"Boy or not, the Admiral claims the monk saved his life, and once he returned to England, it was soma that helped him break free of opium."

We fall silent as the captain of the main mast climbs over the futtock shrouds on his way to the cross trees.

"Does Captain de Clery know what's in *Durness*'s hold?" I ask.

"He does. de Clery's an associate of the Admiral. He's known the purpose of this voyage all along. Only a few people in all of England do."

Eight bells ring out. At the binnacle, Midshipman Moon turns the glass, and the sand begins running out on the first half hour of the next watch.

"Something else I must tell you, Mr. Harriet. Lieutenant Slotter's regaining his strength. Says Enoch regrets admitting his crime."

"Will he recant?"

"He knows it's too late for that." Madrid leans in. "I believe the man intends to jump ship."

*

I join Midshipman Zenith as he stands his watch at the binnacle.

"Mr. Zenith."

"Sir?"

"Have you given much thought to what ship's boy the Captain might promote to acting midshipman?"

"I have, sir. None of them are ready. But Gravy Walters is the oldest. He's learning his letters well enough, but he still confuses his numbers. Switches them around. You're a wizard with numbers, sir. Will you help him?"

"Send him. I'll do what I can."

"Oh, and his mates say he talks in his sleep."

"Does that disqualify him to be considered for midshipman?"

"Oh no, sir. It's just that he keeps them awake, what with their hammocks being slung so close."

"They'd best get used to sleeping in close quarters. And I can't think a ship's boy can make all that much noise in his sleep."

"It's not the noise, sir. It's just that his mates claim his eyes are open even when he seems to be sleeping. It unnerves them, sir. And when they wake him, he says he claims no knowledge of it. Says they're making it up."

"I'll ask Mr. Madrid."

"If you will, sir. Because if Gravy's ever to become a midshipman he should at least sleep with his eyes shut."

That night I lie awake, and with my eyes open, thinking of Gravy. Maybe it's not so bad for him to sleep with his eyes open. A good trait for a lad who might become a midshipman. But even so, Gravy's still a ship's boy who needs his rest, and with eyes shut.

I find Madrid asleep in his birth and hesitate to wake him. But as I'm about to leave he sits up.

"Are you ill, Mr. Harriet?"

"No. Midshipman Zenith has a concern for one of the ship's boys."

"Would that be Gravy Walters? The one who sleeps with his eyes open?"

"Yes."

"Ah. His condition intrigues me."

"Will you come with me to see if it's so?"

"Of course."

As we move along the gun deck every long gun broods in its carriage, each dull beast dreaming of battle. Madrid holds his taper high as we approach the ship's boys, all of them swaying in their hammocks to *Eleanor*'s somnolent motion. All asleep. Perhaps Gravy Walters, as well, except his eyes are open. The lad next to him wakes up, gives a start, and is about to call out, but I motion for him to remain silent.

I whisper to Madrid. "Do you think Gravy's sleeping?"

Madrid studies him for a moment. "Probably. His breathing's steady and even."

He passes his taper forth and back, but Gravy's eyes fail to follow. We step away.

"You've seen this before?"

"Only read about it in a journal. Nocturnal lagophthalmos. Comes from the Greek word for hare. Lagoos. The myth that rabbits sleep with their eyes open."

"Shall we wake him?"

"No. Let him be."

*

On Captain de Clery's desk lies a square wooden board, about once inch thick, and twenty inches on a side. Incised on the board are nineteen horizontal lines, and nineteen vertical, all crossing to form a grid consisting of three hundred sixty-one squares. Two wooden bowls rest beside it. One contains a collection of small, black lozenges, each the size of a halfpenny. The other bowl is filled with white. On the board, a dozen black pieces, and eleven of the white, are positioned on the intersections in what seems to be some sort of counterintuitive fashion.

"What is this, sir?"

"The game of Go, Mr. Harriet. A Chinese puzzle, if you like. More of a mare's nest, really. The black and white pieces are made of glass, but they're called stones."

"A board game? Like chess?"

"A board game? Yes. But not at all like chess. In Go, preeminence is measured differently than in chess. No such thing as checkmate, for there is no king, no rank and file. The object is to surround and capture your opponent's stones, while at the same time avoiding such a fate for yourself. I learned the rudiments from Admiral Wynyard, to remind me that the English play chess while the Chinese play Go. But no one wins the opium war, Harriet. It's a war between empires. The Chinese claim to be oldest civilization in the world, and far superior to all others. And Great Britain's the most dominant power the world has ever known. Very different points of view, except they're both blinded by their arrogance."

He sweeps the stones into their bowls and puts away the board.

"Now then, Madrid has already told you what he knows about this mission, and now I shall tell you more. Any knowledge of this undertaking is limited to a very few. First and foremost, there's the Queen, may God bless her. No one's quite sure what the Queen knows. But she has a network of informants, and the Privy Council, of course. But the Councils' been kept in the dark, along with the Prime Minister, who's being blackmailed. Something to do with spanking sessions and aristocratic ladies. So he's been left out of the coterie forged by Admiral Wynyard. As for Lieutenant Ramsey, he served with distinction on his last ship, and I believe he'll do well as my First Officer. However, the Admiral did not recruit him. Besides, Ramsey's next in line for post captain and the promotion board might pass him over if they knew his involvement in this action. So the Admiral chooses to spare him the risk. The only ones aware of the Admiral's quest are a few unnamed sources in Admiralty House, me, you, Madrid, and the Admiral's agent in Canton."

"The Admiral's quest?"

"Yes, Harriet, you hear me right. The Admiral's mission is nothing less than that. A test, as it were, in hopes that his efforts will help overcome the opium addiction of ten million Chinese, by first curing the Emperor's retinue." de Clery stops, perhaps wondering if he should go on, but then sets his jaw. "The Admiral intends to introduce vedic soma to the Daoguane Emperor's court in the Forbidden City. And the moment is ripe. The Admiral believes Daoguane is about to appoint one of his mandarins as High Commissioner charged with ridding China of opium. Bai Guang's his name. It means Clear Light. Except he's called Sangshu. That's for the colour of a brick. A red one, I think. A moniker given to him by the Emperor because of the brick-red birthmark covering half his face. They say you can see it from a long way off." de Clery's been gazing out the stern window but now turns to me. "Questions, Mr. Harriet?"

Many. But they remain unasked.

After a slight pause, de Clery brings forth a glass jar, its wide mouth stoppered with a cork. Within it, a spray of tapering stems, a dozen or so, with each stem about ten inches long. When he uncorks the container, the pungent scent of dried herbs pervades the cabin.

"This is Vedic soma. It's an herb that's been in use since the first Vedic Hymns ever chanted in India. For over three thousand years it's been consumed as medicine, or as ritual, or by those in pursuit of eternal life."

The marine sentry looks in. "The purser says you wish to see him, sir."

"Tell Mr. Dumfries I'll see him shortly." de Clery turns to me. "We'll continue this discussion later. But just now I'll hear your report on the Indian Gyer."

"Yes, sir. As of yesterday, the thermoscope holds steady. Lieutenant Oliver and I will take the next sounding after noon line tomorrow. I think the findings will indicate we're now in the gyer and will soon enter the horse latitudes. But, current or not, I suggest we get off the fortieth parallel. We've been running on the wind for almost a month, sir, and the sailmaker tells me he has no choice now but to use storm sail to reinforce the clews."

"Yes, so I've seen. Very well. On you way out, send in Dumfries, if you will."

*

The next day, after shooting the noon line, Lieutenant Oliver and I sit in the jolly boat, recording the latest results of the thermoscope.

"The blue bulbs rise, Mr. Harriet! And the red bulbs sink."

"Indicating the presence of a current. Have you ever reported to the Captain?"

"No, sir."

"Then this will be your first time. And you're in luck. Far better to report good news rather than bad. Go you now. Tell de Clery it's time for us to bear north."

5. The Horse Latitudes

Gravy Walters stands before me in the chart room.

"Mr. Zenith tells me you're having trouble with your numbers. That you're mixing them up, and such. Let's try something. Take your pencil and foolscap, and write out the numbers, one through nine."

Gravy writes them out.

"Now then, why do you suppose you mix them up? I mean, why would you write one number instead of another?"

"Mr. Zenith, he says I don't know when I mix them up."

"Well, here's something that might help. When I was your age I began to think of each numeral like it was a person." I point to the first number he wrote down. "So let's think of this character, number one, as the baby. That's because he's small, and he can't take care of himself. But next to him comes two. She one's older sister, don't you see. She's very kind, and her job is to protect her little brother. Especially from three, who's next in line. Three's most angular, and it makes him a bully. No one knows why that's so, only that he always tries to pick on one. But sometimes two needs help defending her little brother against three, that's because two's not as big as three. So that's when four comes along."

I pause to watch Gravy's reaction. A glimmer of interest stirs in his eye, so I go on.

"Four is lovely. She's kind, same as two, only kinder. That's because she's bigger. And what's more, she makes three most jealous, because three's smaller than four. But then comes five, who's angular, same as three, only bigger. He thinks overmuch of himself, and he likes to cause trouble."

I watch Gravy's eyes cloud over.

"Let's stop there. But first, try and tell it all back. I mean all of what I've just told you. Think of it as a play. Or like acrobats on a stage."

He hesitates, scratches his head.

“Start with one,” I prompt. “Who is he?”

“The baby.”

After which Gravy repeats them all back.

“Good. Think you can keep it straight?”

A nod, if only slight.

“Good. One more thing. Do you know you sleep with your eyes open?”

“Yes, sir.”

“Why do you do that?”

“I don’t want to close my eyes, sir. ’Cause that’s when I see me Saucy drowning.”

“I’m sorry, lad. Come back in a few days. We’ll visit the acrobats again.”

*

That night we traverse the equator for the second time on this voyage, and on a heading of north, by northwest. But this time there’s no marking the occasion, and I make reference to the event only by noting we’re now two thousand miles from Purba Island. We’ll soon enter the horse latitudes, and as I stand on the quarterdeck considering how long we’ll be in them, Lieutenant Ramsey joins me.

“A steam vessel would make short shrift of the horse latitudes, Mr. Harriet. Wouldn’t you say?”

“Yes, I’d say that. But steaming to China would still take as long as it takes us. A steam vessel would need to stay close to its fuel source. And I ask you, Ramsey, is there any coal here in the Indian Ocean?”

He chooses to ignore my question, but instead, presses on. “I’ll make you a wager. No doubt you’ve heard of HMS *Nemesis.* First iron-clad steam vessel built for the Royal Navy. Recently commissioned and was scheduled to deploy from Liverpool shortly after we left Greenwich. I served with a lieutenant who’s now on Nemesis. He told me they’re headed for China, same as us, and I bet you a sovereign they arrive before we do. What say you?”

“It’s against my nature to gamble, Lieutenant.”

"Or maybe just not wager more than you can afford to lose." Ramsey grins and walks off.

I find the sailmaker, Bill Cheddar, cutting sailcloth on a section of the spar deck cleared for his work. Cheddar's an old salt, having learned his craft from Wat, the first sailmaker *Eleanor* ever had. He looks up as I approach.

"Oye, Mr. Harriet. Been expecting ye. Horse latitudes coming up. What say yer nose?"

"Dead air about to settle in. In a fews days we'll have nothing but the gyre to make headway." I study the topsail he's repairing. "This is the third time you've patched that sail."

"Aye. A month on the roaring forties been wearin' the sails thin. They can't take much more of it."

"Captain de Clery won't like that. We have to be off Purba Island on a certain date."

"With all due respect, Mr. Harriet. The captain, he been driving *Eleanor* hard. Now he pays the price."

*

At dawn the next day as I stand on the maintop observing the sky and sniffing the wind, Madrid joins me. This morning he's brought a tin of sardines in mustard sauce, and a few biscuits. We share his meager ration and sit for a while before he speaks his mind.

"Captain de Clery hopes to arrive off Purba Island a few days ahead of schedule. But I think our rendezvous at Purba will be catch-as-catch-can."

I nod in agreement. "Always a rare chance to rendezvous with ship at sea. Easy to pass unseen."

"Is that the reason we carry so many signal rockets? Madrid asks. "So we might be detected even from below the horizon?"

"It is. But *Durness* might sail on even if they saw our signal. The East India fleet is notorious for doing as they please."

"All the more reason to arrive on station before Chittagong Thirty-seven arrives. If we're delayed, and they get there before us, they're likely to sail off."

"Maybe so, Madrid. But if *Eleanor*'s not there when they arrive, the captain of *Durness* is under orders to break from the convoy and wait for us."

"For how long?"

"No longer than forty-eight hours. But even two days could leave *Durness* vulnerable to piracy, so if we don't show within the time allotted, he'll turn back for Calcutta."

"What then for us?" Madrid asks. "Quit and go home?"

"No. If *Durness* returns to Calcutta, then we go there, too. That's where the mission will resume. Where did you get the sardines?"

*

That evening, Gravy recites his numbers, one through five.

"Good." I bring out my lodestone. "Know what this is?"

"A walnut?"

"Looks like one. But no, it's magnetite. Just a small piece of rock used for a compass, for when there's no compass to use."

I suspend it above the chart table so that it can swing free in its sling. When the lodestone begins to rotate, I use a pencil as a pointer. "Look right here, at this little brown smudge. Be sure to watch it. The stone will stop rotating in a few minutes, and when it does, that brown spot will come to rest in the direction of north."

After the lodestone stops, Gravy studies it for a good while. "How does it know where north is?"

"Magnetism."

"Like magic?"

"Yes, after a fashion."

"Where did you find it?"

"My teacher gave it to me That was a long time ago."

"Where did he get it from?"

"Likely from his teacher." I take the loadstone down and put it in Gravy's hand. "And now it's yours."

"To know the way north is?"

"No. To hang above you hammock every night before you climb in."

"Why?"

"So you can watch it. Because when you watch it, then you'll know your eyes are open, but you're not sleeping."

*

I listen to *Eleanor*'s port watch as they sing in the jolly boat, and in the cutter and barge, as well, where every man jack pulls hard at his oar. Onboard, the starboard watch mans the ratlines and yards, forming a bucket brigade to douse the sails, better to catch even the lightest breath of air the horse latitudes might begrudge us.

oh the work was hard and the wages low
leave her Johnny, leave her

Bosun Stoner sings the verse, and the oarsmen sing the refrain.

I guess it's time for us to go
and it's time for us to leave her
leave her Johnny, leave her
oh leave her Johnny, leave her
oh the voyage is done and the winds don't blow
and it's time for us to leave her

Eight bells of the forenoon watch ring out. I observe Midshipman Abbot as he logs the noon line on the chalk board. He brushes the chalk dust from his cuff, and steps away.

"Ninety degrees, East, by seventeen degrees North. How much longer, do you think? I mean before we make clear of the doldrums?"

"A few days more, Mr. Abbot."

"But the men have been rowing for three days now. And this morning I saw a squall line on the horizon. A good sign."

"But a false sign, nonetheless."

Abbot sighs, then turns to the sea.

"Look there!" he shouts, pointing at a streak of silver skimming across the water. We watch as it swarms over the barge.

"What's that!"

"A school of flying fish," I answer.

The bow men waste no time using a landing net to gather in as many fish as they can.

I call to the deck officer. "Lieutenant Andrews, you might want to sway out the longboat and retrieve their catch. Looks like Cookie will be serving fish tonight."

Andrews scowls. "Not for me. I won't eat a fish that can fly."

"Then I'll take your share. They're most toothsome."

*

Noon Line
5 July 1839
16ºN x 7ºE
Bearing north by northwest
Purba Island, not far.

Six days of rowing *Eleanor* through the horse latitudes, with only the Indian Gyer providing a slight measure of relief from the oarsmen's arduous task. Yet they row on, if only at one meagre knot, until the calm finally gives way to light, intermittent winds. I make note of the occurrence, just as Zenith finds me in the chart room.

"My father believes in the age of enlightenment, sir, and he has great faith in natural philosophers. But in spite of that I know he'd agree with you."

I blot the ink and lean back. "Agree with me?"

"It's when you told Gravy that magnetism is magic. Because if you ask a natural philosopher to explain phenomena such as magnetism, at some point he's bound to admit he simply doesn't know. Gravy kept asking what makes the thing work, until I had to admit I just didn't know."

"How is the lad?

"His mates say he doesn't sleep with his eyes open anymore."

"And his numbers?"

"Still switching them about, sir. But not all of them, at least."

"Still having a problem with six, seven, eight, and nine?"

Zenith squints, trying to recall. "That's exactly so. I wonder why."

"It's because he hasn't met those acrobats yet."

"Well I should like to meet them, too!"

"And you shall. Only wait until his next lesson, then Gravy can introduce them himself."

*

The next morning a lookout hails the deck. Land. Two points off the starboard bow. I turn to Captain de Clery, who's pacing the windward quarterdeck.

"It might be Purba Island, sir."

de Clery looks relieved. "Very well. Lieutenant Andrews, bear us away. Keep that island well below the horizon. Start the leadsman sounding for that sea mount and keep the watch ready to reduce sail."

For the first ten soundings, the leadsman calls out monotonous. "No bottom."

But on the next sounding his voice calls out lively. "Sixteen fathoms!

Followed close on by a rush of calls. Fifteen fathoms. Fourteen and one-half, thirteen and three-quarters. There's no doubt the bottom is rising over quick. At ten fathoms, de Clery orders Andrews to reduce sail, and *Eleanor*'s headway falls off. The leadsman continues to call out, but with less depth at every cast. At six fathoms, de Clery orders the helmsmen to alter course.

The sails start to luff, just as the leadsman calls out, "Seven and one-half fathoms." And then nine.

de Clery turns to me. "What do you think?"

"It may be the seamount noted in the apocrypha, sir. Seems we've just passed over it."

de Clery nods. "Note the time. Try to determine our exact location. Prepare a note for the Navigational Almanac, and I shall enter the information in the ship's log."

*

A big sea that night. Heavy weather coming from the north, building steady to a fresh gale, with the combers shouldering up to send foam and spindrift running before the wind. I visit Bill

Cheddar who kneels on the foredeck, busy with his needle and sailmaker's palm as he makes a new grommet for a staysail.

"What say you, Cheddar?"

"Me arthritic bespeaks this blow be dying out by first light." He ties off his last stitch with a double reef knot and then looks up. "Men say you the salty one … knowin' just where that sea mount be at. Could 'a run aground of it, 'cept you knew it were there. But the Captain … why he still be stormy?"

"Because this squall will carry us far south of where we need to be."

"Off Purba?"

I nod. "We need to keep station off that place, and now it'll take time to claw our way back."

Cheddar says nothing, just signals his mate to lay out the next sail to be mended.

Just as Cheddar's arthritis predicted, the wind dies before first light. I try to establish our position by stellar observation. Inaccurate, but just the same, I report my findings to de Clery.

"That storm blew us about twenty miles off station, sir. We should make Purba by this afternoon."

de Clery turns to Ramsey. "Have Lieutenant Dovecote set up the tripod on the quarter deck, then make ready the first batch of Congreves."

"Aye, sir. But if may ask, why do we carry ninety-six rockets, and most of them blue?"

"I commend you for your patience in not having asked before, Lieutenant. But up to now you've had no need to know. And now there is. I intend to use them as signal rockets. When we're back on station the gunnery officer will see to it that he fires one rocket off the stern every half hour, for the next forty-eight hours." de Clery tugs at his waistcoat. "One last thing. Madrid informs me that Slotter has recovered well enough to no longer be his patient. Troublesome, I think, because Madrid believes Slotter intends to jump ship. Maybe try to swim for the East Indiaman convoy when we rendezvous. Possibly ask for asylum."

6. Burning the Bridge Before You Cross It

But even before the watch changes, a lookout hails the deck. He's sighted a three masted ship. Dead astern, bow on, with the Union Jack flying from its staff. And atop the foremast flies the pennant of an East Indiaman charter. The wind shifts a point, to reveal the mizzen topmast in splinters and hung up in the shrouds just above the cross tree.

de Clery observes the vessel through his glass, then turns to Lieutenant Dovecote. "It could be *Durness*. Have Mr. Moon fire a signal rocket."

Dovecote nods, and Moon applies his smoldering punk to the Congreve's quick fuse, and with a devil bird's howl the rocket screams off the deck, climbing to a thousand feet before bursting in a blue cluster.

"Now we shall see," de Clery declares. "If that ship is *Durness*, then she'll send up her own blue rocket."

A minute passes. Then another. Still no response.

"Fire another one."

But before Moon can touch off the next rocket, a trail of white smoke streaks off the cargo ship's stern, and same as our own rocket, climbs to a thousand feet and explodes in a blue cluster.

"Ah, there you have it. *Durness*." de Clery remarks. "And I must say it's our good fortune to have met her at all after being blown off station. A minor miracle, I think, thanks to Colonel Congreve." He turns to the signal midshipman. "Mr Abbot, make a hoist for *Durness* to close on us." de Clery studies the wind. "She has the weather gauge, so we'll let her come down."

Durness is a Dutch-built freighter. A ship known to sailors as a butter box because its blunt bow can only push aside the sea rather than cut through it. She makes her way ponderous slow, taking her own good time to close within hailing distance. de Clery summons the bosun, Stoner, who owns the loudest voice onboard *Eleanor*, to stand ready with a hailing trumpet.

"Ask what ship."

Stoner brings the trumpet to his mouth and barks overloud. But the hands onboard *Durness* remain idle, for it seems no one has had the foresight to bring a hailing trumpet on deck.

de Clery speaks under his breath. "Just like an Indiaman to be caught unprepared."

But soon, a plump man wearing a light blue bicorn adorned with a white plume saunters to the rail. He's managed to find a hailing trumpet and calls out in a high-pitched squawk. "I say, would you be so kind as to lend me your carpenter? Mine's been knocked on the head, and not quite himself."

By now the ships have closed to within a hundred feet. Close enough for de Clery to cup his hands and answer back. "You are *Durness*?"

"Of course."

"Very well. I'll send our carpenter. Should I send my loblolly, too?"

"Why yes. Very thoughtful of you. Oh, by the way, you are HMS *Eleanor*, are you not?"

"Yes."

"Very good. And you, sir? You are?"

"I'm Captain de Clery."

"And I'm Wick, principal owner and Master of *Durness*. I have a passenger who wishes to speak with you, so I invite you to come onboard. Your sailing master is Mister Harriet?"

"Yes."

"Then bring him with. Please join me in a light repast. I dine within the hour."

*

Captain de Clery calls Madrid and me to his cabin. "A word before we depart for *Durness*. Except for Admiral Wynyard there's no one in the Royal Navy who knows *Eleanor*'s whereabouts. So the passenger on *Durness* who wishes to speak with me can only be him. He's been planning this undertaking for several years so it's no wonder he's onboard *Durness*. What's more, the Admiral stays in communication with his people in Canton, so expect to hear the latest developments along the China coast. Questions?"

None. At least not voiced.

"Then let us proceed."

Madrid leaves, but I stay.

"What is it?" de Clery asks.

"I do have a question, sir. When was the last time you saw Admiral Wynyard?"

"Six months past. In India. He invited me to his estate in Bengal. That's where he's been conducting an experiment. Something called grafting."

"Grafting? What's that?"

"Don't quite know, to be honest. The Admiral's kept his activities below the horizon up until this spring. But now it seems he's had some success." de Clery pauses to gaze out the gallery windows before going on. "You remember him as a young man, Harriet, but over the years the Admiral's service to the Crown has aged him. Still a vital man, mind you, and I know he's determined to complete this mission, but even so … "

On deck, Stoner calls for the watch to sway out the longboat, and we come through the companionway just as the carpenter, Bunny Shotwell, takes his place in the bow with his sack of tools secured in his lap. Jesus Madrid joins him, his medical kit held firm in hand. And then me, bringing nothing but my own self. As soon as de Clery takes his place in the stern, the coxswain calls out. Six strong backs pull hearty as we cross the gap and tie on at *Durness*'s entry port, where we're met without protocol. Shotwell's brought to the damaged mast. Madrid's led below decks to treat *Durness*'s carpenter, a boy in livery escorts Captain de Clery aft, and I'm left to follow on.

The light repast to which we've been invited is no such thing, but rather a banquet served in the most resplendent of great cabins, with Wick, squat as any toad, seated at the head of the table and devouring a lobster tail drenched in drawn butter, with a flute of champagne near at hand. The sideboard has barely enough room for a standing rib roast, a small vat heaped with steaming mashed potatoes, a pot of gravy and a silver bowl brimful of ripe cherries. Wick looks up, his watery blue eyes bulging as he's about to insert the next fork full of lobster into his gaping mouth.

"Ah! There you are." He sweeps a pink, effeminate hand over the table. "Be seated, if you will."

The Captain and I take our place across from each other far down the table.

de Clery wastes no time. "Who's the passenger who wishes to speak with me?"

"Admiral Wynyard, of course."

"Will he join us?"

"After I've dined. The Admiral has no stomach for haute cuisine. Claims a tin of bully beef and a few biscuits are all he needs. Lobster?"

When de Clery forgoes the offer, so do I. Wick takes no notice, but only calls for his steward. "Grahams, bring the roast and decant the Madeira. Care to try it, gentlemen? From Câmara de Lobos. Their finest vintage."

We both abstain.

"As you wish. Grahams! I'm quite peckish. Serve the potatoes and gravy, too. And tell the cook if I find any lumps in it I shall have him shot." He winks our way. "I wouldn't, of course. But don't tell him that. An anxious cook makes the best cook, don't you see. Sure you won't join me? No? Very well."

Wick tucks in and we can only sit back and witness the onslaught.

"What happened to your mizzen top mast?" de Clery asks.

Wick quaffs his Madeira before answering. "Lost it in that last storm. We hit something hard enough to impede our way."

"What's your draft?"

"Grahams!" Wick whines in mock despair. "You neglect me. More wine." He watches eager as the steward refills his glass. "What was your question, Captain? I forget."

de Clery asks again.

"Oh yes. Twenty-nine feet."

de Clery raises a brow. "What did you hit?"

"Don't know," followed by a nonchalant shrug. "Can't know everything."

"Do you at least know the coordinates?"

"Oh, somewhere off Purba. I was there waiting for you to arrive, I might add."

de Clery ignores the slight. "You may have struck an uncharted seamount. Have you examined your hull?"

"The carpenter sounded the hold. Said we were taking on water. Nothing serious. Began the repairs but then hit his head. Cherries? I swear they're the size of golf balls."

Again we decline.

"A snifter of cognac, then, while you wait for the Admiral. No?"

*

Captain de Clery and I are still waiting in Wick's great cabin as six bells sound in the afternoon watch, when we hear a distinctive thump on the deck. The cabin door swings wide, and there stands Admiral Wynyard. An old man now, at least seventy, but even so he emanates the air of command, his military bearing to the forefront as he steps in with head held high and shoulders thrown back. A shock of white hair, high forehead, his face weathered by decades at sea. He wears the uniform of a retired Admiral. Left pant leg bloused above a heart-of-oak wooden peg that begins just below his knee.

de Clery and I stand, come to attention and salute. The Admiral returns our obeisance, and with steel-grey eyes regards me with the glint of recognition. Then, without so much as looking at the man, he tells Wick to leave. Although the cabin belongs to Wick, he departs without a word.

"Captain de Clery," the Admiral begins, "we are well met and ready to proceed with the expedition."

"Yes, sir. We are."

Wynyard turns to me. "Mr. Harriet, thirty-five years ago and far up the Mekong you knew me as Semyon. You were a fledgling midshipman then, lost in the jungle. And I was an agent of the Crown, shot in the ankle and left to die of gangrene."

A silent moment ensues, providing time enough for us both to shed the specter of memory. He then points to a slatted wooden container set alongside the bulkhead. About three feet wide, two feet deep, and two feet high.

"You're familiar with this. It's a chest used to transport poison from Calcutta. Each chest contains approximately one hundred seventy-five pounds of opium. The Canton exchange is always adjusting to the market, but last month a chest of opium traded for about three hundred Spanish Reales. An East Indiaman can transport about five hundred such chests. Do you have any idea how much money that is?"

"One hundred and fifty thousand Reales, sir."

The Admiral stares at me unblinking. "Still quick with your numbers, I see. An uncanny gift. And you're correct, of course. However, that's just one shipment. But in Canton at least ten vessels under contract with John Company offload their cargos every month. Month after month. Gentleman, I do not exaggerate when I tell you the opium traders in Canton are the richest men in the world. But in terms of their souls, they're the poorest creatures on earth. English and Chinese alike." He bends down and opens the chest to reveal an array of exquisite porcelain. "Beneath this Wodenstoke porcelain lies the source of their wealth."

I count a dozen rounded moulds, but not charcoal grey, as with opium, but a bit lighter. Pearl grey. Each about six inches in diameter. A pungent must rises from the chest, remindful of the soma Captain de Clery keeps in a jar.

"Except this isn't poison," Wynyard explains, "although it's made to resemble the opium exported to Canton. What you see here is the result of a complicated and time-consuming process."

"A graft?" de Clery asks.

The Admiral nods. "Begun as an experiment by my colleague, Mister Chowdry. A natural philosopher. A botanist. I invited him to experiment in the green house on my estate in Bengal. It's required all his knowledge and skill to produce a seed pod derived from the poppy plant and soma. He calls it a hybrid, and its pod exudes the same milky latex as the poppy. But with a critical difference. The hybrid contains very little opium, only about twenty percent. But at the same time it yields a worthwhile amount of soma's healing properties."

The Admiral turns my way. "You remember soma."

I think of Quay, the boy abbot of a silent order of monks. "I remember Quay. He used soma to relieve your pain."

The Admiral nods. "de Clery, have you told Harriet about vedic soma?"

"I told him it helped you overcome the demon serpent and break free of opium."

"Demon serpent? I doubt there is such a thing. But nonetheless, opium is the black hole of Canton. The descent into oblivion. I became addicted to it when I used it to overcome the horror of amputation. Except once you've fallen prey to opium, you might never climb out. But for some, vedic soma may provide a way. And in the last year the botanist's graft of poppy and vedic soma has shown promise. So I provided him with as many villagers as he needed to cultivate the harvest. Finally there's enough to fill *Durness*'s hold with false opium."

A comber takes *Durness* on her beam end and sends her sliding down the backside of the wave. The sudden motion catches the Admiral off balance, but he rights himself with dignity and goes on.

"A century ago the trade imbalance between Great Britain and China evolved into more than a trade war. Since the Chinese refuse to enter into a trade agreement, we chose to reclaim our silver by selling them opium and demanding Reales in exchange. A spiteful act, in my opinion. And the Chinese agree. Just recently twenty thousand chests of opium were confiscated and destroyed in Canton. In response, the Royal Navy's been ordered to blockade the Pearl River, at Hong Kong."

A shift in the wind. Again the Admiral's oak stump sounds on the deck as he makes his way aft to look out the stern windows. "The wind's in our favour. Return to *Eleanor*. Prepare to get underway."

But as we leave, the Admiral thumps his peg on the deck, and I turn to look.

"A word with you, Harriet."

*

In the anteroom of Wick's great cabin, Admiral Wynyard sits at an escritoire, and I take the chair across from him.

"Mr. Harriet, I'm promoting you to the rank of brevet Colonel in the 49th Royal Marine Regiment of Foot."

"Sir?"

"I suggested you be made a general because for the Chinese, the more flash, the better. But Admiralty House wouldn't have it, even though I've chosen you for a critical role for this mission." The Admiral shifts his stump. "At some point in this operation you'll likely come across what looks like an unsurmountable obstacle. I've followed your career from afar, Mr. Harriet, and want you for this undertaking because of your capacity to deny logic. To burn a bridge before crossing it, as it were. Do you understand?"

"Yes, sir."

"Very well. Now then, who's in command of *Eleanor*'s marines?"

"Sergeant Marley, sir."

"Have him fit you out with something that resembles a Royal Marine uniform. It won't have to pass muster, just enough to satisfy the Chinese. Then it will be you, Colonel Harriet, who's in charge of delivering the Wodenstock along with false opium to the Forbidden City."

"How do I get it inside the walls? I don't speak Chinese, sir. How am I to collect one hundred and fifty thousand Reales for the porcelain and a hundred chests of false opium?"

"First, you shall travel with an interpreter who has knowledge of the Forbidden City. And second, you won't collect any payment. The porcelain constitutes a gratuity from the legitimate traders in Canton as recognition of the Dauguang Emperor's efforts to rid China of opium."

"And the vedic soma disguised opium? How will anyone know its's false?"

"Doesn't matter. The Emperor's retinue will use it just the same, and after a few weeks of smoking vedic soma, they won't be as addicted to opium."

"Beg pardon, sir, but I don't think a hundred chests of false opium will go far."

"It won't. There are ten million Chinese addicts. But this shipment is only meant for the Emperor's court. A thousand retainers, at most. And as the Son of Heaven, when he sees his court delivered from their blind misery, he's bound to ask why and then instruct his High Commissioner to introduce it to the population. And my plantation in Bengal will provide it."

7. Noon Line

24 July 1839
13°N x 92°E
Bay of Bengal

As I log the noon line, Midshipman Zenith visits me in my quarters.

"Today I gave the ship's boys their first religious lesson. Based on God's grace, and at the end I asked them what grace meant to them. I must tell you, sir, Gravy's answer was troubling."

Zenith pauses, his eyes expressing the urge to explain further, and my slight nod invites him to proceed.

"The lad told me God' grace is chicken rice soup. Poured from a pot, of all things, and into his wooden bowl. I asked why he'd think such a thing, and he said that one time he saw a drawing of divine grace pouring down from the sky. He said it looked like the chicken rice soup he was eating. But I still can't imagine why he'd say it."

"Maybe he was hungry."

"Very likely, Mr. Harriet. He's a scrawny one. So for Gravy Walters, maybe God's grace is only a bowl of chicken rice soup. I suppose he should be grateful it's not a ship's biscuit chock full of weevils."

*

It's been six days since we contacted *Durness.* And on this day the fat Indiaman sails full and by in our lee, plowing her way through the small seas while *Eleanor* plunges with reefed topsails only. I stand on the maintop, glassing *Durness* with my scope. I train on Wick as he scurries to the quarterdeck with his arms flailing about. Unlike him to be in a hurry, for the man generally moves at a sloth's pace, unless he's stuffing his mouth. Soon a hoist appears on *Durness*'s signal halyard and unfurls on the wind. Blue square on a white field. The prearranged signal for us to close on *Durness.* I come down from the maintop and arrive at the quarter deck, just as we come within hailing distance.

Wick stands at the rail. "Send me your cooper," he whines through his speaking trumpet.

"Imbecile," Ramsey complains. "Does the man actually think we have a cooper?" He calls across the narrowing gap. "We don't have a cooper. What is your problem?"

"We've run out of fresh water. Send someone."

"Bloody hell if I will," Ramsey grumbles.

"I believe we're under orders to honour his request, sir."

Ramsey glares at me. "Then take the gig and go see what's wrong."

"Yes, sir."

I'm brought to *Durness*'s orlop while her bosun explains the situation. "Our water casks were bunged improper and in the last storm we took on three feet of sea water in the hold and it leaked into every cask. Ain't none of it good no more. Serves Wick right for hiring the cheapest cooper in Calcutta."

"What does he expect Captain de Clery to do about it?"

"Don't know. But our sailing master, he says there's an island not far from here."

"North Sentinel."

"That be it. Thinks there might be fresh water there. Worth a try."

"No. It isn't."

"Either that or turn back for Calcutta."

"I'll talk to Wick. Have your sailing master join us. What's his name?"

"Walloon. He be Dutch."

Durness's sailing master and I stand outside Wick's great cabin, waiting for him to arrive.

"You're Walloon?"

"Ja. You?"

I tell him, and then ask, "What do you know about North Sentinel?"

"Fresh water there. Small island surround by a coral reef. But our skiff it make it through good."

"What do your Dutch charts say about the island?"

"Just what I tell you."

"Then I'll tell you this. Don't go there."

Walloon scowls. "Why? Have water there."

"It's also inhabited by an unknown number of primitive natives. And from what I hear, they won't give you water."

"Then Wick buy it. He have much pieces of eight."

"I suspect the good people on North Sentinel don't understand money. What would they do with Spanish silver? And it's been reported they kill people who even try to come ashore."

Wick comes up from behind. "Then tell your captain to send a boat of marines along with us, with orders to shoot anyone who tries to stop us."

"I'm returning to *Eleanor*. I'll tell him what you want."

Upon my return, I walk with de Clery as he paces the quarter deck.

"How long before we reach North Sentinel?" he asks.

"As soon as tonight, sir."

He studies the sky. Clear. "This weather will hold. Tonight will be nearly a full moon. As good a time as any to land a water detail." de Clery calls for the Sergeant of Marines. "Marley, how many men do you have fit for duty?"

"All twelve, sir."

"Form them all in the waist and prepare to act as security for a water party going ashore on North Sentinel. I don't know how many casks *Durness* will have to refresh, or how long it will take to find water, so have your men carry rations for two days. Bring one of your scatter guns to mount on the cutter. Say it back."

The sergeant says it back and then adds, "Permission to speak, sir."

"Speak."

"I served with the Royal Bengal Fusiliers, sir. Us sergeants and their havildars, sergeants they were, same as us, sometimes we talked to each other. One of them, he said once his platoon engaged them people on North Sentinel. His platoon came under attack and they had to kill almost all of 'em because they just kept coming. Didn't understand it was the musketry that was killing 'em. His men was almost out of ammunition and about to be overrun. That's when someone shot off a Congreve."

"Did they break and run?"

"No, sir. When they saw the Congreve explode over their heads, they all put down their spears and long bows. Some of them lie face down in the mud, and some acted like they just saw a vision."

"I see. So the Royal Fusiliers turned the island's false belief to their advantage."

"Aye, sir."

"Very well, take a few rockets with you."

"Sir, should I leave a man behind to keep guard on Lieutenant Slotter?"

"That's not your concern, Sergeant. See to your duties."

de Clery turns to me. "While you were on *Durness* the Admiral sent me a note. Wick believes his first officer is too inexperienced to lead this party ashore, so he's sending his sailing master, instead. What's the man's name?"

"Walloon, sir."

"Yes, that's it. So I'm sending you with Walloon, and I expect you to stay with him at all times. Go you now."

A faint whisper emerges from the past. Perhaps a warning. Never set foot on North Sentinel Island. But I need no forewarning, for I already know the history of this place.

*

Six bells in the middle watch. Three in the morning. A clear night, and in the pale light of a waxing moon, Sergeant Marley and bosun Stoner sit in the stern of *Eleanor*'s cutter as eight oarsmen pull for North Sentinel. The marines sit astride the center line, their muskets held upright between their legs, the tips of their bayonets glinting in the moonlight, with mouths shut tight and eyes cast forward. I sit in the bow with Walloon, who's clutching a satchel while he guides the cutter through the coral reef surrounding the island. Soon he finds an opening and points the way for Stoner to steer us through. I look behind to make sure *Durness*'s skiff follows on. And trailing after the skiff are *Durness*'s longboats, both with empty water casks stacked to the gunnels.

"One hundred and nine casks," I inform Walloon.

"Ja."

"This will take all night. They won't know where to look."

Walloon opens his satchel. "Look see."

In the dim light I see a forked willow branch. "Divining rod?"

"Ja. Water witch."

"Have you ever found water with it?"

"No," Walloon grins sheepish, "but this time maybe ja?"

When the cutter grounds on a bar we all get out. The marines pull it ashore and cover it with fronds, then take up defensive positions. I can't help but feel sorry for them, for when the sun comes up, they'll roast in their red woolen tunics. And most likely they'll be sand fleas along this coast, which will only add to their misery. Such is the life of a marine. Close behind, *Durness*'s skiff arrives, and while its crew offloads, Marley confers with Walloon and me.

"My orders are to stay with the cutter. But you'll find water faster if you split up. Fire one round if you find it. More if there's trouble."

A body of ten men strikes off through the underbrush, with each man bearing an empty water cask on his shoulder. Walloon points to three other men, one with a shovel, and invites me to go with him. I have no faith in dowsing, but like the man said, "Maybe this time." We proceed a hundred yards inland, then stop. A rustle in the brush, nothing more. Likely some animal, for it's doubtful the inhabitants of North Sentinel are stirring in the night. The silence returns, pressing on my ears.

Walloon walks slow, his divining rod leading the way. The moon casts long shadows, but it's still high enough to reveal an opening in the underbrush. Walloon takes us through and soon points to the ground in front of him.

"*Graaf, rechts hier.*"

And the man with the shovel digs right where Walloon points. A dry hole. We move on.

More night sounds. A nightjar's quiet call announces the false dawn. Walloon discovers another likely place. His man digs. From deep within the tree line I hear a chattering sound. In spite of a chill tracing on my spine, I go to investigate. Back at the cutter, at this point a thousand yards distance through the trees and underbrush, Marley's marines fire a tight volley, followed by the scatter gun. I turn to see Walloon and his men sharing a look. Another volley, but this time sporadic, like men firing at will, followed by the wail of human agony. We stand in a bad place, for it seems there's a hostile force between us and *Eleanor*'s marines. Walloon and his men know it, too. They don't wait for me but instead run and leave me on my own. And it's then I realize that, as a sailing master, I can find my way upon the sea, but on this island, I'm dreadful lost.

Once more the chattering, this time sounding more like the clicking of teeth, and coming from the near tree line. I bend low, if only to make myself a smaller target, but if anyone's watching, then surely, they'll see I'm alone. A movement in the brush, and a figure emerges, stumbling toward me. I take aim with my best pistol and set the hammer at full cock. The man hears the snick of my weapon and stops. He studies me and then calls out.

"Harriet? Is that you?"

I return the hammer to half-cock, and demand to know who he is.

"Enoch."

"Lieutenant Slotter?"

"I am Enoch."

I doubt it. "Come you forth, whoever you claim to be."

Slotter bears fresh wounds, as if the surf has rolled him along the coral reef and scoured his face raw. Shirt and trousers shredded and torn. Barefoot and shivering.

"Enoch is cold. What is this place?"

"North Sentinel Island. You jumped ship when you saw how close we were, didn't you?"

Slotter shakes off his chill and stands tall. "Enoch prefers to take his chance here, rather than await execution."

Another ragged volley from the marines, still holding firm on the beach.

"What's that?" Slotter asks.

"I believe *Eleanor*'s marines are under attack."

"Attack?"

"The denizens of this island don't love us overmuch. That includes you, Slotter. And your shipmates hate you, too. They'd consider it good riddance if I shot you where you stand. But if you tell me how you escaped, I might choose otherwise."

"Enoch will explain."

Another volley.

"Say it fast."

"Last night they replaced the marine guarding Enoch with a sailor. When he brought Enoch to the head, Enoch asked for his cuffs to be removed so he could relieve himself. He obliged, and that's when Enoch pushed him down and went over the rail. By the time anyone could fire a musket Enoch was out of range."

"But you're not out range of my pistol."

"Then shoot Enoch where he stands."

"No. If you walk back into the trees and disappear, I won't report seeing you. You'll be left on your own."

"A kindness, for which Enoch owes you his life."

"A kindness you may soon regret. Go. Before I change my mind."

But when Slotter turns to go, an arrow loosed from the trees pierces his heart clean through. The next arrow hisses past my ear, and I run toward the sound of marine musketry, even if there's a hostile force standing between them and me.

As I run, my thoughts chase ahead. Is this how I die? Not at sea, but shot through the heart with an arrow on some God-forsaken island? Not die in my own bed? At home with my cherished family watching over me, with the enumerations dancing merry on the greensward, and the Sukiyama finally put to rest? Please, not like this, not killed by those standing in my way, or overtaken by the ones chasing me. By now I now see the marines, either kneeling or standing rank and file in silhouette against the rising sun, decimating the population of North Sentinel. And then I hear Sergeant Marley as he shouts a command.

"Launch a Congreve."

Oh, I'd forgotten about them. I watch a trail of white smoke as the rocket climbs and detonates direct above the assault. And, just as the good Sergeant foresaw, the warriors of North Sentinel put down their bows and lie face down in the sand, while I'm left to pick my way through the living and the dead, to join the marines on the beach.

*

While I was onshore, Admiral Wynyard has come aboard *Eleanor*, and upon my return he stands in the great cabin, giving full attention to my report.

"The water party managed to refill all one hundred and nine casks, sir."

"And you say Lieutenant Slotter's dead?" the Admiral asks.

"Yes, sir. Shot through the heart with an arrow."

Th Admiral's only reaction is to raise a brow. "Do the inhabitants of North Sentinel have any way of reporting the presence of *Durness* and *Eleanor*?"

"I'm given to understand they have a language of their own making, sir, but no one can communicate with them."

"Let's hope you're correct, Harriet. I'm reducing Wick's dividend. His syndicate already stands to make a handsome profit on these voyages. But his negligence caused a delay. And more critical, he caused us to come within sight of land. An unfortunate compromise. If no one knows our whereabouts, then no one knows our purpose." The Admiral stumps to the stern windows and studies the weather. "The wind backs. But with any luck we'll get underway before nautical twilight. Within a week I expect to enter the Straits of Singapore and stand into the South China Sea."

8. Canton

True to the Admiral's prediction, we enter the Straits of Singapore just one week after departing North Sentinel. Midshipman Zenith stands at the galley funnel supervising a punishment detail at work sweeping a month's worth of soot from the stack. As I pass by, he calls out.

"Mr. Harriet! I gave the ship's boys their first spelling match. And when I asked them to spell, they all failed miserably. But Gravy Walters failed in a grand fashion. You'd never guess how he spelled fish. He spelled it . . . G-H-O T I. When I asked why he spelled it so catawampus, he explained it very cleverly. Seems the lad just sounded it out. gh, like it's pronounced in enough. That's for the f in fish, don't you see. And then o, as in women, so there comes the i. And ti, as it sounds in nation, which is pronounced like . . ."

"Like the sh, in fish."

"There you have it, sir. Oh, father will be amused when I write and tell him."

"It seems your father has a sense of humor much like your own. Save some of that soot for me, if you will. I use it to make black ink."

*

After shooting the noon line on the fifth of August 1839, I record in my log:

> 22°Nx113°E
>
> Approaching the Gulf of Canton

I finish blotting my entry just as Gravy Walters calls from my door.

"It's the Captain, sir. He wants to see you in his quarters." He darts off but returns over quick. "I forgot. He says bring your charts for Canton."

"Very well. By the way, lad, you've a most clever way of spelling fish. How did you think of it?"

"I didn't, sir. It was them enumerations what put me up to it. Once, when three asked five how to spell fish, that's the way five guessed how to spell it. You know how they talk to each other, and all. Always going on about something."

"I didn't know that. Thought they only tumbled about on the greensward."

"Oh no, sir. They talk to each other. Mostly at night, though, when it's gone quiet. Their chatter keeps me awake some. Want to know what they say about you? Except I promised not to tell."

"No. Now be on your way."

But my true answer for Gravy isn't no. It's yes. And I must ask, has Gravy taken command of the players on the greensward of my youth, to become the enumerations who dance the implausible theory of numbers? Has the lad made this a thing of his own, and now improves upon it?

*

When I enter *Eleanor*'s great cabin, the Admiral, Captain de Clery, Jesus Madrid, and Sergeant Marley all stand at the desk studying de Clery's Go board. It appears there's a game in progress, for a string of black stones stretches across the board from one edge to the other. One border is labeled south, and the other's tagged north. At about midway between, a distinctive bulge.

The Admiral clears his throat. "Gentleman, since the onset of this mission we've had little or no contact with shore, or with any other vessel. This has served our purpose. I wish to arrive at Canton unexpectedly because there are many in Canton, as well as London, who would oppose me if they knew my intentions. However, there's a price to be paid for independent action, since we shall arrive off the coast of China not knowing the current political climate. The last contact with my agent was in March, when I was told the conditions in Canton are unstable but could be coming to a head after the Royal Navy destroyed a blockade of the Pearl River. She also says the Emperor's High Commissioner, Sangshu, seized and destroyed twenty thousand chests of opium, which on that day were trading at four hundred fifteen Spanish reales per chest." The Admiral looks my way. "Mr. Harriet, be so kind as to tell us what those twenty thousand chests were worth on that day."

"Eight million, three hundred thousand reales, sir."

"You have a unique trait, Mr. Harriet. And you are correct, of course. This is a fortune. I was also told by my agent that the Emperor praised Sangshu for his actions. But there are some within the Forbidden City, along with the Cohong in Canton, which is something akin to a chamber of commerce, who wish for the opium trade to flourish. Even to expand, since there are fortunes yet to be made, both in China and in England. And due to their lost inventory, along with any subsequent profit from the sale of opium, the Cohong has asked for the dismissal of Sangshu. They also expect to be compensated in full, and to underscore their demands, they've asked the Royal Navy to send war ships into Canton harbour to prevent the Emperor's troops from closing down the market."

The Admiral glances at the Go board.

"No one in the Royal Navy would consider a military operation in terms of the game of Go, such as we have before us. But in order to gain tactical advantage, one must try to understand how an adversary thinks. It's not well known, but officer candidates in the Emperor's Military Academy at Baoding study the game of Go because it was used by Chinese warlords who would lay out small stones on the ground to mark enemy positions. So it stands to reason that many of the Emperor's generals perceive the military occupation of Canton in much the same way."

The Admiral sweeps a hand over the grid.

"These stones represent the coastline of China, from Macao, here in the south, to a few miles north of Hong Kong. This stretch of coast includes Canton, where this mission will come ashore. As you can see, the line consists of black stones, while the white stones, placed here at this bulge, represent the barrier islands that lie between China and the Gulf of Canton. These stones include the islands of Ladrones to the south, and to the north, Lama. Together they define a deep-water channel which is approximately a mile wide, and leads to the Pearl River estuary, called the Bogue. There are forts on two of the islands in the Bogue, built to defend the channel. One fort here, at Chuenpi. And the other directly across from it, at Taikoktau. These installations are manned by Chinese militia, armed only with antiquated matchlock muskets. And their shore batteries are no better. They consist of obsolete artillery incapable of training on a target. The Chinese claim to be the oldest of all civilizations and take pride in the self-indulgent notion that they are superior to any colonial power. Including Great Britain. But the fact is, their army is woefully inferior. As well as their navy, which would stand little chance if it were to engage the Royal Navy. Conversely, there are those in England who believe our own civilization is superior to the Chinese. But is our advanced weaponry the only source of our dominance in the world order? Many would contend our strength is due to our enlightenment and forthright intentions. They would argue that for England to subject the Chinese to the ravages of opium addiction is no less than a sin against humanity."

Most longwinded for the Admiral, and he pauses to gather himself.

"Notwithstanding, the Royal Navy depends on charts, not on some panorama displayed on a Go board." Again he looks my way, "Mr. Harriet, set your chart alongside this board so we can apply our own perspective on Canton." The Admiral waits for me to place my chart, then continues. "About ten miles up the Pearl River there's a stretch of rice paddies that lead to Canton. There are many wharfs along the waterfront at Canton. But they also serve as enclaves built to house British workers and their families employed by the East India Company.

"Much of the trade is legitimate. Tea, porcelain and silk. But there are those who market opium, and upon their wharfs stand the godowns that contain thousands of chests of opium, just waiting to be sold to the Chinese, who in turn distribute it to the population. And this one here, just upstream of Canton, is Jordain Wharf. It's where *Durness* will offload her cargo, because Jordain Wharf constitutes the southern terminus of the Grand Canal, two thousand years old, originally constructed to convey the annual rice tribute to the capitol, a thousand miles to the north. Over the past two millennia the Grand Canal has evolved. Its network of lakes, rivers and excavations can now bear any cargo transportable by water." The Admiral steps back, better to take us all in at a glance. "And it is the Grand Canal we will use to deliver vedic soma to the Forbidden City."

*

9 November 1839
Canton
First light

I blot my entry, snuff the taper and step on deck. The wind is near calm as we steal in on the tide, and enter the outer roads of Canton. Lights along the waterfront begin winking out, as well as the lights on the Chinese junks already making their way along the Bogue. One is a most ponderous junk, with its yellow sail panels asserting it belongs to the Son of Heaven. Another with pale blue panels, no doubt a junk owned by some over rich mandarin. But most carry the grey, weathered sail panels of working junks plying the coastal trade. Amid the junks, a host of sampans skimming the surface like so many water bugs. And, just as Admiral Wynyard predicted, two Royal Navy frigates lie at anchor in the Bay of Canton. *Andromeda* and *Imogene*.

At the base of the fort on Chuenpi island there squats a stone hut, with a flag flying from a short staff. Harbour Pilot. At its dock, two skiffs tug at their lines. One skiff painted red, one green.

On *Eleanor*'s quarterdeck Lieutenant Dovecote gives an order. "Mr. Abbot, hoist the flag requesting a pilot."

Soon two mates board the green skiff and wait for a third man to join them. In not five minutes they hook on at our main chains, and a man's bald, nut-brown head appears at the entry port. He's met by Midshipman Abbot, who brings him to the helm.

"I'm Labarth, harbour pilot. Your draft, sir?"

Captain de Clery arrives to answer the question. "Twenty-six feet. And the Indiaman close astern is *Durness*. Twenty-nine feet."

"Victualing?"

"No. We'll be escorting *Durness* to Jordain Wharf."

"That will be three pounds. One pound per mile, paid on delivery. Plus tuppence a mile for each of my oarsmen."

"Very well"

Labarth calls for his oarsmen to secure the skiff, then takes the helm and brings us into the ebb flow of the Pearl River. Fore staysail and spanker only, with *Durness* following in our wake. On shore, the flash of red streamers. A yellow pennant flying at some imperial ministry. But mostly, a sea of drab colours worn by a population of peasants. The smell of Canton carries on the wind. Steamed rice. Noodle shops. Vendors grilling meat on every pier. A thousand joss sticks. The sweat of hard labour, both human and beast. The stench of night soil. And a multitude of sounds. Men shouting over the bray of donkeys, or goats bleating mournful. And no children, who in England would be racing along the shoreline trying to keep pace with a warship. But in Canton, the children are kept hidden from foreign devils."

As is my daily practice, I go aloft to stand on the maintop. But when I come through the lubber hole, Lieutenant Ramsey's already there, glassing the entrance to the Bogue. He hands me his telescope and points.

"Look there."

I train on a sleek warship, not under sail, but moving under steam as she enters the Bogue.

"I owe you a sovereign, Mr. Harriet."

"How's that?"

"That ship is *Nemesis*. I bet you she'd arrive in Canton before us, but she didn't. Don't you recall?"

"I recall not taking the bet, sir. But if you insist, then give a sovereign to Midshipman Zenith. Have him buy a bolt of number eight duck cloth and fit out the ship boys in proper fashion."

By six bells in the afternoon watch, *Durness* and *Eleanor* lie alongside Jordain Wharf. Captain de Clery pays off Labarth and his oarsmen. The Chinese dockworkers start offloading *Durness*'s cargo, working long into the night. After the last chest is swayed on to Jordain Wharf, the Admiral comes aboard *Eleanor* and orders a lantern with red-tinted glass to be lit and displayed at the maintop.

Seven bells in the middle watch. Three-thirty in the morning. A light mist. I've offered to stand a watch and lean into the night trying to identify a sound on the river. A cutter emerges, bows on, its oars shedding a faint glimmer of water with each stroke. Behind me, I hear the Admiral's oak peg treading the deck. I turn to him.

"As you were, Mr. Harriet. The red lantern has summoned my agent. Join me at the entry port."

*

A figure steps through the entry port dressed in the quilted jerkin and dark trousers of a common peasant. And not until she speaks do I understand that this is no man, but a woman. And hardly a Chinese peasant, for she's most abrupt in her manner.

"Admiral Wynyard. I'm Cyd Jordain."

The Admiral's slight bow. But instead of a curtsy, she extends her hand. Not to be taken, but to present a canvas pouch.

"My report."

"Come below. You as well, Harriet."

"A word with my crew." She steps to the rail and speaks but a word. "Dengdai."

I don't know Chinese, but from her gesture, I think she's told them to wait.

She joins the Admiral, and I follow on. Only then do I see that this woman walks with a pronounced limp. In the great cabin, Captain de Clery stands at his desk while his steward lights a lantern, and then two more. I close the door and stand in place. A place better to observe Cyd Jordain's image in the cheval glass. About fourty. Auburn hair parted down the middle, just brushing her shoulders. Five feet six or seven, and most thin.

The Admiral makes introductions. Captain de Clery calls for ginger beer. Cyd Jordain brings out a clay pipe, stuffs it with latakia, and sets it to burning with a punk. The smoke veils her face, but still I note her high forehead and arching brows. Dark brown, wide-set eyes. Focused and clear.

The Admiral begins. "You're here in part because you know Chinese. How well do you know it?"

"I read Chinese and understand most of what I hear," she replies. "But don't speak it well, so I don't say much. Which is to my advantage. If people don't hear me speak Chinese, they assume I don't understand it, either. That can lead them to say things they might not want me to know. Although at some point it may serve my purpose to let people know I understand what they've been saying all along."

Eleanor's hawsers pull up short, sending a shudder through the hull that catches Miss Jordain off guard. Her right ankle folds under. Captain de Clery steps in to help. But she shakes him off and stands tall, waiting for the Admiral's next question.

"Do you know the Forbidden City?"

"No subject of Great Britain has ever set foot in the Forbidden City. I do know it's a sprawling expanse of gates, though, and a pageantry of halls. However, as a correspondence secretary for Jordain Bank, it's my responsibility to know exactly what gate to send any bank business meant for the Emperor."

"Your brother is Robert Jordain, the Principal shareholder of Jordain Bank. A bank that underwrites the opium trade."

"I regret it is so."

"He brought you to Canton to be his secretary."

"His correspondence secretary."

"A trusted position. Yet you would betray your brother's trust."

"I betray the man he's become. Not the brother I knew as a child."

Her pipe gutters out, and we all watch her hobble to the stern window and scatter the ashes into the river.

"For two years you lived in Calcutta with Iris Ashford, your cousin."

"On mum's side. We grew up in Stirling. We were close until she married and moved to Calcutta. But she was lonely there, and she invited me to visit, and I stayed."

"I know her husband. Captain Ashford. We served together on *Defiant*. A few years back he wrote and told me that Iris took laudanum for her gout, and over time she fell prey to it. He didn't know about my venture until I told him. And then he asked for my help. So when my botanist was at the stage in his grafting where he believed it was ready for a trial, Iris was our first test. It seems to have worked."

"I think it has. That's why she told me about your proceedings. She thought I should contact you."

"To become my agent?"

"I remind you, sir, I didn't ask to work for you. It was you who asked me. Iris just thought I should contact you because my heart ached for my brother, and I wished him to be free of his addiction."

"To opium?"

"Not opium. He knows better. He's addicted to the profit acquired from trading opium, whoever pays the price."

Bare feet pad on the deck. One bell rings out. Four thirty, and the morning watch begins.

"In your latest report you said the Emperor was probably going to dismiss Sangshu and appoint a new High Commissioner. Did he?"

"He did. But not before Sangshu threatened to have everyone in the Chohong consortium put to death, starting with Howqua, the wealthiest Chinese broker in Canton, if they didn't quit trading opium. At first the Chohong agreed to his demands. But their losses mounted. A hundred thousand reales in the first month. It wasn't long before they petitioned the Emperor to have Sangshu executed."

"But he didn't."

"He did not. The Emperor's fond of Sangshu, mostly for when he destroyed those twenty thousand chests of opium. He spared Sangshu and just removed him from his position. He's now Viceroy of some province."

On the quarterdeck, Bosun Stoner prods the morning watch hard at work holystoning the deck. "Put yer backs into it, me beauties! Lest I take names!"

Cyd turns pensive. "But it may be our good fortune that Sangshu is no longer High Commissioner. He still has the support of the honest merchants in Canton. And the man's greatly admired for his sangfroid. And now that the Cohong no longer feels threatened by him, they've dropped their guard." A bent smile. "That was a mistake. While they weren't looking, Sangshu stole a march on them. Managed to procure transport for your vedic soma." She looks out the gallery windows, and points. "See those two junks across the river? They're watching for your signal to come alongside and load your one hundred chests. The signal is one lantern on the fore top, and another on the mizzen top. What time is it?"

"Almost five.

"I have to changes clothes and be at the bank before it opens."

"One more thing." The Admiral takes a leather drawstring purse from his waistcoat and hands it to Cyd. "Open it."

A hundred Spanish reales.

Then he hands her a Jordain Bank chop carved out of jade. "Take the money and the seal with you on this mission, Miss Jordain At some point you may have cause to use them."

"I am in debt."

"Come back tonight, Miss Jordain. I'll have your report read by then. Now I must pay a visit to that frigate in the bay. Their captain's been observing us through his scope. No doubt he's curious about why we're here."

"What will you tell him?" Cyd asks.

"Only that we're here on an independent action."

Captain de Clery gives the order for two lanterns to be lighted and hung in place, and by first light the two junks lie alongside *Eleanor*. The largest of the two is about fifty feet long. Two masted. With red Chinese calligraphy painted across the transom. And in English, stenciled just below it, *Shilong*. I count a dozen crewmen. The smaller of the two, *Foshan*, is about forty feet long, with a single mast. Eight crewmen. I keep count as the first sixty chests go into *Shilong*'s hold, and the remaining forty into *Foshan*.

*

Later that day I oversee the midshipmen as they shoot the noon line. I'm nonplussed, because for the first time on this voyage they've all derived our true co-ordinates, including Mr. Zenith, who asks for a word with me after I dismiss his mates.

"Sir? Who is Tate?"

His question takes me unprepared. "Why do you ask?"

"It's Gravy Walters, sir. He says you called him by that name. I mean on the day his brother drowned. Has he gone woolly?"

"I'll talk to the lad."

But what do I tell him? Some lie? No, because if you must lie, don't. The truth, then. Yes, the truth. Or a half-truth? But Gravy's the clever one. Likely to see through a ruse. And he deserves better. A solid tap on my door.

"Enter."

Gravy steps in. "Mr. Zenith sent me, sir."

Stop thinking overmuch. Just begin. "You remember when I called you Tate, and now you want to know why." A good start. "So I'll tell you." Now what? Stall. "But first tell me what the enumerations say about me."

Gravy recites, almost as if by rote, and with eyes following the lantern rocking in its gimbal to *Eleanor*'s motion.

"One, he doesn't say anything at all. That's because he's the baby. And two, and four, and eight. They all say good of you. It's because you give us ship's boys the horehound. And because Mr. Zenith says it was you who bought the duck cloth for our Sunday slops. But three, and five, and six and seven, they all none of them like you. It's because you don't like them, either." He looks at me undeterred. "You called me Tate. Who's that?"

The truth, then.

"Tate was younger than you."

"How old was he?" Gravy asks.

"No older than ten. He was a stowaway. We think maybe it was his mum who smuggled him onboard *Eleanor*."

"Why?"

"Maybe she couldn't take care of him, or didn't want to. We won't ever know. That was a long time ago, and I was a ship's boy, same as you. It didn't go well for Tate. He came to a sad end because he wouldn't do what someone tried to make him do. And for that, he died."

“"Drowned?"

"I won't say."

Gravy scowls. "Nine. He's the judge. He says if you called me Tate, then you must tell me how he died."

Of course. Because nine would never equivocate. Out with it, then. I take a deep breath.

"He was beaten, stuffed in a gunny sack and thrown over the rail. Already dead."

There it is. The still point in time. Isn't it time for the watch to change? Why doesn't the watch change? The moment quickens until Gravy backs away and runs. Just as Bill Chester, the sailmaker, arrives holding a large bundle secured with a red sash.

"Beg pardon, sir. I just stitched together your Marine uniform. Tunic, breeches. Epaulettes with one pip 'neath the Crown, regimental insignia, and belt plate. Had to embroider them pips, but if you don't look too close, they'll pass. And Sergeant Marley, he has a shako and boots that will fit. You'll look a right smart colonel, Mr. Harriet!"

"You do me proud, Chester. How much for your efforts?"

"Two bob, sir."

*

When Cyd returns that night, I'm ordered to the great cabin wearing my Royal Marine Colonel uniform. I step in as she's addressing Admiral.

"I arrived in China two years ago and lived in my brother's residence in Macao. After Sangshu seized those twenty thousand chests of opium, the conditions in Canton improved. It's now safe for foreigners to live there year-round, so I've worked at Jordain Bank ever since. As my brother's correspondence secretary, I know he has informants along the Grand Canal, all in his pay to intercept dispatches to and from the Forbidden City by way of the canal. They're in three cities. Wuxi, Jining, and Dezhou. One of my responsibilities is to date a record these intercepts. Information travels fast on the canal. From Canton to the Forbidden City in about three weeks. But I must tell you, much of that information is misleading. You must realize the Chinese will alter the facts in order to please the Emperor. Or just as likely, to save their own skin. Don't kill the messenger, as it were. The first time I noted the disparity was in a missive regarding the recent Battle of Kowloon. It was meant for the Emperor, but first it was read by my brother's informant at Wuxi. He sent the report on, of course, shortly after copying it out. The commander of the Chinese ships at Kowloon claimed a great victory over British forces, including the sinking of enemy ships and inflicting fifty casualties. A deception perpetuated solely to please the Emperor. The fact is, the Royal Navy routed the Chinese at Kowloon. None of our ships were lost, nor were any sailors killed or wounded."

She looks my way. "The uniform becomes you, Mr. Harriet. Or is it now Colonel Harriet?"

"It's Colonel Harriet," the Admiral responds, "and will remain so until he returns from Peking, a journey that begins tomorrow morning. *Eleanor*'s marines have already boarded *Shilong* and *Foshan*. Sergeant Marley and eight marines will be with you on *Shilong*. Corporal Penny and four marines on *Foshan*."

"I assume an interpreter will go with us."

"Yes, Colonel Harriet," Cyd replies. "Me."

9. The Grand Canal

At first light I come aboard *Shilong* and stand amidship appraising the junk. Cyd joins me at the rail.

"Colonel Harriet. I'll introduce you to Hop. Sounds like hope. He's the captain."

On the way aft, Cyd briefs me. "Sangshu owns the *Shilong*, and the *Foshan*, too. And his broker's seen to our provisions. About three weeks of food, which *Shilong*'s cook will make for us." She points to a deck cabin. "That's where Hop lives. There's a partition that makes a smaller compartment to accommodate one passenger. I'll take the cabin. You take the compartment. Hop has offered to sleep on the roof of the deck house."

We find Hop. Average height for a Han Chinese, although with a slight stoop. Rope thin. Muscles knotted hard. Hard to know his age. Certain he's not a young man. Judging by his weathered face, maybe fifty. Black hair chopped short, with a long, plaited queue.

After the proper bows, I ask Cyd to translate. "Please thank Hop for his kind offer."

But Cyd speaks to him harsh.

"What did you tell him?"

"That you're insulted by not being offered the best quarters."

This woman begins to remind me of my daughter-in-law. Rachel's most independent and bound to say as she sees fit. It took years for us to come to terms. And only then by me refusing to rise to the bait but just posing the unforeseen question. While all along enjoying her most wondrous cooking.

"Miss Jordain, can you cook?"

"What?"

"Never mind. I don't seen any artillery on *Shilong*. Ask how he defends his ship."

Cyd doesn't bother to translate, just answers on her own. "The *Shilong* doesn't have artillery. No room for it. A canal junk has to make use of its space. But I'm sure Hop has a pistol. All the captains do. There are dacoit to deal with."

"Bandits?" I ask."

"Yes."

I study the junks's top hamper. "Ask him what the sail panels are made of."

She asks, and Hop replies, "Yama bu"

"Linen," Cyd translates.

"Do the sail panels take the shape of a foil?"

"A foil?"

"Yes. On a square-rigged ship the sails are cut for the wind to shape them into a foil so they fill proper. Is that so on a junk?"

"I don't know how to ask that. Besides, you're supposed to be a marine colonel. I don't think a marine colonel would ask about sails."

Hop's called away. Cyd tends to her own affairs. And I'm left to consider how Cyd Jordain and I will get along. We'll be several weeks on this junk. Best set things in order straight away. So I call for Sergeant Marley.

"Yes, sir."

Spoken a bit sardonic, since the sergeant knows me as the sailing master on *Eleanor* and now must regard me as a marine colonel.

"Report, Sergeant."

"Eight marines onboard, sir. Eight rifled muskets, powder and shot for a hundred rounds each, a scattergun on each junk with powder and grape for ten rounds each. A ration of biscuit and biltong to last a month. The watch is set. Corporal Penny has just boarded *Foshan* with the rest of *Eleanor*'s marines. I told him to keep his men below decks unless they're on watch, and when topside, remove their tunics. No need to draw attention to a marine's red coat spotted on a junk."

"Very well. Mount your scatter gun on the bow but keep it under cover, and the ammunition locker nearby."

Marley and I both cock an ear. No matter in what language, the sharp call of *Shilong*'s crew can only mean we're about to cast off.

It will take some time before we pull away from the wharf, so I find Cyd and ask her to join me in the hold.

"Count the number of chests with Wodenstoke Porcelain stenciled under the latch, if you will. I counted sixty chests brought onboard. I want you to verify it."

"Of course. Wouldn't want any gift meant for the Emperor to go missing."

"One more thing. I don't think Hop should sleep on the roof. Why don't you tell him to move back into his quarters. You sleep on the roof."

*

By the next morning I've replaced my marine tunic with a *hanfu,* a cloak common to the Chinese. Best not to draw attention to myself while I stand at *Shilong*'s stern, making sure to stay clear of the helmsmen. They struggle with the tiller, a solid timber eight feet in length, with a ten-inch diameter. It's secured in such a way to allow the helmsmen to raise or lower the rudder, which is a heavy wooden board, about three feet square, and four inches thick. A most ponderous way to steer a ship. But a junk's rudder and tiller haven't changed in a thousand years. And the sail panels haven't changed, either. They're of a most clever design, for they provide a junk with the means to sail close to the wind, with panels spread wide between the battens like some prodigious big fan.

Such as now, when the Grand Canal presents the long procession of canal junks with a headwind. Ten junks in line ahead of us, and ten more behind. All making about three knots. Most slow, yet they press steady on, along with a thousand sampans, propelled by men sculling their yuloh rudders en route to the floating villages that line both banks the canal. Where countless sampans lash together to form a wide sprawl of rafts, all of them rising and falling on the water. A waterborne culture where people bear their children, live out their lives, and die. Never going ashore. So the world has made them.

I feel eyes upon me and turn to watch Cyd and Hop approaching.

"I removed myself to the roof," Cyd begins without so much as a good morning, "and Hop's back in his quarters."

I never guessed she'd actually do it. Best not say it, though. Better just to have Sergeant Marley pitch her a tent on the roof.

"Ask Hop if he keeps a chart for the Grand Canal."

When she asks, he answers with tap on his head.

Admirable. I bring out a blank sheet of foolscap, about fourteen by eleven inches, and two pencils. One pencil for Hop, and one for me.

"Ask him to sketch it out."

"He's never seen a pencil."

"Then I'll show him how to use it."

"Why? He can't read or write."

"No need of that." I demonstrate how to use a pencil, then watch him trace a line. "Good. Now ask him to draw the canal from Canton to Peking. Have him mark the important places, then say their names. Oh, but first ask him how many miles from Canton to Peking."

"How many miles," Cyd asks.

A long reply.

"He doesn't know. But he says it takes about a month. Depending on how long he has to wait at the lock gates. Or stop where they're dredging the canal. Or to make repairs."

"Does he have a carpenter?"

When she asks, Hop taps twice on his own chest.

I smile and say, "Quite right."

I spread the foolscap on the roof of the deck cabin and tell Cyd to write the name for the Grand Canal at the top of the page, both in Chinese and English.

Jing–Hang. Grand Canal.

"Now, how do you say north?"

She has to think for a moment. "Bei."

I put an arrow near the top, then say "Bei." Now tell him to place an x for where Canton would be on this map, and another x for Peking."

When he complies, I say for him to trace the canal route.

A long string of Chinese from Cyd.

And Cyd's reply. "He says the canal doesn't go all the way to Peking. It ends one day south. At Tianjin."

Hop understands what I want and starts to draw lines, explaining to Cyd what they mean.

"These lines" she translates, "are the different stretches of the canal. They're all connected. This one right here, that's the Yellow River. And this one's the East Zhejiang Canal. Here's the Jiangnan Canal. The Yang Canal. Middle River. Huitong River. And the longest is the Southern Canal, where it joins the Wei River. And here, where the Northern Canal ends at Tianjin."

Hop draws several broken lines. "Hee."

"River," Cyd explains.

He draws three circles.

"Huu."

"Lake."

Another long string of words.

"He says the canal makes use of the Yellow River, the Huitong and the Wei. And also these lakes, drawn as circles. Nabshui, Dongjiang, and Liuki."

"Very well. Tell him to place a square for the cities along the way, name each one and say how long it takes to reach them."

By instinct, Hop starts in the south and edges north as he places the cities.

"Yangzhou, San tian."

I look at Cyd.

"Three days to Yangzhou."

I smile. "Go on."

"*Zaozhuang, shi tian. Linqing, shiwu tian. Cangzhou, ershier tian. Tianjin, sanshi tian.*"

"Ten days to Zaozhuang. Always stop there for one day, maybe two. Take on rice." Cyd goes on. "Thirteen to Linquing. Twenty-three, to Chngzhou. And after thirty days, Tianjin."

"Ask how many lock gates along the way, and where they are. Put a dot by them."

Hop places a dot just south of Zaozhuang and Linqing, and north of Chanzhow.

"Good. Now ask where the dacoit are."

Another long explanation before Cyd replies.

"The lakes. They attack on the lakes because soldiers are at every x and dot. But the lakes are hard for soldiers to defend. Too many places for dacoit to hide and wait. And sometimes the dacoit pretend to be a dredge barge. When you pass too close, they attack. That's why canal junks travel together. First and last defense. Also the best."

Hop is called to his duties, and Cyd makes a point of what he's just said.

"Sangshu, the owner of these two junks, thinks traveling in a group is also the best defense for us. And they fit nicely in this line. The *Shilong* and the *Foshan* are both very common junks. Not too big. Not too small. That's why Sangshu chose them. We'll go unnoticed. All the better if no one pays attention to us because they won't know what our cargo is. If the Chohong in Canton knew what we carried, they'd try again to have Sangshu executed. So would my brother."

"Will your absence be noted by your brother?"

She stares at me. "Another surprise question."

"Thought it was time to ask." A half-truth. Certain I've thought of it but never thought to ask before now.

"I won't be truant, if that's what you mean. My brother's on his way to England, so I suggested to the regents at Jordain Bank that this would be a good time for me to visit a sick friend in Macao. But it's obvious I didn't go there." A thoughtful pause. "You might as well be the first to know. I've resigned."

*

19 December 1839
26°Nx113°E
onboard *Shilong*
nautical twilight

I blot my entry, close my log and call for Sergeant Marley to join me in the cramped partition I now call my quarters.

"I see that you've pitched a tent for Miss Jordain."

"Yes, sir."

"It would pass a marine muster, but did it pass hers?"

"I don't know, sir. But she did like the canvas awning I rigged."

"Very well. Come look at this." We stand over the small table Hop has sent in. Spread before us is the foolscap chart for the Grand Canal.

"This is a crude rendering of the Grand Canal. I want you to pay close attention while I copy this chart onto another piece of foolscap. Are you good with charts?"

"Yes, sir."

"Good, because I want you to use this copy to make your own chart and explain each detail to me as you go."

After I'm finished, the Sergeant draws his own chart. When he's done, he checks his work, then hands it to me.

I make a note on his chart. "These co-ordinates are our present location. Twenty-six degrees north, by one hundred thirteen degrees east." I point to the nearest mark, which is a square. "What does that square represent?"

"A city, sir."

"What city?"

"I believe it's Zaozhuang, sir."

"Correct. And from our present location, how far to Zaozhuang?"

"About twenty-four miles."

"Not miles. Express the distance in hours. That's how the captain of *Shilong* measures distance, so we'll do the same. Making three miles in every hour, how many hours to Zaozhuang?"

"Eight hours, sir."

"That gives you more than enough time to copy out another chart before we reach Zaozhuang. I believe we'll stop there, at least long enough for *Foshan* to come alongside. Have a chart ready to give Corporal Penny. Go you now."

10. People Are Dying Who Never Died Before

That night I stand at *Shilong*'s stern with Hop, both of us pointing out constellations.

Hop points to Draco. "De la ke."

I point to Virgo, and name it.

Hop names it in Chinese, "Chunu zuo," then points to Ursa Major. "Beidouxing."

I'm about to point out Polaris when a shout rings sharp from the hold.

"Toudu zhe!"

Hop runs toward the cry just as a *Shilong* mate comes from below, gripping a small, struggling figure who's complaining most indignant.

"Leave me be! You woke me and I was asleep."

A familiar but unforeseen voice.

Once more the call. "Toudu zhe!"

Cyd joins us, and I ask her what it means.

"Stowaway. A boy, I think."

"Gravy Walters," I say under my breath.

Hop unleashes a long tirade.

Cyd explains, "He says the boy snuck on and as soon as we reach Zaozhuang he's going sell him."

I step forward and take Gravy in hand. "Tell Hop he can't do that. The boy's English. I'll take responsibility for him."

Gravy squirms like some cat fighting to get away. But I hold tight, recalling when he once slipped from my grip while onboard *Eleanor*. Hop tries to grab him, but he thinks better of it when Sergeant Marley arrives. There are eight Royal Marines onboard *Shilong*, all armed with muskets and bayonets. They're outnumbered by *Shilong*'s crew of ten, but the junk's crew carries no weapons and don't look eager to fight.

"Sergeant Marley, take the boy to my quarters and stand watch over him. I'll be there shortly. First, I'll have a word with Hop." I turn to Cyd. "Tell him the lad's a ship's boy serving on a frigate at anchor in Canton harbour. I don't know how he came onboard *Shilong*. And this time, Miss Jordain, I'll oblige you not to put words in my mouth."

She tells him. And in reply, another stream of hot words from Hop, followed by Cyd's interpretation.

"He says he doesn't care where the boy came from or how he got here. The boy's a stowaway, and if he does nothing about it, he'll lose face with the other canal junk captains. His family will disown him. He'll become an outcast and die as a leper. Therefore he must sell the boy."

"Then tell him I'll buy the lad."

When Cyd tells Hop, his eyes brighten in expectation.

"*Ershi yingbi.*"

"Twenty coins. Reales, I think."

"Fifteen."

"*Shiwu.*"

"Now he wants twenty-five."

"First he said twenty."

Cid relates my words, then translates Hop's reply. "He says when you lower the price, he raises it. I suggest you pay the twenty-five. And don't wait too long. He might raise it again." She lays a hand on my arm. "If I've put words in your mouth, it's because they're the right ones."

"Tell him I'll pay twenty-five. But first I need to go ashore at Zaozhuang to get the money."

When she explains, Hop nods and walks away, looking most pleased with his windfall.

I turn to her. "Come with me to my quarters."

On the way, I confess the unpromising facts. "Truth is, I won't be finding twenty-five reales in Zaozhuang, or anywhere. When Hop realizes it, I might have to commandeer his junk before he sells the boy."

"I don't think it will come to that. Before we left Canton the Admiral advanced me money from his own purse. It's for me to use as needed. Especially if needed to buy an English subject out of slavery. It's in my trunk. I'll get it."

I open the door to my quarters and light a glim. I expect to see Gravy cowering in the shadows, but he stands defiant in the middle of the room

"That man, he was going to sell me. I heard the lady say it."

"He is going to sell you."

"Can he do that?"

"He can. This isn't England. It's China."

Gravy slumps and groans low. "You said you'd take care of me. But you left."

"I did. But now I'm buying your freedom."

Gravy stares at me.

"Hops's selling you to me."

He breaks down in a sob, weeping uncontrollable. "I saw you leave *Eleanor* and I followed you here. Me and Sauce . . we was the last of us. He said if I come with him, he'd watch out for me. But … but then he become drownded, and thought I'd become drownded, too." His defiance returns. He breaks the cord around his neck that holds the lodestone I gave him and throws it on the deck. "I don't want this."

"When was the last time you ate?"

His shoulders sag, and once more the child comes forth. "*Eleanor*."

"Then you've been on *Shilong* for two days without food." I give him the last of my Stilton and a chunk of stale bread.

Devoured whole! The lads's learned the first lessons of the sea. Eat when you can. Drink when you can. You don't know when you'll get the next chance.

"When was the last time you slept?"

"*Eleanor*. I mean when I got here, I was trying to stay awake. But I was tired and fell asleep behind some boxes. That's when I got woke up and brought on deck."

"I'm confining you to quarters. Try and sleep."

I pick up the lodestone and leave.

*

When we reach Zaozhuang the next afternoon, *Shilong*, *Foshan* and several more canal boats depart the line and tie up at a wide pier, upon which stands an open-sided godown made of bamboo poles and thatched over with woven fronds. A horde of dockworkers come aboard *Shilong* to offload any cargo marked for Zaozhuang, watched smart by the marines to make sure none of the Admiral's chests are taken off. The dockworkers then carry on one hundred sacks of rice, a small portion of grain tribute destined for the capitol.

At noon, a large sampan comes off the canal to lay alongside *Shilong*, and the man working its yuloh gestures for permission to tie on. No doubt this sampan serves as a dwelling, for it has a roof running its entire length, where stands a woman and a boy. The woman holds a speaking trumpet in her right hand, and a cymbal in her left. The boy holds a bowed instrument. Hop gives them permission to tie on, which the man does before ducking into the sampan's cabin. The boy starts to bow his instrument in some high-pitched whine. The music attracts some of *Shilong*'s crew, along with Cyd, who hobbles to the rail and joins me.

"Oh, they're going to perform *bian lian*."

"What's that?" I ask.

"A mask play. Very ancient. Many different kinds, and it looks like this one will be a painted veil performance. That's when the main actor wears several masks, all of them rolled up in the headband he wears throughout the play. Actually they're silk veils painted to show an emotion. Fear, anger, happy, sad. And the actor switches them many times during the performance. A skilled player can make it look like magic." She looks around at the men gathered at the rail. "Magic. That's why these men love this kind of play. It's very popular on the canal. They like to jiayou and boo how."

I give her a questioning look.

"Jiayou, is cheering," she answers, "and boo how is a catcall."

The woman brings the trumpet to her mouth and makes an announcement. Cyd translates.

"We are a humble troupe. Father, mother and son. We are honoured to perform this mask play for you. Behold! The Secret Hidden Treasure of The Wind."

The onlookers energetic jiayou as she clangs on her cymbal with her speaking trumpet. And the same man who asked permission to tie on springs from of a hatch cut in the roof that's now become a small stage. His hair's tied back. He wears a rolled headband and a dark blue robe. Another clang. He turns away, and of a sudden jerks his head back to face us, wearing a white, silk mask, like a veil that spreads from ear to ear, and hangs from his headband to just below his chin. The veil portrays the thoughtful expression of a young woman.

The woman with the trumpet and cymbal steps forward. "Here is the beautiful Feng-shiu," Cyd translates, "Secret Hidden Treasure of the Wind."

The sailors cheer. "Jiayou! Jiayou!"

Another clang and the man's veil becomes the face of a dragon. Bright green scales and ruby red eyes. A frantic wail as the boy saws away on his instrument while the woman narrates the tale.

"And here is Fucanglong, Dragon Seeker of the Secret Hidden Treasure!"

Boo How! Boo How!

A clang, and once more the veil depicts the girl, Feng-shiu. But this time expressing surprise and terror.

Ohhh! moan the sailors.

But then comes another clang and the veil becomes the Dragon striding across the stage with a red silk stringer hanging out like a fiery tongue.

The woman warns. "Feng-shiu! Dragon Seeker of the Secret Hidden Treasure knows you hide a treasure. The secret of the wind! Huff, Feng shiu! Huff and blow the dragon away."

She begins to huff most courageous. The dragon staggers back but then gathers his strength and comes on stronger. Another clang, and the silk veil now becomes the face of a young man. Fierce and determined.

Ohhh!

The woman goes on, while Cyd interprets. "Ah! Here is Jun Di, Lord of Handsome Virtue. Watch out, dragon. Jun Di loves Feng-shiu and has come to save her."

Jiayou!

Clang! And the dragon's veil reappears. But now its scales are pale grey, and its red silk tongue falls off. The dragon crouches low and backs off, until he reaches the stage hatch and tumbles below, followed by a puff of white smoke and the thud of an unseen drum.

Jiayou! Jiayou!" howls the audience.

The boy saws away, and the woman clangs her cymbal most lively.

"Yes! Yes, good people. Feng-shiu's hidden treasure is safe. Hah! And now she wants to share her treasure with you."

The man climbs back through the hatch and stands with his players. He looks away, and then turns back, once more wearing the happy veil of Feng-shiu, Secret Hidden Treasure of the Wind.

Cyd translates as the man speaks for the first and last time. "The Secret Hidden Treasure of the Wind is love!"

Ohhhhh, the sailors groan sentimental.

Cyd only scoffs. "Nonsense."

But when the players pass the hat, she puts in a reale from her own purse.

*

That afternoon Cyd invites me to join her for a meal of mangos and rice.

"Miss Jordain, I can't help but notice. Your ankle gives you a great deal of trouble. It appears to be something you've lived with a long time."

A nod. But nothing more. I press on.

"An old sailmaker onboard *Eleanor* claims his arthritic hurts more when the weather's about to change. Is that true for you?"

"Tommyrot." She rests her foot on the deck, just so. "This is not arthritis. I've lived with this condition since I was ten, when I fell from a horse. My ankle wasn't set properly. It's hurt for thirty years, in all sorts of weather."

"Can you find relief? The Admirals's vedic soma?"

"The Admiral carved me a chuck of it from one of his moulds. Wrapped it in waxed paper and tucked it in my satchel, just in case I wanted to try it. But so far, I haven't. Owen. May I call you Owen?"

"Yes."

"Then you may call me Cyd. The truth is, I was addicted to opium once, when I lived in Calcutta. I took it to relive the pain. But its enslavement was far worse than the pain. So I don't dare think what would happen if I took vedic soma. I might become addicted again. And besides, the Admiral's unsure the hybrid soma can overcome everyone's habit."

"But you're not enslaved now. How did you free yourself?"

"I found something stronger." A pause. A pensive look. "I hope it's not just another addiction." She changes the subject. "I have business in Zaozhuang. One of my brother's agents lives there. No one knows his real name, probably not even his first wife. But he goes by Xi. I have letters for him that need to be delivered in person."

Shilong's cook, Johnny Biscuit, comes to clear our meal, then speaks to Cyd.

"He says he bought a sack of cobras and asks if you'd like to drink cobra blood. He has whisky to wash it down."

"Tell him no."

She grins at Johnny's reply. "Johnny wishes to know if it's too late for cobra blood, or too early for whisky."

She sends him away, then turns to me. "You told Hop you had to go ashore to get his money. But now that I've given you enough to buy the boy's freedom . . . what's his name?"

"Walters. Gravy Walters."

"Yes. So now you don't need to go with me ashore. But you should."

"I don't think so."

"Xo has timely information concerning the Emperor."

"Just the same, I told Hop I'd take responsibility for Gravy Walters. I can't just leave him here on his own."

"Then bring him with us."

"No. The conditions onshore are always in flux. To put the boy at that much risk would be unconscionable."

"More unconscionable than a boy serving on a war ship?"

She raises a brow, waiting for my answer.

"I'll take him along."

"Good. But there's no reason for us to stand out more than we already do. You must wear a hanfu. The boy can wear his slops. I'll braid my hair and wear a quilted peasant jacket. Do you know how to kowtow? Because fifty years ago Lord Macartney's refusal to grovel at the feet of the Ruler of the Celestial Empire was the source of this current state of affairs."

"I doubt I'll ever be in the presence of the Emperor. And it's unlikely a Royal Marine Colonel would kowtow."

"Nor would a certain Sailing Master."

*

We find the rickshaw drivers dicing at the pier. Cyd waves to them, and the next driver in line trundles forward.

When he arrives, Cyd says nothing, but only gestures toward a low hill brimming with shop fronts and lodgings. The drive holds up four fingers.

"He wants four taels. But he expects me to haggle. I think he'll settle for three."

When she holds up three fingers, the driver nods.

"Still too much. But at least I've shown him he can't take complete advantage of every foreign devil, and a woman, to boot. Besides, I always make sure of the fare before getting in. With my ankle, a rickshaw is problematic."

I offer to help her climb in, but she won't have it. The rickshaw tips back, and we begin.

Gravy sits between us, wide-eyed and pointing at a woman with a pole balanced on her shoulder to carry the duck pens suspended on each end.

"What's that?"

"A choggi pole." Cyd brings his hand down. "Don't point. The Chinese are superstitious."

Gravy sniffs the air. "What's that smell?"

Time to step in. "Shut your mouth, boy. You're still under strict discipline."

Our driver trots along, calling to the other rickshaw drivers as we fall in with donkeys burdened with bulging wicker baskets, oxen drawing carts stacked high with ponderous loads, and an endless stream of foot traffic.

Cyd laughs. "The driver's crowing. Says he's charged us twice the normal fare."

"Are you going to tell him you understand what he's saying?"

"No. I prefer keeping the upper hand, especially with rickshaw drivers. They're informants."

"For who?"

"Depends on who pays the most."

When we reach the crown of the hill, Cyd calls for the driver to leave us on a busy corner, and hands over three taels. She nods toward a building with the sign of a printing press displayed over a window. An exposed flight of stairs clings perilous to the side of the building. The steps lead to the second floor, and a landing with a closed entrance.

"Xi lives up there. Let's hope he's home."

This time she accepts my help as we navigate the stairs while she explains that Xi lives with his family in one large room above the shop. When a young girl opens the door, the smell of steamed rice, strong tea, and tobacco smoke rolls out.

"I wish to talk with Xi," Cyd asks in Chinese.

The girl's blank expression makes it plain she doesn't understand. A young woman comes to stand behind her. Cyd asks again. Same blank stare. An ancient arrives. Same result. In the end, the girl, the women, four ancients and a toddler stand at the door. From somewhere in the room a voice calls in English.

"My family is from Xinjiang. They do not understand Chinese. Come in."

The family goes their separate ways into a room consisting mostly of empty space. Bare wooden floor. Two windows facing each other across the room. Beneath one window, the ancients have returned to their game of mahjong, each of them squatting on the floor and hovering over the tiles. In one corner, a small stove with a tea kettle. Sleeping mats rolled up and stowed against a wall, along with two chairs.

At the far end of the room a man sits on a divan smoking a long yellow cigarette. Black hair tied back in a queue. A rounded, pockmarked face. Slitted eyes. Wide cheekbones and a flattened nose. Pencil thin mustache , a few facial hairs sprouting from his chin. This is not a Chinese with Han ancestry. He's Mongolian.

Cyd introduces me in English. "Xi, this is Colonel Harriet."

I have my half-lie prepared, and step forward. "An honour, sir. Miss Jordain is accompanying me to Peking where I'll have the privilege of presenting one hundred chests of Wodenstoke Porcelain to the Emperor. A humble gift from the British traders in Canton."

Xi waves for the girl to set the two chairs before him, then gestures for us to sit.

"You are wise not to wear your uniform, Colonel. As an interloper your presence was noted as soon as you stepped off the pier. I am sure you are aware that your country's shameful attempt to colonize China is an open wound. An atrocity made worse by opium."

Xi's interrupted by a squeal of delight from the girl as she runs to a window, where the head of a dragon floats by, its papier mâché body trailed by some dragon-dance parade. Soon the procession moves on, and Xi continues.

"It would have been better for you to pose as a missionary. The Chinese consider missionaries as irrelevant, so they are mostly overlooked, unless they are involved with Chinese Christian militants. But if the inhabitants of Zaozhuang learn you are a colonel, some will confront you for defending the opium trade," an unreadable shrug, "and some for interfering with it. Such is the duplicity of this war."

"I assure you, sir, England is not at war with China."

Xi scoffs. "At least not declared." He gives me a studied look. "On second thought, you do not have the look of a missionary. Your military bearing cannot be easily erased by a cleric's collar. As for Mr. Jordain's gift, I am the one who suggested the Wodenstoke. It is well known the Emperor is quite fond of it. An irony not lost on his retinue, since Wodenstoke is one of the few trade goods he consents to be imported from England. However, you will not be allowed in the Forbidden City to present Mr. Jordain's offering."

From the print shop below, a leather mallet strikes twice on a galley, preparing for the next job.

"Who is the boy?" Xi asks.

Gravy chimes in, "I'm Gravy."

"What is he doing here?"

"He's in my charge," I reply.

When Xi scowls, Cyd intervenes. "I have your stipend, Xi, and instructions from my brother. Tell me about the current conditions."

Xi draws deep on his cigarette, then stubs it out. "There are nine warships and twenty-seven troopships in Canton Bay. All there to save China from the Chinese."

"My brother's on his way to London to lobby Parliament. He'll be pleased to know they've sent more ships."

The clicking of mahjong tiles, and a dry cackle from the ancients.

"I do not think your brother will be pleased. The increased military presence in Canton has encouraged the opium traders to import even more. As a result, they have flooded the market. Four days ago a chest of opium sold for two hundred reales. Yesterday, one hundred fifty. Today? Who can know?"

"And the Emperor's current state of mind?"

"His intelligencers tell him only what he wants to hear. Therefore he remains unaware that his army and navy are defeated whenever they engage British forces." A long sigh. "I regret to say the Emperor is much given to fantasy. Such as the belief that the greed of opium dealers will lead to their extinction. The dragon consuming its own tail."

"Do you believe it?"

"No. Not until China rids itself of its addiction and the English stop importing it. I, myself, think this and that."

"What do you mean?"

"Your brother pays well. I think that if his bank quits the opium trade," a raised brow, "I will lose a major source of revenue. But …" a reverent bow of his head, followed by a prolonged silence.

"… but what?" Cyd finally asks.

"People are dying who never died before."

From below, the start of a press shakes the room. The toddler begins to fuss. The tea kettle whistles. A squabble erupts at the mahjong tiles, and the girl comes to roll another cigarette for Xi. We let ourselves out.

11. Fix Bayonets

When we return to *Shilong* I no longer restrict Gravy to quarters, and late that night he calls from his deck space in the bow.

"Are we going back to *Eleanor* now?"

"That's a question a ship's boy has no business asking."

"Can I have the lodestone back? Because I shouldn't of flung it."

"We'll see."

"How much did you buy me for, sir?

"Twenty-five Spanish reales."

"How much is that?"

"More than you'll ever earn as a ship's boy."

"I'll pay you back, sir. I will."

"I'm not the one you need to pay back. The ransom came from Miss Jordain, so you'll have to make arrangements with her." A thought arises. "How far have you progressed with your education?"

"On *Eleanor*, Mr. Zenith, he says that in ragged school I'd be in fourth form. What's ragged school, sir?"

"A school for the less fortunate. And fourth form is the rating for a lad about your age."

"It's good being four. Four's me favourite number. But I don't much like becoming educated."

"Even if education could provide you with the means to buy your freedom?"

Hop calls for all hands on deck, where they stand ready to take in the mooring lines. A sure sign we'll be departing Zaozhuang soon.

"My son, Albert, didn't think much of education, either. Not until I showed him a way for knowledge to make him money."

Gravy perks up. "How?"

"It started when Albert was about your age. I'd give him an assignment. Some sort of problem. Or a geography. If he completed it in on time, and it was correct, I'd give him a few pence. He liked education after that."

"I should like it, too! Will you give me a problem for me to make a few pence?"

"Do you know what a backstaff is?"

"No, sir."

"It's a navigational instrument. Hop doesn't have a sextant, and it would be difficult to make one for him. So tomorrow I'll show you how to make a backstaff. When you get it to work, I'll pay you."

"A few pence?"

"No. First I'll give you back your lodestone. We proceed from there."

*

I find Cyd sitting in the shade of her awning, scraping the cake from her pipe.

"Cyd, I want you to ask Johnny Biscuit if he'll give me four chopsticks."

"He won't."

"Why?"

"Four is unlucky. To the Chinese it sounds like their word for death."

"Will he die if you ask him for three?"

"No. He'll be happy. Johnny's a Buddhist, and for Buddhists, three stands for the three jewels. Why do you want chopsticks?"

"To teach Gravy how to make a navigational instrument."

We visit Johnny in his galley and Cyd asks him for the sticks. I collect my building materials, then call Gravy to my quarters.

"Stand near and watch how to make a backstaff. We have three bamboo chopsticks, one foot of lanyard, and a penknife. First, I'll use the lanyard to make a taut line hitch for a hinge knot. That will connect two of the chopsticks end to end. The whole thing has to end up looking like upper and lower jaw bones connected by a hinge that allows it open and shut."

I tie the hinge, then take it apart.

"Now you try."

But Gravy's first attempt comes undone.

"Try again."

Again it fails.

"Again. This time go slow."

He succeeds. And the two chopsticks open and close like a jaw. A jaw that's about six inches long, for both upper and lower.

"Set that aside for now and lay the third chopstick flat on the deck. My thumb is about once inch long, and I'm going to use it to scribe an index bar on the chopstick."

I set my thumb alongside the chopstick, and with my penknife score it just beyond where my thumb ends. I scribe six marks, with each mark one inch apart.

"Now take the index bar we just made and secure one end to the lower jaw. Use a taut line hitch, same as before, and tie it snug so the index bar can't slide."

I watch while he makes the knot.

"Now tie the other end of the bar to the upper jaw. Only this time keep the knot open, so the upper jaw can ride along the bar."

Not perfect, but usable.

"Good." I give him back his lodestone. "When I take the noon line today, I'll teach you how to use a backstaff, then enter our observations in a logbook. Go you now."

I find Cyd and show her what Gravy's just made. She holds it in her small hands, turning it this way and that.

"This is a navigational instrument?"

"A backstaff."

"I've never seen one."

"I'm not surprised. Not many of them around. They're obsolete. Simple, but not as accurate as a Newton's sextant. I just showed Gravy how to make one."

"But if they've fallen into disuse, why would you teach the lad how to make one?"

"I'm not just teaching him how to make a backstaff. I want him to learn the sea."

"Learn it like a sailing master?"

"No, I suspect Gravy has a certain quality beyond that of a sailing master. He has a mercurial nature. A condition that will serve him well in the Royal Navy."

"I hope you're not encouraging him to pursue it."

"I don't believe the mercurial can be encouraged or pursued. It just is. But those who possess it can go far in the Royal Navy. Because they're unpredictable."

"Even to themselves?"

"Particularly to themselves. If the commander of a warship can't predict what he himself is likely to do, then how can the enemy possibly know what to anticipate?"

"You have expectations for him?"

"No. Just a glimmer. And it's nothing the lad's aware of. But as for just now, he wants to give this backstaff to Hop."

"He can't."

"Why not?"

"Because Hop will lose face if a mere child gives him a gift."

"Of course. Don't want Hop to die as a leper."

Cyd's bent smile. "You begin to understand. But Hop considers you his equal. So if you're the one who gives him this backstaff, then the gods won't take offense."

"I also showed Gravy how to make this as a way to start paying you back. I told him you bought his freedom, don't you see, and now he wants to repay you. Tomorrow, I'll show him how to us the backstaff. That's when he can start repaying his debt."

"A clever way to demonstrate the velocity of money. You pay him. He pays me. I replenish the Admiral' purse, from whence Gravy's ransom was obtained. All while he's learning the backstaff, even if it's disused."

"It's not the use of a backstaff I'm teaching. It's to get him in the habit of recording the observations derived from it. It's a practice he'll need if he's ever to advance beyond able seaman"

"How much will you pay him?"

"Tuppence."

"He'll never pay me back at that rate."

"That's why I need your help. Gravy can read, but I want you to give him lessons, so he reads better. He can use those lessons to pay you off faster. Tuppence per lesson. Paid upon completion."

"Why don't you teach him?"

"I don't have any books with me, only charts and manuals, and such. But you read books that don't look over much like any manual. Could you try one on him. Just to see if he's able?"

A squint. "I have one in my trunk that might do. Wait."

She returns with a book in hand.

"Original Stories From Real Life, With Conversations Calculated to Regulate the Affections and Form the Mind to Truth and Goodness" by Mary Wollstonecraft.

"What do you think? Cyd asks.

"I think you can lead a horse to water, but you can't make him read a book."

Cyd laughs. "A break down in logic, however true."

*

At noon line I call Sergeant Marley to the bow. "We're about to enter Dalu Lake. Hop tells me this lake is favoured by dacoit posing as a dredge barge. They stay below deck and wait for a likely looking junk to come near. Then they grapple on and send across a boarding party to plunder the unsuspecting junk. That's why these canal junks try to stay in groups. Something like a school of small fish looking like a large fish in order to discourage predators. So as long as *Shilong* and *Foshan* remain in line, we'll be protected."

"How well are these dacoit armed, sir?"

"Pikes and machetes. But their leader will have a matchlock musket, and maybe pistols. But what they lack in weaponry they make up for in numbers. Hop says twenty or more dacoit have been known to attack a canal junk."

"Not this junk, sir. We'd slaughter 'em."

"No doubt of that, Sergeant. But Hop also says that where the lake narrows it's even more perilous. The dacoit have sampans they keep hidden in the trees along the shoreline, or behind the dykes, and attack before a junk can react."

"I'll mount a guard, sir. Two men forward and two astern. Two along the starboard gunnel, and two more to port. Place a scatter gun in the bow and remind the men to stay out of plain sight. I'll instruct Corporal Penny to mount a guard on *Foshan*, with his scatter gun ready."

I call for Gravy, who arrives most eager with his backstaff.

"I worked it out, sir. At tuppence a lesson it will take me two hundred lessons to pay back Miss Cyd."

"Then let's begin. First, mark the time."

"Twelve, sir."

"Which way is north? Use your lodestone if you need to."

But with no need for his lodestone, Gravy points north, straight up the canal.

"Now open your backstaff wide as it will go. Align the bottom edge, remember, we call that edge the lower jawbone, align it with the horizon, then point the upper jawbone to a point just above the sun. Mind you, don't look at the sun."

Gravy proceeds with great care.

"Now go slow and adjust the upper jawbone by drawing it down to where it points at the sun and stop there."

He does so.

"Now then, look at the number we scribed on the index bar, and call it out."

"Seventy. What does seventy mean, sir?"

"It means on twenty-third December 1839, at noon, and just about to enter Lake Dalu, the sun is approximately seventy degrees above the horizon."

I give him a small pad of foolscap and a pencil stub. "This is your ledger. Don't lose it. Enter today's date, the time, the place, and the angle."

Gravy scratches away most diligent, with his tongue lolling out until he's finished.

"That will do for now." I hand him his first payment. "Now go give this to Miss Jordain."

"When's my next lesson, Mr. Harriet?"

"Tonight. Stellar navigation, if the night sky permits."

*

But the night sky does not permit. Instead, it brings heavy rain, strong winds, lightning and thunder. At dawn, the conditions moderate, but by noon another storm finds us. *Shilong* starts taking on water, and Hop sends his men to the bilge pump. After ten minutes, I tell Sergeant Marley to spell *Shilongs* crew. The marines pump steady for ten minutes, and then five more before the *Shilong*s take over. They pump for fifteen minutes, and then another five. This has become a test of wills! Each shift outlasting the other at each turn. The marines are bigger and stronger but not used to the demanding work of a bilge pump. And during their fourth stint, they begin to slow. The *Shilong* gloat and stand ready to take over. Lucky for the marines, because now the deluge as stopped, and the grand test of will ends in a draw.

But within a minute we hear and feel a solid thunk coming from *Shilong*'s bow. Hop races forward.

"*Sihutong*!"

I look into the water, and need no translation, for *Shilong*'s been struck bows on by a deadhead, the trunk of some big tree that's fallen into the canal after the storm. As I watch it drift by, Cyd comes to join me.

"What was that sound?"

"We've been hit by floating debris."

Hop gathers his crew and calls out.

Cyd translates. "He's swearing. I won't relate that. But he says to lower the lug sail."

"We're pulling out of line, Cyd."

"Is it wise to lose our place?" she asks. "This stretch is favoured by the dacoit."

"Dacoit or not, Hop needs to assess the damage before going on."

Foshan hauls her wind to stand in behind us. Both junks now hug the near bank. The marines stand guard, muskets primed and ready at the half-cock, with their scatter guns aimed at the embankment. I look to the sky. Not long before dusk. I go below, first to make sure of the Admiral's consignment of vedic soma, then to inspect the damage caused by the deadhead. The chests are dry and secure. The tree trunk's smashed on the bow and caved in several strakes just above the waterline. But *Shilong*'s framework remains undamaged. Two inches of water in the hold. I don't know how much this junk needs for ballast, but two inches seems about right, along with the pig iron astride her keel.

I return to Cyd. "Someone will have to go in the water to find out the extent of the damage. Ask Hop if any of his men can swim."

She asks and then translates Hop's reply. "He says one of his crew knew how, but he drowned last spring."

"Outstanding."

But there will be no one drowning in the canal, for the damage is minor, and Hop begins his repair without in need of going in the water. At the bow and stern of each junk the crews drive stakes into the embankment and secure mooring lines. But the repair work is slow, and the file of canal junks soon leaves *Shilong* and *Foshan* to fend for themselves.

In the middle of the night, Sergeant Marley finds me. "I believe the dacoit are close, sir. Before dark I spotted a stretch of shoreline that looks suspicious."

"Where?"

"Not far. On the right bank, where the lake joins the canal. The foliage was a bit off colour there. Camouflage, I think, put in place to conceal some sort of encampment. If the dacoit make an attempt, it will come from there."

"When?"

"Soon. An hour ago I sent my best scout to reconnoiter. He's just returned. He found their bivouac. Impossible to make an accurate count, but he heard many voices, and machetes whetting on a stone. They're getting ready to strike, sir. But we should strike first."

"What do you have in mind?"

"The dacoit have only one approach. They have to walk the dykes and then come across the dry rice paddy. I still have three Congreve rockets. White star clusters. At the right moment I'll use them to light up the field of fire and catch the dacoit in the open." Marley pauses to identify a sound. Likely some night predator moving about, nothing more. "Last month, sir, that skirmish on North Sentinel?"

"Yes?"

"It was no more than idle fighting. My men are eager for a proper dust up."

*

Cyd stands with me at the rail, smoking her pipe. Hop is still in the hold, but the sawing and pounding have tapered off. He sends word, and she translates.

"All that remains is to caulk the staves. Then we go." She rests heavy on the rail. I know her ankle hurts overmuch at night. She point to a star low on the horizon. "Sirius, the Dog Star."

"Its Latin name is Canis Majoris," I reply. "Soon it will take its turn as the Southern Pole Star."

"How soon?"

"In the year sixty-six thousand, two and seventy. Anno Domini.

Her crooked smile. "Are you sure?"

"No one's quite sure of the exact time."

"Well are you sure of the time right now?"

I withdraw my dirk and reflect star shine off its blade to shed light on my pocket watch.

"Three in the morning. Where's Gravy?"

"I sent him to the hold. He asked if he could do something, so I said go help Hop fix the damage."

"Hop will refuse."

"Maybe not, Owen. I taught Gravy to say, 'It's my honor to help.' The boy says he wants nothing more to do with Mary Wollstonecraft. That if he has to learn his letters by reading that woman, then he'd rather go thirsty. So instead I'm teaching him Chinese. Tuppence a lesson."

"More useful, I should think."

Cyd nods. "If he speaks to Hop in Chinese, it will impress him, and he might let Gravy help. Or at least watch. Either way, it should keep him from thinking too much."

"Is he scared?"

"He says he isn't, but he is."

"Are you?"

Cyd nods at the dark shoreline. "I hold no value for the dacoit. Too damaged to sell as a concubine. If they capture me, they'll rape me to death. But I have a brace of pistols, so make sure to say your name before entering my tent. Or I'll shoot." She limps away.

Marley comes to stand with me, and together we study the night. The Sergeant has better night vision, but I hear better. And between us we detect movement. Marley points at a shadow.

"There, do you see it moving?"

"No."

"Look away, then back."

"Yes. There on the dyke."

I hear a faint sound, almost inaudible, but it's out of place. A machete easing out of its sheath.

"They're here," I whisper.

"Give them time to leave the dyke and come across the paddy."

When we hear the snick of a pistol locking back, Marley levels his musket and fires. The shot is the signal for his marines to fire a Congreve, and in not one second a rocket shrieks over *Shilong*'s bow, leaving a trail of flame that detonates overhead, catching the dacoit unprepared, like figures frozen in time. Every marine on *Shilong* opens fire, each choosing his target and taking careful aim. Eight dacoit fall in the first volley, with never a scream or a moan. Just the silence of the dead. The marines on *Foshan* fire, and more dacoit go down. The Congreve burns out, but by then the marines on *Shilong* have reloaded. Now they wait. Once more a rocket lights the night sky. Again the marines take aim and the dead lie heavy on the killing ground. *Foshan*'s marines fire. More dacoit add to the count. The second rocket burns out. But instead of more silence, there comes an unexpected sound.

Marley explains. "Bamboo sticks. They tap them to regroup."

Soon the tapping multiplies, comes closer. The third Congreve goes up. When it detonates the rice paddy teems with dacoit.

"Good God, there's more than I can count. Hop said there's usually no more than twenty."

Marley replies. "Bad information is worse than none."

I draw my pistols and make for Cyd's tent, ready to defend her life. I have two rounds, and so does she. If the dacoit storm her tent we can only hope the four rounds between us are enough to turn them.

Marley calls out. "Prepare to repel boarders. Engage with scatter guns."

The scatter guns take down more dacoit, but still their numbers swell. They throw lines and grapple on to *Shilong*. The marines shoot the first boarders off the rail. But before they can reload the next wave swarms on, wielding their machetes.

Hop screams from the hold, "Kaishi Ba!"

The marines close ranks and charge with fixed bayonets. But in tight quarters a bayonet is no match for a machete. A marine screams in agony. Blood splatters my tunic, a tooth lands on my boot, a shako rolls across the deck. One by one the marines go down. Before I reach Cyd's tent the next wave of boarders comes over the rail. It's too late to stand and fight. Time to make my way aft to cut the mooring line, no matter if *Shilong* is ready. At the bow, Marley does the same. Both lines fall away. The current catches the junk and brings her mid-channel. The marines on *Foshan* fire one last volley, decimating the dacoit standing on the embankment. One's shot dead in his tracks, nine more in retreat. They've had enough.

12. A Mandarin's Greed

As it turns out, Hop's cry from the hold was for us get underway. And within the hour Sergeant Marley presents me with the butcher's bill.

"One dead, sir. Private Brodmin. Three with machete wounds. I've done what I can for them."

"Are you wounded, Sergeant? Your hand's bleeding."

"Not my blood, sir."

"And Hop's crew?"

"Sent below before the assault began. Just as well. They'd have gotten in our way. I'm going ashore now to bury Private Brodmin."

A brief ceremony. Just enough time for his mates to dig a shallow grave, say the Lord's Prayer, leave a marker.

After the service I find Cyd and Gravy standing in front of the marines. Gravy's found a tarred rope shaped into a circle to make a portrait frame.

Cyd calls out. "Shingqui."

Gravy thinks for a moment, then replies, "Angry." He squints his left eye over tight, while keeping the left side of his mouth open to portray some fearsome snarl. The marines laugh grim at his antics.

Cyd calls out again. "Shangxin."

Again Gravy thinks, and then replies, "Sad." And pulls his face doleful long while peering through the frame. Once more the marines laugh.

"Kuaila!"

Gravy thinks for a bit, then responds. "Happy," he says, while looking through the frame with an over bright smile.

Again the marines laugh, for they're all familiar with Gravy's antics. He's playing make-a-face for them, a pastime common to marines and sailors alike. And these men laugh, if only to smooth over the loss of their just buried mate. A simple lot, looking for a brief reprieve from the misery in their lives.

When the game ends, I stand with Cyd. "You just let Gravy keep working off his debt. Learning Chinese words to play make-a-face for the marines."

"I did. He likes it far better than wading through Mary Wollstonecraft's book."

"How much did he just earn?"

"Tuppence a face." She turns and points up the canal. "That village is Changzhou. Before we left Canton, I told Hop I wanted to stop there."

"Why? It's not much more than a landing with a godown."

"Hop knows that, and at first, he didn't want to. But the situation changed last night. He wants those wounded marines off his junk so he's agreed to make the stop. There's a mission outpost at Changzhou. Tongqing. That's the Chinese word for compassion. For years it was just a small Buddhist monastery and orphanage. But recently they've become a mission hospital and school. I know the doctor there. Rohit Pandya. I'm sure he'll take the wounded marines."

"I didn't think the missions operated this far up the canal. A Christian order?"

"Not Christian. It's Bahá'í. But Tongqing isn't an official mission, just a sect of Bahá'í who feel compelled to help free ten million people enslaved by opium. Doctor Pandya's also a Bahá'í, and he came to Tongqing to start a hospital. His wife, Darshana, also came with him to start a school. I know them from Calcutta when I lived with my friend, Iris. She introduced me to the Bahá'í faith, and to her dear friends, Rohit and Darshana. But then they went to Tongqing. And before I left for Canton, Iris wrote them a letter and asked me to deliver it, if I had the chance."

"A good reason to stop there."

"There's another reason. Do you recall what I told you once? That for me, vedic soma might not work, and would only be another form of addiction? Well, there's something more promising at Tongqing. Stronger. More fulfilling."

By noon, *Shilong* and *Foshan* lie alongside the landing at Changzhou. Once ashore, Gravy and I join Cyd and together we walk the slight rise leading to a gathering of small buildings.

Gravy nods at the buildings. "What are those?"

"That's a *siheyuan,*" Cyd explains. "It's a courtyard surrounded by households called hutongs."

At the *siheyuan* a weathered flag flies at the entrance of a two-story structure. Cyd translates what it says. "That's Chinese for Compassion." And then gestures to a symbol above the portal. Gravy says it looks like a row of square knots.

"Not quite. It's the Eternal Knot of Samsara. The endless cycle of birth, death and rebirth."

She taps on the blue lacquered door. A young nun opens it, looks down and smiles at Gravy.

Cyd asks in Chinese. "*Yisheng Pandya, qing.*" And then in English. "Doctor Pandya, please."

The nun understands, either the Chinese or the English, or maybe both, and invites us into the foyer, motioning to a wooden bench. When we sit, she offers us several joss sticks and nods to a stone Buddha sitting in a corner. Then she's off, presumably to find the Doctor.

But instead, an older nun appears. "I'm Quan Duc," she says in English, "Abbess of Tongqing. Please tell me who you are."

"My name is Cyd Jordain."

"Jordain?" Quan Duc cocks an eye. "You are related to Robert Jordain?"

"My brother."

The Abbess stiffens. "What is your business here?"

"I have a letter for Doctor Pandya written by his good friend in Calcutta, Iris Ashford."

Quan Duc looks most distrustful. "Let me see it."

Cyd hands it to her. She studies it for a moment before deciding how to proceed. "I'll give this to the Doctor. I believe he'll want to see you. But he's with patients. It may take a while."

I step forward. "I'm Colonel Harriet. I have three wounded marines in need of the doctor."

"Where are they?"

"On the junk moored at the landing."

"Can they walk?"

"No."

"I'll send stretcher bearers. The Doctor will see them when he can." She looks at Gravy. "Is this boy an orphan you intend to leave with us? Because if you do, we have barely enough room as it is. The nuns are out collecting alms, but there will be no food to spare."

"The boy is my responsibility."

"Very well."

Cyd lays a hand on Quan Duc's sleeve. "It would be my honour, Abbess, to give Tongqing one hundred pounds of rice. I have it stored on the junk and can send it today."

Her eyes soften, if not over much. "You are welcome to wait here for the doctor. Would you care for tea while you wait?"

"That would be fine."

"Very well. A votary will serve it. Now I must tend to duties."

As she departs, I speak low to Cyd. "I don't think the Abbess of Compassion is fond of your brother."

Cyd shrugs, "My brother's respected by very few in China." A deep sigh. "Although at one time he was admired at home. He followed after father and became a doctor." A deep sigh. "I'm convinced becoming a doctor's why Robert changed."

"What do you mean?"

"As a doctor he didn't make much money. But Robert accepted that, until he signed a contract with the East India Company. The remuneration was meagre, but officers on John Company ships are permitted to conduct their own trades. In Canton, Robert soon realized he could make far more money in the opium market than as a doctor. Fifteen years ago he resigned his commission and started his own joint-stock company. And to corner the opium market, he established Jordain Bank. Now he's one of the richest men in the British Empire."

The same nun who let us in returns with fresh brewed tea. Gravy looks after her most fond as she leaves. The entrance hall is in its second or third reincarnation, and in need of a carpenter. A rice paper, saffron-yellow globe hangs high from a vaulted ceiling that accommodates four octagonal windows. They all leak, and water stains discolour the blue plaster walls. The floor is made of teak parquet, but the floor runs slightly downhill on its way to the corridors that meet in the foyer. One passage leads to living quarters, from which emits the noise and chatter of an active order. The other passage leads to chapter and meditation, and the source of a crystalline chant.

When Gravy begins to cry, Cyd asks him why.

"I'm not crying."

"I see. But if you were crying, why would that be?"

"Because that abbess woman, she was right. I'm a orphan. Because Sauce, he was all I had."

Only after all our joss sticks have burned down does Doctor Pandya come to see us. A squat, bald headed man whose pate shines like a buffed acorn. He wears a long, high-collared white coat, spotted with blood.

When he sees Cyd, his eyes beam merry. "Ah, it is you, Miss Jordain. I did not think for this surprise, and you have even brought me the letter of Miss Iris. We shall have a jolly good chat, but first I must speak with the colonel." He turns to me and bows. "I regret it, sir, but one of your men is dead before ever brought to me. But I am pleased to say the other two will not be dead, although both are having the bad machete wounds. I ask them how this can be, but I do not understand what they say. So now I ask you. How is this happening?"

"Last night we were attacked by canal bandits. We fought them off, but our information was incorrect. There were more than we were led to believe."

"Yes, more dacoit have come this year. There is famine on the steppes. The tribes of the Gobi are moving east to find food. Most are honest peasants, but hunger drives them to madness. I am very sorry to not save your soldier."

"Thank you. Are the others fit for duty?"

"No-no. They must rest."

"For how long?"

"One week."

"We can't stay that long. Cyd and I have business that can't wait. But we intend to return by way of the canal. I'll take charge of them then. Is that possible?"

"Yes."

"Doctor Pandya?" Cyd asks, "we were lead to believe that Tongqing's run by the Bahá'í."

"Such is so," the Doctor replies, "and also not so. The monastery and orphanage, they are Buddhist. But along the back wall Quan Duc has allowed our little flock of Bahá'í to build a small hospital and a school. I run the hospital. And my dear wife runs the school. I am the only doctor, and Darshama is the only teacher. We have named it Compassion. Oh, and the Abbess gives us the use of a cottage. Two rooms!" The doctor presses his small, delicate hands together. "Oh, it's of goodness to see you! I invite you both to have the lunch with us."

"Thank you, Doctor. However, we must leave. But as the Colonel said, we'll return for the marines. Then we'll have more time."

The Doctor looks at Gravy. "Who is this boy?"

"I'm not a orphan."

"His name's Gravy Walters," I say. And while explaining that Gravy's with me, I begin to wonder. Could Gravy stay at Tongqing while Cyd and I proceed up the canal?

I take him aside. "Gravy, if the Abbess will agree, I want you to stay here until I get back."

"But I don't belong here."

"No. But you're obliged to obey orders. Mind you, I'm not ordering you to stay, but it will be best if you do. Besides, Miss Jordain's gift of one hundred pounds of rice could put you in good stead with the Abbess."

We rejoin Cyd and the Doctor. "Doctor Pandya," I ask, "do you think the Abbess would allow Gravy to stay at Tongqing while we continue our mission?"

"The orphanage is full. There is little food. It would not be a good thing to ask the Abbess for something she won't do. But the lad, he is welcome to stay with me and my wife. The Bahá'í in Canton send us our rice, don't you see, and if my wife and I eat less, then there will be enough for the lad. Oh! And he can attend school." The Doctor bends down. "Gravy, do you wish to be staying here with me?"

"Mr. Harriet, he says it's my duty to stay."

I place a hand on Gravy's shoulder. "Then it's settled."

We depart. Gravy remains.

*

On the way back to *Shilong*, Cyd takes my arm. "Can I use you for support? Walking downhill is harder than uphill."

"Are you in pain?"

She just tightens her grip and changes the subject.

"Poor Gravy. First's he's a ship's boy and he watches his brother drown. Then a stowaway on a canal junk. He said he was an orphan, but then he told Doctor Pandya he wasn't."

"Orphan or not, he's still a sailor. He belongs on *Eleanor* and I don't intend to leave him for long at Tongqing. Where will you get the rice?"

"I'll buy it from Hop."

"That rice is bound for Tienjin. Are you sure he'll sell it to you?"

"He will if I pay him more than he'd get in Tienjin."

Once onboard, Cyd conducts the transaction straight away. After we watch the rice carried ashore, we sit in the shade of her awning. She rests her foot on a low stool as we watch the junks making their way down the canal, headed south to Canton.

"I thought of telling Doctor Pandya about the vedic soma. He can be trusted to keep it to himself, but I don't want to jeopardize his position at Tongqing. If the Chohong suspected the Doctor of complicity they'd send him back to Calcutta."

I just sit and watch the farmers on shore working in the rice paddies. "I wouldn't want to be a rice farmer. Bent over permanent, eyes cast down. Same as a farrier."

"You were a farrier before going to sea?"

"Father was."

"But you chose another path."

"Not chosen by me. Mother was a weaver. Her income brought in money for the family, but she died giving birth to her fourth child. Without her earnings father went into debt. My Uncle Cedric, mum's only sibling, was a Captain in the Royal Navy. He heard of our misfortune and offered to take one of us to sea and serve as his cabin boy. I was the youngest of three sons and chosen to go with him."

"Did you want to go?"

"No. Newbury was hearth and home. It was all I knew. But I didn't want to stay, either. There are a good many horses in Newbury, and four times as many hoofs for a farrier to trim. But every horse has just one owner, and most are stingy when it comes to paying farriers a fair wage. It was difficult for father to feed us. But if I left there'd be one less mouth to feed. Besides, my older brother was a rotter." I touch the scar on my forehead. "When I was ten I got this when he threw a horseshoe and hit me in the head. He was a mean one. Always flying into fits of rage."

"Did he cause that scar near your left eye, too?"

"That happened on Minorca. Creased by a pistol shot fired by the same man who did this."

I hold up my left hand.

"He shot off your little finger?"

"At Monrovia. I was twelve, and too young to take heed of the Sukiyama's omen."

Cyd looks at me askance, no doubt waiting for me to explain, but just then the sail battens luff. And like a camel who sticks his nose under the tent, an errant gust steals under the awning and disrupts the moment.

"Hop says we'll make Tianjin in three days," I tell Cyd. "He'll wait there for his next cargo. That takes about three more days. Let's wish it won't come to this, but if Hop's still in Tianjin he's offered to transport the marines back to Canton if they have to go back without us. Says he owes the marines for saving his ship."

Cyd agrees. "But we still don't know how to get the Admiral's vedic soma into the Forbidden City. And the Grand Canal ends at Tianjin. That's where the junks transfer cargos, and carts carry it the last twenty miles to Peking. After Teinjin, we have no plan."

"Better than making a plan that comes undone."

*

The jetty at Tienjin is three hundred feet long, with six canal junks tied alongside, end to end, while another four, including *Shilong*, await their turn. We start offloading at two in the morning, and by first light the carts stand ready for my signal to proceed. I summon Sergeant Marley.

"You're provisioned?"

"Six days on full rations, sir."

"Very well. Your men have had little opportunity to maintain their fighting trim, so march them with full packs all the way to Peking. When the carters stop to rest the mules, have your men patrol the road ahead. And when we reach Peking, I want you to bivouac near the Forbidden City. Miss Jordain tells me there's a large parade ground at the front gate. Camp there. Do your men play football?"

"Not football, sir. Cornish hurling. We're from Cornwall."

"I see. Then I want your men to play Cornish hurling on the parade ground."

"Sir?"

"I know it's an unusual request, Sergeant, but the arrival of Royal Marines in Peking will likely put its citizens on edge. So for them to see the marines playing at some sport might make your presence seem less threatening."

"Beg pardon, sir, but have you ever watched Cornish hurling? Much gouging and scraping, and no rules. Might frighten the fine citizens of Peking."

"Or it may amuse them to watch foreign devils knocking each other about."

I meet Cyd at the carts that carry the chests of vedic soma. She declines my offer to help as she climbs onto the lead cart. I sit next to her as she lists more of her concerns.

"The Admiral was unsure of how we should distribute the vedic soma once we arrive in Peking. He admitted it would be a problem. Or as he put it, a bridge we needed to burn before we cross it. Seems a break down in logic, if you ask me."

"Illogical, yet counterintuitive," I reply.

Cyd looks at me curious. "If you say so. But either way, there's a problem with the Forbidden City itself. It's one thing to deliver vedic soma to Peking, but another thing to introduce it into the Emperor's court. And I'm not sure the next twenty miles will give us enough time to plan. Or make a start."

"Start with what you know."

"One thing I know is that all correspondence and goods enter the Forbidden City through the East Glorious Gate."

"Who's in charge of that gate?"

"His name's Lo Ting. He's a correspondence secretary, same as me . Well, actually, he's a low ranking mandarin appointed by the Emperor to record incoming correspondence and freight. It all comes through the East Glorious Gate. And if Lo Ting finds contraband, he confiscates the entire shipment and sends it to a godown. But informants tell me he also has a warehouse of his own. That's for anything he doesn't want to report. I've never been able to confirm it, but I have an address. Dongtanze Alley, at Jinbao Street."

We make unsteady progress, with the mules more interested in stopping to graze the median between the tracks.

Cyd shifts her ankle, then goes on.

"And there's another gate. The West Glorious Gate. All outgoing traffic leaves through there. It's overseen by another correspondence secretary. A mandarin named Darvish."

"The Son of Heaven needs matching secretaries?"

"At first, I thought it was redundant. But it's an ingenious system. My correspondence must always be addressed to Lo Ting, which he then sends on to the Emperor. And the Emperor's replies always come through Darvish" Cyd's crooked smile. "The left hand unaware what the right hand is doing. And only the Emperor knows what's coming and going. When we arrive, I'll meet Lo Ting at the East Gate and conduct business."

"Does he know what's hidden under the Wodenstoke?"

"I don't think so. But if he finds out, he'll take it for himself. Some believe he's the opium dealer who controls the market in the Forbidden City. But he won't know that what we have is vedic soma. He's never heard of it, and it looks, and even smells like moulded balls of opium. So to him it's just more opium he can smuggle into the Forbidden City."

"No turning back if Lo Ting discovers what's in the chests, Cyd. He might have us arrested."

“Not if I show him a copy of the letter I’ve left behind at Tongqing, with instructions for Doctor Pandya to forward it if we go missing. But the letter will implicate Lo Ting.”

“Who would the doctor forward it to?”

“The Viceroy of Zhili. He’s here in Peking.”

“Will he read it? The Emperor’s retainers usually dismiss letters coming from foreigners.”

“They do. But the Viceroy won’t dismiss this one.” Cyd’s crooked grin as she removes the Jordain chop. “Back in Canton the Admiral told me I may be in need of this chop. So I affixed it to my letter. The Viceroy will recognize it and be eager to read the letter. If Lo Ting confiscates the Admiral’s false opium, the profit will be his alone. But not if the Viceroy gets wind of it. A mandarin’s greed is how he gets rich, but it can also be his ruin. It’s a matter of using a mandarin’s greed to our advantage.”

“The Admiral said to burn the bridge before you cross it and then gave you a that chop. But what he gave me is the freedom to do the unexpected.” I halt the cart, open a few chests and shatter the porcelain within.

Cyd glowers steady on, asking why.

“I destroyed it for Lo Ting. When he discovers this broken porcelain, he’ll be obliged to examine every last chest. That’s when he finds the fortune hidden under it.”

Cyd nods. “And then we let him do our bidding?”

“He’ll go on to peddle what he thinks is opium, while all along he’s introducing vedic soma to the Emperor’s court.

Finally a grin from Cyd. “He’ll burn his bridge while he’s standing on it.”

13. The East Glorious Gate

At mid-afternoon, the carts turn left at a crossroads, and soon the outliers of Peking line both sides of the widening road. We pass an increasing array of siheyuans placed haphazard among a great many shops displaying their wares. And carried on the breeze, the smell of steamed rice, the sizzle of pork cooking on open braziers. A stable with a braying donkey who wishes to remain in his stall. Women scurry about. Men stand idle. All watching as two foreigners and a column of marines pass by.

I turn to Cyd. "Back at Tongqing you told me you wouldn't be returning to Canton."

"I won't. That's the bridge I've burned. Sooner or later my brother will discover that I've been working against his interests. He's a spiteful man. At the very least he'd send me back to Calcutta. That's why I intend to stay at Tongqing. I plan to teach at the mission school. There're so many children in the orphanage."

"And not enough food," I remind Cyd. "I don't think the Abbess would allow you to stay."

"She wouldn't. Not unless I bring more."

"More rice?"

"Not rice. The canal junks heading back to Canton carry millet. It's grown in the north, but not in the south. And at the market in Tienjin it's far less expensive than rice. I can afford to buy an entire shipment of millet bound for Canton."

"Are you sure you want to do this?"

"I am. For three years I've been no more than a pawn in my brother's schemes. But as a child, father taught me the value of a pawn. He'd say, 'Cyd, the value of a pawn is that no one pays them much mind, until it's too late."

*

Sergeant Marley musters his men and barks out a command. "Corporal Devoran, begin the match."

The corporal stands on a stone bench, and while holding a six-pound cannon ball, he proclaims. "Town and country do your best, for in this parish I must rest," and then he throws the ball to the men waiting eager in the field of play.

Sergeant Marley joins Cyd and me. "The Corporal's just started the match."

"It's played with a cannon ball?" I ask.

"Not in Cornwall. A hurling ball's made from sheets of sterling silver that have been peened into hemispheres and shaped around a wooden core. Usually weighs about twenty ounces, and just about the size as that lead shot the men are using in its place. Corporal brought a hurling ball with him on *Eleanor*, but he left it back in Canton. Never guessed we'd be playing Cornish hurling in Peking."

"What's the purpose of this game?" Cyd asks.

"To take that ball and carry it across the goal."

"Where's the goal?"

"Good question, ma'am. Back in Cornwall it depends on if you live in town, or in the parish. But the match always starts in town. Not much rough play in town, though, or at least until someone decides to take the ball and run through the parish trying to reach the next village. If he makes it, then he's made a goal. And in between, that's where most of the tackling and smashing takes place. But here in Peking, we'll limit the play to this parade ground."

"Why are they all bunched together like that?" Cyd asks.

"That's a scrum."

"What's that?"

"It's when they huddle together and decide what to have for elevenses."

"Are you're making this up?"

"I am. That's because there are no rules. Only allowances. Such as now. Do you see Private Chancewater there? He's the bloke holding the ball over his head. When the player with the ball holds it over his head, then the others must allow him space."

"How very kind of them," Cyd mocks. "But why's he doing it?"

"He's showing the other team that he wants the spectators to hold the ball for a short spell. It brings good luck to both sides, don't you see?"

"No, I do not see. It's a lot of bunkum."

"But entertaining," I add. "The Chinese seem to enjoy holding the ball."

But when Chancewater takes back the ball, two rivals tackle him, scraping his face along the gravel. The balls squirts away. Which leads to another scrum.

"Now I suppose they're deciding what to have for afternoon tea," Cyd derides.

Marley plays along. "Yes. Well no, not actually. They're watching for the ball to roll out from under the pile."

Soon the ball comes out, and a marine nearby picks it up and runs. But then someone drives a shoulder into his stomach and knocks the breath out of him.

Cyd screams. "My God! They've killed him."

"Not likely. That's Lance Corporal Fowey. He's a tough old jack. But if you want, I'll call off the match."

"Do that. I can't stand to watch anymore." She turns to leave but then looks back. "I need to gather my correspondence for the Emperor. I told Lo Ting we'd be at his gate at eight o-clock tomorrow morning."

Sergeant Marley blows his whistle, and the contest ends. After he dismisses the men, I call him to me.

"Well played, Sergeant."

"A pleasure, sir. Marines like to cuff each other about now and then."

"I'm sure they do. Your first duty in this mission is about to end. It was to make sure Robert Jordain's gift to the Emperor arrived safely in Peking. That's been achieved, so your presence here is no longer needed. Return to your bivouac and remain there until tonight. Then under cover of darkness, break camp and double march back to Tienjin." I look to the sky. "It will rain tonight. Just as good. You might be mistaken in the rain as a band of dacoit out on some raid and be given a wide berth. Say it back."

Marley says it back, and I go on. "You should arrive in Tienjin before first light. Make camp at the jetty and wait two days for Miss Jordain and me to join you. If we don't, then find Hop. He'll probably still be waiting on cargo and told me he'll transport you to Canton."

"Beg pardon, sir, but how am I to pay for it?"

"Hop says he owes you for saving his ship. So take him up on that. Once in Canton, report to Admiral Wynyard that we're likely being detained in Peking. Go you now."

*

The East Glorious Gate may be glorious, but at eight in the morning it looks much the same as any of the lesser gates that give entrance to the Forbidden City. The portal consists of three arched bays leading through the oxblood red walls of the inner sanctum, with the centre arch offering a glimpse of the Hall of Literary Glory. A pavilion stands atop the East Gate, providing the mandarins who assemble there an elevated platform from which to review those arriving to pay homage to the Emperor.

As the footmen lead our carts to the gate, Cyd explains. "The mandarin sitting in the sedan chair above the centre arch, that's Lo Ting. He speaks fluent English, so that's how we'll communicate. He still doesn't know I speak Chinese."

Lo Ting may be no more than a low-ranking mandarin, but nonetheless, he's tricked out smart in a flowing robe of green silk. An obese, effete personage, with overlong fingernails, his queue oiled and braided tight, shaved brows, sunken eyes. With an indifferent gaze the man looks down upon us, and for a brief moment his eyes meet mine, no doubt wondering why a Royal Marine wearing the epaulettes of colonel would call at his gate. But then he goes on to Cyd, acknowledging her with a slight nod before summoning his lackeys. Four liveried servants hurry to his chair and bear him away.

Soon Lo Ting's entourage comes through the middle arch of the East Glorious Gate. He calls for his bearers to stop at our cart. But not set his chair on the paving stones, for that would place him beneath us, and the look in his eye flaunts his intention to remain above Cyd and me. Without a word he extends his hand, not for Cyd to take, but to receive the letters she brings for the

Emperor. He tucks them away in a yellow silk purse encrusted with pearls. Yellow, the royal colour of the Emperor. And pearls, to denote the Ruler of the Celestial Empire. Only then does Lo Ting address me.

"Do you speak Chinese, Colonel?" he asks in English.

But before I can reply, one of his minions cries out, then comes scraping toward his lord to offer a broken piece of Wodenstock.

"Now we shall see if he rises to the bait." Cyd says under her breath.

"The point of no return," I add.

Lo Ting scowls, then orders his bearers to convey him to an open chest, just as his inspectors uncover the vedic soma. He wastes no time in calling the Palace Guard.

"*Ba tamen! Guan jìn jianyu*!

"He just told them to take us to jail. Now I won't have the chance to threaten him with my letter." She turns to me. "If there ever was a time to for me to speak Chinese, it's now. Or we might die in a Chinese jail." She grabs my hand for reassurance and calls out. "*Wǒ zhīdào nà shì chou nǎlǐ! Jiēdào!*"

Lo Ting stares at her in disbelief, then gathers himself and shouts to the guard.

Cyd sighs in relief. "He told them not to take us to jail."

"What did you say to him?"

"That I know all about his stinking godown."

"Does he believe you?"

"Stinking sounds very convincing in Chinese."

"A good start," I reply, "but I can't guess we're free to go."

"We are not. He's taking us to his godown. That may be good, or bad. But either way, he'll soon see a copy of my letter to the Viceroy."

*

The hush in Lo Ting's godown lies heavy as he sits across from us at his black, lacquered desk. The godown is one large room with a wide, thick timbered portal and a half door built into it. A heavy teak plank bars the entrance. Dark walls, twenty feet high, one small window near the ceiling. Slanted beams of morning light reveal the dust motes adrift in the close air. The scent of perfumed incense meant only for the Emperor's nose. A round table made of walnut dominates the middle of the room, and upon it, a glass display case, twelve inches by ten, eight inches high. And within the case, a gleaming timepiece rests on a blue velvet cushion. The case is gold, the face is carved nacre, the hour and minute hands crafted in silver, with twelve sapphire studs to denote the hours. Was this watch destined for the Emperor, and is now in the hands of his corrupt gate keeper? I feel my own timepiece ticking lively in my pocket. Beyond the walnut table, a pile of overlarge Persian rugs stacked six high, the savour of opium, where in a corner I count four chests of it while Lo Ting sits reading Cyd's letter.

January 1840
To the Honourable Viceroy of Zhili, Qishan Suu
Your Most Eminent Sir,

You may wish to know that the Emperor's Keeper of the East Glorious Gate, Lo Ting, maintains a private warehouse at the junction of Dongtanze Alley and Jinbao Street. Jordain Bank has long suspected Lo Ting of storing ill-begotten goods at that location, and further suspects he's storing opium there, which he eventually sells to the Emperor's court. Lo Ting has detained me for threatening to expose him. So this letter has come to you by way of a missionary who I've entrusted with sending on to you if he doesn't hear from me by a certain date. But I have not been in contact with this missionary because I've been taken into custody. I hope this note will be of use to you, and you will take appropriate measures.

I Remain Your Most Humble & Obedient Servant,
Cydney Ellice Jordain
Correspondence Secretary, Jordain Bank

I thought Lo Ting would be most upset with what he's just read, but he just asks Cyd a simple question.

"How long have you known Chinese?"

"Long enough," she replies.

He emits a dismissive sound, then waves the letter in her face. "You are a fool if you think this will be a problem for me. The Viceroy of Zhili is a friend. He will not take measures." Lo Ting points to the Persian rugs. "These were woven for the Emperor and sent through the Kyber Pass. But the Ruler of the Celestial Empire has no need of them. So they will go to Qishan Suu's residence to honour our arrangement. I fill his house with fine things, and in return, he overlooks my private affairs." He slides opens a drawer and removes a humidor and a glass water pipe. "I could have you beheaded and fed to the pigs for trying to smuggle opium into the Forbidden City. Or send you to the Gobi to live with the wild asses. Either way, your opium is now mine, to do with as I please. But is it not," he pauses to stuff the water pipe, then uses a stick of the Emperor's fine incense to light it. "But is it not better to make use of your failed ploy?"

Cyd and I exchange a look. Oh yes! Far better! Lo Ting leans back, exhaling a long stream of smoke.

"I will give you one hundred silver reales for your opium. No doubt this is a great loss for you. But I also offer you the chance of returning to Canton with your lives, where you will invest your silver for opium and have it sent to the East Glorious Gate. If I fail to get my first shipment in forty days, my hashish-eater will kill you." He places his tiny white hands on the black desk and repeats his demand "Silver for opium."

14. I Choose to Stay

Ting claps his hands twice. The lower half of the service door swings wide, and a young man with no legs pulls himself through on a small pallet with wheels. When Lo Ting speaks to him, the man bows, then leaves.

Ting turns to us. "Remove your belongings from the cart and follow him."

The man uses a set of grappling hooks to pull himself along as he leads us through a warren of streets teeming with vendors. It seems he knows where he's going. And I know he's going in circles because twice I smell the offal coming from a wet market and hear the same steady rhythm of a smithy's hammer.

"He's leading us in circles," I tell Cyd. "What did Lo Ting say to him?"

"He called him Yang. But at one point he called him *erzi*. That means son. Lo Ting spoke very fast and I didn't understand all of it. But I caught the word gong ding. That's a vault. I think he told his son to take us to a safe."

When we come to a noodle shop, Yang enters and takes us through the kitchen to a small office, but large enough for a parlour safe. He motions for us to stay back while he works the combination, then removes a velvet purse from his jerkin, and we hear the chink of coins. I count one hundred, after which he closes the safe, spins the dial, hands me the purse and points at the door. Certain his gesture needs no translation. We turn on our heels and depart the noodle shop. But, when we re-enter the lane, we stop.

"Are you lost as me?" Cyd asks.

"Yes."

"Well, lost or not, I'm famished. Let's eat some noodles."

We go back in, but don't eat noodles, though, for Cyd sees on the chalk board that they have what she calls hot pot.

When the cook hears Cyd's halting Chinese, he comes to gawk at the *waiguo* before he speaks.

"He says foreigners must pay first."

I put one silver reale in the cook's palm. The coin pleases him over much.

"I'll order a pot of beef brisket and ginger," Cyd explains, "and a second pot of oyster and pork. We can share."

As we sit waiting, we discuss what just took place at Lo Ting's godown.

"At least we got the vedic soma past his gate," Cyd remarks. "This is turning out better than we dared hope, since now he demands we send more. Seems he's fallen prey to his own avarice. I just wish we knew our way out of here."

The pots arrive piping hot and we tuck in. Just as we finish, a small cannon fires. It's not far off. I look at my watch. Twelve noon.

"When we were at the Forbidden City I saw a signal gun on the rampart. That gun we just heard is probably the same one, marking the noon hour. Let's head that way. Maybe we'll end up at the square where the marines played Cornish hurling."

"I hope so. At least then we'll know where we are, and where to go from there. I suggest we find a carriage and driver to take us back to Tianjin."

"We will. But my mission has changed, Cyd. I'm no longer a Colonel of Marines. I stand out wearing this uniform. So if you see a tailor's shop along the way."

"I'll watch for one. We should go now."

The lane widens into a street jammed with small carts and rickshaws and ends at a broad avenue that borders a square, a thousand feet long, three hundred wide, and thronging with people. I stand on a bench to see better. And there, at the far end, the Forbidden City abuts the square.

"We're in luck. There it lies in all its glory."

"But we can't go near the place now," Cyd warns.

"No. We'll stay on the side streets and look for a coach and driver. But first let's find a tailor."

In not overlong we spot a sign hanging over a shopfront. Caifeng.

"Tailor," Cyd translates.

But the door's locked, and when she knocks, a tiny man peeks through a curtain and whines in a thin voice.

"Likai."

"He says go away."

We keep going, and in the next block we find another tailor. Closed.

"Must be bank holiday for tailors," I carp.

But at the next shop the door stands open. When we enter, a man looks up from his cutting table.

"Shi de?" Yes?

Cyd explains that I want a simple shirt and am willing to pay extra if he can make it while we wait.

The man nods, then holds up two fingers.

"He wants two reales," Cyd tells me.

When I pay, the tailor sizes me up, and then points to an old chesterfield that's somehow found its way to Peking.

"*Yi xiaoshi. Zuó*," he says. One hour. Sit.

When we sit, Cyd massages her ankle.

"Does it hurt?" I ask.

"I have to keep moving," she says, and steps outside.

The tailor talks to himself while making my shirt. I hear a slight stir and turn to the beaded curtain hanging in a doorway, where a girl peeks through. I can't read her young face, but in her eyes, I sense an ancient soul watching me. She comes forward, takes my hand, and tugs. She wants me to come with her. We tread down a tight passageway and stop before a broken door. I know what's on the other side. I smell it. The decay of one empire, the disgrace of another.

I've smelled opium before, but only when it's being transported in a chest, and never when smoked. It smells much of a poppy flower. Not unpleasant at first, but the opium den I've just entered reeks of it, and the smell soon turns my stomach. I don't know how large this room is because its grim walls recede in the shadows. The space is lit by just one small lantern, with its wick turned low, barely shedding enough light to perceive the human figures sprawled on pallets, or in bunks stacked three high. Silent and still, no more than living ghosts. And for the first time in years, I choose not to count what I see.

Each dreamer has his own pipe. A thin bamboo stem with a small clay bowl halfway along, and a metal fitting for a mouthpiece. Amidst the filth on the floor, an opium lamp burns, used to heat the opium before inhaling the vapor. Some manage on their own, but most need the assistance of an old woman who prowls like a spectre. She stops where a man lies motionless, nudging him with her foot. But he doesn't stir. She tries once more, and when there's still no response, she brings up a gob of phlegm, spits it on the floor, and moves on. I suspect that's what I'll remember about this place. Phlegm pooling on a squalid floor. The fate of ten million lives lost to opium, the poison brought here by Robert Jordain and his ilk. And all while our Queen, God Bless Her, remains indifferent to the trade. The woman returns, bringing the tailor with her to help drag away the corpse. When he sees me standing there, he cries out.

"Chuqu!"

I don't know what that means. Nothing good, I don't think, so I depart the den and return to the shop, where my new shirt rests on the cutting table, folded just so. I try it on.

"A good fit," Cyd remarks as she steps in from the street. "I've just hired a coach and driver. We should go."

*

The carriage is a hackney drawn by two small horses. A grey, and a piebald. I watch as the driver kneads the grey's left foreleg with liniment while the piebald nibbles at his straw hat.

"These horses make a good team," I tell Cyd. "But they're small. They can't go all the way to Tianjin in just one day. It's thirty miles."

"The driver's name is Harbin. He told me we'll stop at Langfang. That's about halfway. His sister lives there, and she'll take us in for the night. We can't be on the road after dark. Highwaymen."

Cyd allows me to help her step into the coach, and after I climb in, the driver takes his seat and we set off.

"Sergeant Marley and his men carried light packs for this mission," I tell Cyd, "and he quick-marched them to Tianjin so they may have already booked passage to Canton. A good thing they don't carry over much. I don't, either. A bedroll and a brace of pistols. At least Lo Ting let us keep our possessions. What does chuqu mean?"

"It means 'get out.' Why?"

"That's what the tailor said when he found me in the opium den behind his shop."

"Why were you there?"

"A little girl led me there. I don't know why. She seemed a mysterious child."

Cyd dismisses the notion. "She's probably the tailor's daughter, and her job is to bring in business. Sometimes you make a mystery out of nothing."

"My daughter-in-law thinks so, too. Except she doesn't know the mystery of her own daughter."

"Such as?"

"The Sukiyama."

Cyd thinks for a bit while observing the way ahead before she replies. "You've said that before. Why not tell me more? We have time."

The horses plod along. A magpie circles overhead and cries out, seeming to mock our slow pace while I try to think of where to begin. If there's ever a time to start in the middle of something, then certain this is it. So I tell Cyd about the whispered forewarning at Jamaica Station. And the incident at Volus, along the Aegean coast. I muse over what to say next and am relieved when we stop at a stream to water the horses and give them a rest. Once more underway, I choose to go back to my great grandmother, Sara Cedric, and the rustling leaves of an oak tree.

Cyd looks at me dubious and asks, "Like the Oracle at Delphi?"

"Or a thing just as ancient as that. But with ancestral lineage. Legend has it that Sara Cedric was kin to Morgan y Dylwythen Deg. Welch for Fata Morgana. Not all in my family have that premonition, though. My sister and my son don't. But I suspect my granddaughter does."

"Did you have a premonition about this mission?" Cyd asks.

I've talked overlong, so I choose not to reply. Besides, it's approaching nautical twilight, and the hutongs of Langfang come in sight. We stop at the entrance of a small courtyard, where Harbin leads the horses through. A woman steps from a hut to greet him, and after a long exchange, Harbin explains to Cyd.

"His sister says we can stay here tonight. But her house is just one room, and we have to sleep on the floor. She'll cook rice for us. But she expects us to pay for it, and grain for the horses, too."

Late that night as we shared a narrow space on the floor, Cyd asks me again. "Did you have a premonition about this mission?"

"No. The risk was clearly understood. As a military attaché I was allowed to travel to Peking on my own, but it's likely our troops will come ashore soon, and in great numbers. I'm certain the local militias have been alerted, since they eye us over much as we pass. I hope to fetch Gravy and return to *Eleanor* before the fighting begins."

Cyd speaks low. "I hope the hospital and orphanage at Tongqing don't get caught between."

"You still intend to stay at Tongqing?"

"I'm cold," she replies. "Come warm me."

*

At first light the horses stand patient in their traces while we finish our bowls of rice.

"Are you sure this is rice?" I ask Cyd.

"It's congee. Rice soup. What peasants eat."

"About last night . . ." I begin, but Cyd cuts me off.

"Harbin says we won't get to Tianjin before the grain markets close. That suits me fine, because then we can book passage on a canal junk already loaded with millet. I intend to offer a good price for the millet and pay extra for the captain to stop at Tongqing and unload. Now then, what about last night?"

"I hope you don't ask me to marry you."

For the first time ever since we've met, Cyd laughs merry bright. "Only if you don't ask me to marry you." She extends her hand. "Shake on it?"

We do. But she doesn't let go. Instead, she plants a wet kiss on my forehead and then goes on just as before.

"I have a recipe for flatbread made from millet flour. Bhakri. I learned how to make it in Calcutta. Doesn't taste too good though, but when you're hungry, like at Tongqing.

We get underway. This morning Harbin keeps a better pace. The horses are willing since they know they'll rest well this evening. After two brief rest stops, we reach the outliers of Tianjin and make our way to the wharf. Cyd pays Harbin, and I reward each horse with an apple. Chinese horses. Chinese apples. But no matter where in the world, the sound of a horse crunching an apple is always same.

Once on the wharf, Cyd points to a shed with a sign. "*Matougongren*. I think that means stevedore. I'll ask the headman if they've loaded any junks with millet."

"I don't see Hop's junk. Maybe he left with Sergeant Marley."

"I'll ask about him," Cyd replies.

But the headman fends her off. He stomps his foot and screams and she screams back while pointing at me.

"Say something about me," she tells me.

"What?"

"I don't care. Just say it."

"You … you're a wild mare ruled by the moon."

"Good. Because I just told this man you'd shoot him if he won't talk to me."

The headman considers me for a moment before he replies. Then Cyd explains.

"First, he said a woman can't be on this wharf and told me to leave or he'd have me carried off. But then I pointed at you and told him what you'd do if he didn't talk to me. That's when he pointed at third junk in line. *Changshaw*. It's carrying millet and leaving in the morning. Oh, and he says the *Shilong* left yesterday."

"I wouldn't have shot him. You've put words in mouth again."

Her crooked grin. "Only when they're the right words. Did you really mean that? I'm a wild mare ruled by the moon?"

"Yes. No. I mean it's the first thing that came to mind."

A raised brow as she lights her pipe and draws in. "Let's go find *Changshaw*'s captain and strike a deal."

The captain and owner of *Changshaw* sells Cyd his entire shipment of millet, six hundred pounds, and agrees to offload at Tongqing. But I have my doubts about *Changshaw*. She's a benighted old tramp in sore need of fresh paint and new rigging. Yet upon inspection, I find that her hull is sound, and her cargo hold is dry. However, there's only one passenger cabin, which currently serves as the chain locker. But since it's only one day to Tongqing, Cyd and I book deck passage, and hope it doesn't rain.

But the next morning, even before we leave Tianjin, the rain begins and continues all the way to Tongqing, where Quan Duc stands inside the open-sided godown built on the small wharf, watching *Changshaw* cast her lines. We join her, both of us soaking wet, but most relieved to be out of the rain. Quan Duc's mood is as fowl as the weather, which is to say, unchanged.

"Doctor Pandya has been expecting you," the Abbess begins, "but we weren't expecting a junk to stop here. They hardly ever do, so I came down to find out why."

"They stopped to unload six hundred pounds of millet, all of it meant for the orphanage." Cyd explains.

"Tell them to leave it on the junk. I don't have the money to buy it."

"I bought it. It's for Tongqing."

Quan Duc's blinks once and then responds, "I will inspect it."

Cyd and Quan Duc leave to inspect the millet, leaving me to ask why the Abbess would look a gift horse in the mouth. Soon Doctor Pandya comes scurrying along with a small yellow parasol held high.

"Oh, you are here in the very drenching of rain."

"How is Gravy?" I ask.

"Oh, he is very good. But there are matters, you see. The boy, he is talking in his sleep."

"Yes, I know."

"And while he is doing the talking in his sleep, he is also doing the walking in his sleep. But Quan Duc, she is saying this is the very old thing calling this the kinhin. The meditations walk."

"Where is he?"

"He is in school with Darshana. Come."

I hear Gravy's voice as we stand outside the classroom. When I peek in, I can't help but laugh, for he's standing at Darshana's desk while she sits with a look of wonder colouring her face as he speaks.

"And nine, he's above all the rest, and the other numbers, they don't dare talk to him. Except eight. She's not afraid of nine and reminds him to be kind. And that's how I keep me numbers straight."

Darshana clears her throat. "I see. But what about naught?"

I step in and Gravy shouts my name as he runs to give me a hug. It's only been a few days since I last saw him, but today he stands tall as my chin. Soon he remembers his place and steps back and comes to attention. I hold back a grin while telling him to report.

"I obeyed all of your orders, sir."

"Very well. Gather your kit. We depart soon."

"The boy's leaving?" Darshana asks. "I wish he weren't. He's a good student, when he has an interest in the subject."

"Gravy's in the Royal Navy, ma'am. His place is onboard *Eleanor*."

"Of course. I hope you'll see to his education. He says it was you who taught him this queer way of keeping his numbers straight."

Doctor Pandya joins us and asks me to come with him to his humble dwelling, where we are met with the aroma of curried chicken.

"I have the question, sir. I am wondering why you are not wearing the uniform."

"I apologize for not telling you sooner, Doctor Pandya. I'm not a colonel. I'm a sailing master in the Royal Navy. I can tell you no more."

Just then Cyd steps in and Doctor Pandya brings his hands together.

"Oh Miss Jordain, it is so very good to be seeing you and be looking very well on top of all that. And I wish for us to have the long chat."

"You're very kind, Doctor Pandya, and we'll have a chat. But first I must have a word with Mr. Harriet." She turns to me. "*Changshaw*'s captain says he staying in Tongqing until tomorrow morning, but he'll let us sleep on board tonight."

Doctor Pandya cries out joyous. "Oh! But you must stay here. We will share the meal of curry chicken and basmati rice. Oh, and now I remember to give Mister Harriet the letter with his name on it that was coming here some days before now."

The letter's from Captain de Clery. I break the seal and begin reading.

> 3 February 1840
>
> Harriet,
>
> I advise you to close ranks. On 7, January, twelve hundred Indian sepoys and a hundred British marines came ashore at Canton and laid siege to Fort Tycocktoa. The action routed the Chinese but only escalated the hostilities between Great Britain and China and further encouraged the opium trade. Therefore it remains paramount for you to succeed with your mission. What's more, Admiral Wynyard's health is in decline. It's not been very good for the last year, but after he received a letter from his botanist, he hardly eats. I asked him what was wrong, but he wouldn't say. I've sent this missive by way of canal junk. An unreliable method at best, so I can't know if it will find its way to you.
>
> de Clery

That evening, after curry chicken and rice, we sit at the tiny kitchen table. Doctor Pandya and Cyd have their chat while Darshana and I listen, and it's not overlong before Cyd asks a leading question.

"Darshana, how many students do you have?"

"Today I had thirty-one students in the morning. They are the oldest. In the afternoon I had twenty-seven of the little ones. But the number of students changes every day."

"But it's always a lot. Yes?"

"Yes."

"Too many?"

"No, never too many."

"Oh!" Doctor Pandya intercedes, "Yes, too much many. My dear wife, she will not say it, but this many students are making her very tired. I worry for her health."

I'm certain of what Cyd will say next.

"Darshana, I wonder, would you consider me being your assistant?"

"But are you not leaving to Canton on one day after now?" the Doctor asks.

"No, Doctor Pandya, I'm not going back to Canton."

"But where then will you be going?"

"If you permit me to stay, I'd be honoured to be part of your mission, and to teach. But there's something more. I wish to live my faith as a Bahá'í, and to serve the poor. Here, in Tongqing."

"Oh my. Oh my. Do you hear this, Darshana? Do you not think this a fine thing?"

"I do. But we have no place for Miss Cyd to say."

"Then I will ask the Abbess to make the place for her."

I withdraw Captain de Clery's letter from my vest. "Before you do that, Doctor Pandya, I want to tell you what's in this letter. It seems the hostilities between Great Britain and China have recently spread. British troops have come ashore at Canton, and the Royal Navy maintains a large presence all along the coast. Given the incendiary climate, I wonder if it's wise for you and your wife to remain in Tongqing."

The Doctor sits straight and tall. "I will tell you a thing, sir. Many years before now my wife and me, we are making the vow to live here. So then we will be staying here."

I turn to Cyd. "And you, Miss Jordain?"

"If the Doctor and his wife choose to stay, I choose to stay with them."

*

That night the sky over Tongqing reveals an infinite expanse of stars while Gravy and I stand on the wharf and resume his lessons in stellar navigation.

"Let's begin with a review," I point to Polaris. "What star is that?"

"Beijixing."

"What?"

"It's Chinese for North Star. I learned it in Miss Darshana's school."

"Outstanding."

I go on to point out more stars and constellations, then give Gravy my telescope and tell him to train on two amorphous shapes low in the southern sky."

"Do you see them?" I ask.

"Yes, sir. What are they?"

"The Nebeculae Magellani. The Magellanic Clouds. Difficult to see, but astronomers have observed them for thousands of years. The first record of them was found in pre-historic petroglyphs, somewhere in Chile."

We hear footsteps on the wharf and turn to see Cyd walking toward us.

"I couldn't sleep," she announces.

"Your ankle?" I ask.

She hands me a sealed envelope. "I think you should stop at Zaozhuang and call on Xi. Give him this note. He might have information depicting the proper course of action. I'm telling him in this note that he can trust you."

"Recent information?" I ask.

"No. Intuition from two thousand, BC. From the markings on the back of a tortoise shell."

"Nonsense."

"Possibly. But no more misleading than the tripe believed in Parliament and the Forbidden City. You'd do well to pay Xi a visit.

And there's something else." A brief look at Gravy. "Something we should discuss in private."

I tell Gravy the lesson is over and dismiss him.

"Owen, we might not meet again, so there's something you should know. Over the last past few years I've wanted a child. Never a husband. But yesterday, when you called me a wild mare, well, I don't know what will come of it, but two nights ago, at Langfan, this wild mare was in oestrus."

15. The Hexagram

We depart Tongqing at first light. I stand at the rail thinking about Cyd's last words for me. If I've quickened her, would she let me know? But why would she? She wants no husband. And what's more, I'll be husband no more. Only the widower of my beloved Rebecca.

By sign and gesture I learn that *Changshaw* will stop at Zaozhuang to take on more millet. That will give me enough time to call on Xi and deliver Cyd's note. Gravy's enthused when I tell him he's coming with me. It seems he remembers the young girl who rolled Xi's cigarettes when we visited him the first time.

As we climb the stairs, Gravy asks "Do you think she likes me?"

"She might."

"Because I learned how to say you're pretty. Ni henmei."

"Well then, there you have it."

I knock on the door. The one who opens it is the same girl as before. She looks first at Gravy, whose blushes, then me. She and Xi are the only ones there. I hand her Cyd's note with Xi's name etched in Chinese. She brings it to him, and from his divan he invites us to sit. He reads the note and sets it aside.

"Why are you not in uniform?" he asks.

"Because I'm not a Royal Marine. I'm Sailing Master Owen Harriet, serving on HMS *Eleanor*, currently at Canton. I wore the uniform of a Marine Colonel to assure the save arrival of Robert Jordain's gift of porcelain to the Forbidden City. And perhaps, as a colonel, gain access to the Emperor to thank him for his existence."

"You were sent on a fool's errand."

Not quite, I say to myself. But not to Xi.

"Miss Jordain's note says I can trust you. She says you can reveal the proper course of action."

"Not reveal. But perhaps portray."

"Something to do with markings on the shell of a tortoise?"

"That is the origin. But the practice has transformed itself many times and is now called the Book of Changes. The I Ching."

Xi nods at the young girl, who brings a low table with a thick book and a wooden bowl set upon it. Three bronze coins rest in the bowl.

Xi explains. "These coins are used to summon the I Ching. The ancients used yarrow sticks. That is complicated and can lead to misunderstandings. But the coins are simple. They do not equivocate. One face is yang-hsiao, the male principle, and assigned the value of two. It is represented by the unbroken line. The other face is yin-hsiao, the female entity, with the value of three. It is represented by the broken line. Is this clear?"

No, even though I nod.

Xi looks doubtful of me, but he goes on. "Now think of what is on your mind, take the coins, and toss them on the table."

"It's unclear what's on my mind."

"Then the I Ching will tell you."

I throw the coins and they come up. One male, two female.

The girl chalks them on a slate. Two, three, three. The total value is eight."

"Eight! Me best number!" Gravy chirps.

Xi continues. "The number eight is ruled by the female principle. Therefore the first line in your hexagram is feminine and is represented by a broken line." Xi looks at the girl, who records it.

He goes on. "To compete the hexagram, cast the coins five more times."

I comply, and the girl records the results.

He studies the hexagram, refers to the book, gives it a name. "The Thai Hexagram." He shows it to me, and then recites what's written beneath it.

	HEAVEN	WIND	FIRE	LAKE	EARTH	THUNDER	WATER	MOUNTAIN
HEAVEN	1	9	14	43	11	34	5	26
WIND	44	57	50	28	46	32	48	18
FIRE	13	37	30	49	36	55	63	22
LAKE	10	61	38	58	19	54	60	41
EARTH	12	20	35	45	2	16	8	23
THUNDER	25	42	21	17	24	51	3	27
WATER	6	59	64	47	7	40	29	4
MOUNTAIN	33	53	56	31	15	62	39	52

"No state of peace will remain undisturbed. Even the superior man vacillates and is unsure of his sources. He will engage his forces but will regret it."

I study the hexagram, not knowing how to decipher it. Gravy tugs at my sleeve.

"What does it mean?"

I take a guess. "It means never interrupt the enemy when he's making a mistake."

Xi' s eyes open wide. "You quote Napoleon Bonaparte."

"You knew the God of Clay? Even here in China?"

"He sent an expedition to the Mekong delta. No one knows what became of them, though some believe they were turned to stone."

He gathers the coins and returns two of them to the bowl, but hands the last one to me, and with a cryptic grin, he says, "Time to return the beggar's coin."

*

That afternoon Gravy and I stand on the wharf at Zaozhuang watching the last of the millet swayed into *Changshaw*'s hold. He stares at me most puzzled when I address him as boy, rather than Gravy.

"Boy, I've been too lax with you. You may be in line to study for midshipman, but you're acting as if you're no longer a ship's boy. This junk will take only three more days to reach Canton where you'll resume your duties on board *Eleanor*. So from this point on you will act accordingly, including the proper form of address for an officer. To begin, come to attention and salute."

Gravy salutes, and I return it.

"Next, never speak to an officer unless he speaks to you first, or unless there's information he needs to know. Say it back."

Gravy says it back.

"Now, as for when you jumped ship in Canton. That will have consequences."

"But I . . ."

"Shut your mouth and listen to me. You won't be flogged for that offense. You're too young. But Captain de Clery may order the bosun to cane you."

Gravy slumps.

"Stand at attention."

"How many times will I become caned, sir?"

"That depends on what you say in your own defense. I suggest you look Captain de Clery in the eye and tell him the truth. He needs to hear it from you. But I want you to tell me first. Begin with why you left *Eleanor*."

"When I saw you leave, sir, I wanted to come along because I wanted to learn the navigation. I came ashore on a lugger that just brought stove wood and I saw what ship Miss Jordain and you got on, so I snuck on and hid in the hold. I only left *Eleanor* to find you, sir. And when I found you, I never tried to run. Even when you left me at the orphanage."

A cry from *Changshaw*'s captain, calling for the crew to muster in the waist and prepare to get under way.

I pat Gravy on the shoulder. "I'll attest that you never tried to run from me. But you made a mistake, lad. You must pay for it."

"Will Miss Jordain become caned? Because she ran away, too. I mean from her brother."

I'm about to tell Gravy it was a different situation for Cyd, but think twice, and ask him instead.

"What number does Miss Jordain remind you of?"

He thinks, but not overlong, before answering. "Two. I think she's two. Because she's watchful of me, sir. And her brother. He's three. Because he bullies her. I don't think she should be caned, Mr. Harriet."

*

Three days later, at Canton, Jordain Wharf teems with activity as *Changshaw* ties alongside. I search the outer roads for *Eleanor* and find her at anchor amid twenty-one warships. Among them is the splendid third rate, *Cornwallis*, flagship of the British Squadron.

I hire a bum boat to row Gravy and me out to *Eleanor*. As we draw near, I study her lines, watch how she swings to her anchor, see that her gun ports are open, with the long guns run out. Close ranks, Captain de Clery forewarned me in his note. It appears the entire fleet is now on a war footing. When we tie on at *Eleanor*, Peter Zenith is midshipman of the watch, and meets us at the entry port, along with the master at arms, Corporal Penny, who takes Gravy by the collar and frog marches him away.

Zenith shakes his head rueful. "You found him, sir."

"Rather the other way around, Mr. Zenith. The lad found me. Where's Captain de Clery?"

"In his quarters."

The marine sentry stands his post at the great cabin and knocks once before stepping in to announce my presence. Captain de Clery sits writing at his desk. When I enter, he puts down his quill and strews a bit of sand across the parchment.

"Mister Harriet, you received my note?"

"Yes, sir. At Tongqing."

"Then you know the drums of war grow loud. There's much to discuss, beginning with your mission. Were you successful?"

"Yes, sir."

"Make your report."

Six bells in the afternoon watch ring out, then seven, before I finish my account, ending with Gravy Walters.

de Clery stands from his desk and starts pacing, then stops at the stern gallery windows to observe the harbor. With his back to me, he says.

"Last week Doctor Bryant, the fleet surgeon, came to examine the Admiral."

"How is he, sir?"

“No one knows but the Admiral himself, and he won’t say. So to better see to his needs, Bryant transferred him to the flag ship. The Admiral expects a written report from you, Mr. Harriet, and for you to deliver it in person.” de Clery turns to me. “Perhaps the Admiral will tell you why his ennui has eclipsed his well-being. Dismissed.”

I go below to my quarters, which are much the name as I left them, but for the orange cat who wasn’t here before I went on the mission. It lounges on my berth, and I disturb its repose when I set my ditty bag next to her.

“My apologies,” I say, then look around to discover a few charts that have been used but not replaced exactly as I filed them. But nonetheless, my desk is order, and I begin writing my report, until Jesus Madrid knocks on my door.

“You made it back, Mister Harriet. Can I have word with you?”

“Certain you can, Madrid, but make it brief, if you will. The Admiral’s waiting on my report.”

The loblolly steps in. “I know, sir.” He retrieves a tin of sardines from his waist coat and gives it to me. “The Admiral hardly ever eats, but I know he’ll eat sardines. When you see him, give him these. It’s my last tin.”

“I will. What’s wrong with the Admiral?”

“The fleet surgeon thinks it’s a febrile malady. He tries to cup him every day, but the Admiral won’t have it. Thinks it’s barbaric. So do I. It cures nothing, certainly not a fever.”

“What do you think it is?’

“A chronic condition, I think. A malaise aggravated by news from India.”

*

Onboard *Cornwallis*, Admiral Wynyard’s oak peg lies on the mess deck while a surgeon’s mate applies ointment to his bare stump. When he sees me, he dismisses the mate.

His white hair’s turned waxen yellow, his weathered face gone pallid. His obsidian eyes no longer spark before he speaks, and his voice is wafer thin.

“They say one can feel a lost limb after it’s gone. Rubbish. Once I amputated the thing, I no longer felt it. Cast it aside far up the

Mekong, likely devoured by a host of centipedes. But now, after thirty-seven years, I begin to feel it again."

"Does it hurt, sir?"

"Not as much as Miss Jordain's ankle, I wouldn't think. But at least she still has it." A long pause. "Enough self-pity." He bends low to strap on his peg. "You succeeded, Mister Harriet."

"We did, sir."

I hand him my report.

"Later. First, I want to hear it from you." And of a sudden his military bearing returns. "Proceed."

When I finish, he ponders for a moment before responding.

"I followed my instincts when I entrusted you and Miss Jordain with this mission."

"She did well, sir."

"But you say she won't be returning to Canton."

"No sir."

"Just as good. Canton's no longer safe for an English subject, nor is any trade port in China."

I remember the tin of sardines and give it to the Admiral. "Compliments of Jesus Madrid, sir. He thinks you should eat more. And he thinks you don't have a febrile malady, such as what Doctor Bryant says. If I may ask, sir, what's wrong? I thought you might be pleased with our success."

"I am. But as it turns out, it's all been for nothing." He nods at the letter set on a table. "My botanist tells me, as he puts it, 'I am at the very bad place of my work.' He can't get the hybrid graft to reproduce, which is the only hope for producing enough vedic soma to cure ten million Chinese of their addiction." He adjusts his peg, then goes on. "I served the Crown for over fifty years, Harriet, never asking questions, never questioning answers. To be sure I've committed crimes in the name of the Crown, but never have I partaken in a sin against humanity. Now I've used my influence, meager as it is, to make right what my country has done to the Chinese. I don't love these people, Harriet. In truth, I don't even like them. Their self-image is distorted by hubris. Well, at least what the ruling class believes of itself. But no matter how high the Emperor's throne, he still sits upon his ass, same as a peasant."

We both mind the ship's bell ringing four times in the afternoon watch. Two in the afternoon.

The Admiral goes on. "The peasants are the salt of the earth, although they don't have time to think about it. Not quite noble souls, yet enduring. But now the scourge of opium has eroded their souls. I know its power. You watched as opium slowly devoured me when we served on the Mekong. If it hadn't been for that boy monk. Quey. You must remember him."

"Yes, sir."

He pauses long enough for me to reflect upon our time on the Mekong. I was fifteen then. I thought he was cruel. He served the Crown, but only as an excuse to act as he pleased.

He taps me on the shoulder. "Lost in thought, Mister Harriet? Recalling the Mekong differently than me? I will tell you this. If it wasn't for that monk giving me soma, along with the opium, I would have died on the Mekong. The opium masked my pain, but it drained my will. But the soma became the essence of my resolve. A secular epiphany. As it turned out, I still became addicted to opium, but not so profoundly. And when I returned to India to convalesce on my family's estate, I remembered the effects of the soma. It took many years to find a way to combine the two. The opium and the soma. And a few years more to devise a plan to introduce it into China. A way to overcome the corruption of the British Empire and the decadence of the Chinese. And now my botanist sends me news."

On deck, the signal gun barks and we crane our necks to watch for the hoist. All-frigate-captains-report-to-*Cornwallis*-six-bells-afternoon-watch.

I look at my watch. "That's in an hour, sir. I should return to *Eleanor*."

"No. You should stay. I know why Commodore Stirling's called this council, and it involves *Eleanor*. Why don't you open that tin of sardines? I have biscuits."

After we finish, we sit in silence listening to the activity coming from every deck. The banter of the ratings. The squeal of block and tackle, the rumble of a gun carriage as it's hauled across the deck. And from far forward, someone plays a bugle.

*

I stand in the reception line as three captains are piped aboard *Cornwallis* in the order of their seniority. Captain Montgomery, *Redoubtable*, thirty-six guns. About fifty. Tall. Coal black hair and high forehead, with a widow's peak that makes him look taller yet, piercing, sea-blue eyes and a beaked nose. Captain de Clery's second to step through the entry port, followed by Captain Negril, in command of *Rook*, a bomb ketch with a mortar and a dozen twelve-pound long guns. Negril's about forty, with a bald head round as any cannonball. Scant eyebrows. Narrow set hazel eyes, fleshy nose, a cherubic mouth.

de Clery spots me straight away. "Mister Harriet, come. I want you to act as my aid."

Once gathered in the great cabin the discussion turns to the latest news while waiting for Commodore Stirling to arrive.

"Have you seen the Gazette?" Montgomery asks. "It mentions Hornsea for refusing to surrender his bosun to the Chinese for killing a local."

"And he should have refused," Negril responds. "Can't allow an English subject to be tried in a Chinese court. Might give them pretensions."

"To be sure. Hornsea's father lives in Canton and holds shares in the trade consortium. If the Chinese were permitted to have their way there's no telling who they might arrest. Bad for business, don't you see, legitimate, or otherwise."

Soon the Commodore steps in, followed by his adjutant.

"Gentleman, on five July of last year the Royal Navy bombarded the port of Ting-hai, which was subsequently occupied by the Ninety-Eighth Regiment of Foot. Thereafter, the admiral of the Chinese fleet asked for a suspension of hostilities. However, the Daoguane Emperor has ordered the remainder of his fleet to shelter in smaller ports along the coasts." He nods for his adjutant to spread a coastal chart on the table, then taps a gnarled forefinger on three ports. "Shantou, Donghai, and farther up the coast, the offshore island of Xiaman. These ports are deep enough for a war junk, but third rates would run aground and be subject to shore batteries. Third rates, but not frigates. That's why I've convened this council of war."

As soon as de Clery and I return to *Eleanor* he holds a war council of his own. First Officer Ramsey, Lieutenant Dovecote, and I all study the chart for Xiaman.

de Clery begins. "The Commodore has ordered us to sail to Xiaman, enter the harbour and sink every war junk. Mister Harriet, when was the last time the harbour at Xiaman was sounded?"

"Sixteen December 1835. Thirty feet at the entrance."

"That gives us five feet of clearance," Ramsey advises. "More than adequate."

"It should be, sir, but that sounding was logged by Sailing Master Ayr. I've known Master Ayr for years, and he makes the most detailed entries in his marginalia. And for Xiaman he noted that the entrance to the harbour is three hundred yards wide, and an ebb flow was starting to deposit silt across it. That was five years ago. That silt could have built up by now."

"Could have." de Clery to Lieutenant Dovecote. "The gun sections have been idle for that last few weeks. Have Shotwell build a float and we'll have target practice. Five hundred feet seems about right. Whatever gun hits the mark gets an extra ration of grog. It's two days to Xiaman. That gives the men time to improve upon themselves. Lieutenant Ramsey, prepare to get underway. Dismissed."

As we file out, de Clery calls me back. "Mister Harriet, I can't trust a sounding from five years past. So we'll take our own, and you'll oversee it. But you must go detected, so this operation will be conducted in the dark of night. In two days, there will be no more than a quarter moon. Make use of that. Hopefully it will be overcast. Take the cutter and the best leadsman."

A dark blue sea. Light air. *Eleanor* makes her way close hauled under reduced sail. Bunny Shotwell returns from setting out the target he's cobbled together for gunnery practice. Captain de Clery, Lieutenant Dovecote and I stand on the gun deck watching the long guns run out.

"Lieutenant," de Clery asks, "did you know that at one time *Eleanor*'s guns were feared for their deadly accuracy?"

"No, sir, I did not. Unfortunately, I don't hold much hope for accuracy on this day. The crews are eager to do well, sir, but they don't get the chance to unlimber very much. Five hundred feet isn't a great distance, but still, it's a small target. I don't think any gun will hit it."

"But come close?"

"Well, sir, I doubt there'll be an extra ration of grog today."

Midshipman Moon comes to report. "Port battery ready to fire, sir."

Dovecote's stands tall, waiting for *Eleanor* to rise on the swell. He's about to order gun one to fire, but instead, it's gun three that fires, and in an instant the target's blown to splinters. A lucky shot, no doubt, but nonetheless it raises a great huzzah. But instanter comes a cheerless cry from gun three.

"Hell Jesus! The thing went off on its own."

Followed by a scream. "It's smashed 'is 'ead to a bloody pulp."

We all rush forward, and de Clery demands, "Who's gunner's mate on three?"

"Worthing, sir."

Worthing looks most grim. de Clery asks, "What's your mate's name, Worthing?"

"Murphy, sir. The man were a lubber, sir. Didn't know to stay clear of the gun. Breach caught him on the recoil. That gun, it went off premature like. I were about to traverse it, but it went off before I ever even took aim."

"Why did it fire, Worthing?"

"I … I don't know, sir. But I know it weren't no cook off. It were a cold gun, sir. Not been fired in a while."

"Was the gun primed?"

"No, sir. I made sure to check on that before we run out. But there could 'a been powder residue in the primer. I mean, from the last time it were fired. A static spark might 'a set 'er off."

"Very well. Be prepared to give sworn testimony. Dismissed. Dovecote."

"Sir?"

"The gun drill is postponed. Begin an investigation immediately. Start with checking the primer on every piece." He turns to me. "Mister Harriet, join me in my quarters."

In the great cabin de Clery stands at his desk. "I've been putting this off, Harriet, but now I must act. Gravy Walters. I could have him caned. You vouched for him, so convince me not to do it."

I think overlong. "Midshipman Zenith's in charge of the ship's boys, sir. Perhaps he could be asked what to do with Walters."

"Very well." He calls for the marine sentry standing his watch, and the man steps in.

"Send someone to fetch Mister Zenith."

When Peter Zenith arrives, he looks guilty of having committed some gaff. The very look all midshipman have when called before their captain.

"Mister Zenith, you're in charge of ship's boys, and as such you were upbraided when Gravy Walters ran." de Clery begins to pace. "Mister Harriet and I have been discussing punishment for the boy's offense, and Harriet's put forth a suggestion." de Clery stops and faces Zenith. "He has suggested we ask your opinion on the matter. Do you have one?"

All grows quiet in the cabin. *Eleanor* tops a comber and slides down the back side. The tiller, one deck below, creaks in its rudder stock. Zenith frowns, thinking it over. Finally, he breaths deep, and speaks.

"I think, sir, that Walters must be held liable for what he did, but he shouldn't be caned. I would like to put forth what I believe is a suitable disciplinary action. He should be made to muck out the chain locker."

*

The next day after noon line, de Clery calls me to his quarters, where a hand drawn map lies on a table.

"This map was drawn by the Commodore's informant at Xiaman. Two small points flank the entrance to the harbour. One point to the north, and one to the south. At night, both points are marked by fires keepers. Those two keepers will surely see a cutter sounding the entrance and raise an alarm, so they must be dealt with. Which of Sergeant Marley's marines is best with a quiet kill?"

"I'm sure the Sergeant will put forth his own name, sir."

"Then he'll go with you. Who'll go as leadsman?"

"Oren, sir. Eps has more experience, but Oren has the sharper eye for a night operation."

de Clery nods. "Very well. Now then, to insure no one sees what we're doing, I plan to stay below the horizon and put in the cutter five miles offshore. Choose eight strong backs to man the oars and take the bosun to go as coxswain." He steps to the grating and studies the cirrus clouds racing high overhead. "Crossing clouds. Should bring weather tonight. Be ready at twilight."

The sun lies crimson on the horizon, sinking fast. The bosun secures the davits and is about to sway out the cutter.

"Have your men greased the thole pins, Brown?"

"Yes, sir. Slick as a whore's cunny."

"When was the last time this boat was inspected?"

"Nine days ago, at Canton. Wouldn't want it to sink all around us." He checks the sky. "It'll rain tonight. When's the last time you had to bail?"

"Before you ever went to sea, Brown."

Sergeant Marley joins us. He wears all black and has smeared his face with soot. He takes his place and we set off. After the first hundred strokes Brown orders the first two oarsmen to ship oars and rest. After the next hundred strokes, the second set rests, while the first oarsmen resume their steady pull. Always two men resting. Always six men rowing, until I spot one small fire on the still unseen coast. Then another.

"Brown, do you see them?"

"Yes, sir.

"Land us fifty yards short of that nearest fire. Sergeant Marley, make ready to go ashore. After you dispatch the first watchman, return to the cutter and we'll go on."

Marley enters the water, wades ashore, and disappears. When he returns, we go on to the second fire. It starts to rain. It must be slowing Marley because this time it's taking overlong.

"We'll wait five minutes more," I tell Brown, "then you go find out what's keeping him."

It begins to rain heavy. As the oarsman bail, a muted howl comes from the point and then silence.

"Take a mate and go find him."

Soon Brown returns with Marley leaning on him. They help him climb in the cutter, where he bleeds from the gash above his right knee. While he dresses his own wound, he explains.

"He saw me first and sliced me with his parang. I slipped in behind, but he screamed before could I slit his throat."

"We heard the scream. Do you think anyone else did?"

"I don't think so, sir. Not in this rain."

"Then let's get on with what we came here to do."

We begin at the south and sound our way across the entrance to the harbour. Oren calls out low, marking the depth while I record it. Five feet. Six feet. Nine, twelve, twenty, twenty-five feet. At midpoint, the soundings start to shallow up until we nearly run aground, leaving no doubt that when *Eleanor* enters the harbour she must bear south, where there's clearance.

16. Easy Prey

The rain stops and the sky clears. At first light the Eleanors beat to quarters. de Clery makes clear how to proceed.

"They've discovered those fire keepers by now. Likely they've made preparations for an assault of some kind. But the war junks at Xiaman are no match for *Eleanor.* I shall sink every one of them. Let us press on."

We enter on the tide, making sure to bear south with all guns primed and ready. I count nine war junks in two parallel lines, anchored two hundred feet offshore.

"Easy prey," smirks Andrews, standing his watch at the helm.

"I don't like it," de Clery says. "They must have seen us by now, but I see no activity on deck."

"Maybe they've abandoned ship, sir."

"We shall see. Andrews, bring us between those junks to make use of both batteries. We'll make one pass," he looks to *Eleanor*'s banner. "And if the wind holds, we'll come about on a reverse heading just to make sure of any junk still afloat."

A short wait. But for the gun crews any wait seems over long. Soon enough, though, both the port and starboard batteries bear on their targets. And open fire at point-blank range. Impossible to miss. Each round hits home. The masts on every junk crash to the deck. *Eleanor*'s guns blow jagged holes through every hull to reveal fires burning below deck. But no one clears the damage or fights the fires.

Same as de Clery, I begin not to like it. And to like it even less when a lookout hails the deck.

"Sampans making for us. Bows on."

de Clery turns to me. "Go aloft."

I stand on the maintop with my glass and train on the sampans. Twelve in all, each one making for *Eleanor* with two men working the yuloh and one man standing over a keg. A keg with a fuse sticking out, and with the man standing over it with a smoldering punk. Good Christ!

I call to the deck. "A dozen sampans with powder kegs ready to be lit off. Making straight for us."

de Clery reacts instanter. "Steer to port. Bring our starboard carronades to bear."

The carronades fire a ragged salvo that reduces the lead sampan to matchwood, just as more sampans come on relentless.

de Clery thinks it through. "Sergeant Marley, they don't intend to board this ship, just blow it up. Along with themselves, it would seem. Send your men to the fighting tops."

The marines shoot every man off the sampans, and the fuses remain unlit. All but for one sampan that's managed to slip through and now approaches *Eleanor* with its fuse burning.

"Brown!" de Clery calls out, "rig the bilge pump and run the hose to the starboard entry port."

In not one minute Brown brings the hose up the gangway and to the entry port with bilge water already gushing. When the water douses the fuse, a cheer rises from all quarters. But just then a shrill voice calls from far forward. Gravy Walters.

"Another sampan! It's under the bow sprit!"

Gravy runs aft, but he trips on a gun slide, falls to the deck and knocks himself cold. Zenith's first to react, and dares run for Gravy and carry him below. No one risks going forward to try and sink that sampan, except for Captain de Clery, who races to the bowsprit and crawls out on its mast. A lone figure fighting to save his ship. The sight puts me to shame, and I won't have it. I grab the hose and climb onto the bowsprit. de Clery's about to drop onto the sampan, where a man lies unmoving, slumped across the yuloh with blood on the planks.

I call out. "Sir! The hose!"

But by now the bilge is pumped dry and there's no more water in the hose. We watch as the fuse burns short, share a look, and expect to die. The keg detonates, but the powder's damp, and the explosion's less violent. But still, de Clery and I are blown off the bowsprit and into the water. de Clery goes under. I swim for him, bring him up, and we wait to be fished out.

"Your arm's bent most queer, sir."

"No matter. Can't swim anyway." But then he grins. "I shall name you in my report."

"For saving you?"

"No. For being the only one willing to die with me."

*

The explosion damages *Eleanor*'s cutwater. Shotwell repairs it as best he can but says he can do no more until we lie at anchor. That will be at Canton. Now that we've completed our mission, we're expected to return and report to Commodore Stirling.

The only injuries we've sustained are the Captain's elbow, a knock on Gravy's head, and although I didn't feel it until brought back onboard, a five-inch splinter that's pierced my left leg just above the knee. A most gruesome looking thing, as are most splinter wounds, that hurts over much as Madrid removes the splinter and stitches the gash.

"Could have severed an artery, Mister Harriet. Then the sailmaker would be stitching you into a hammock."

"How's Gravy Walters?"

"Just a bump, sir."

"de Clery?"

"I've put his left arm in a sling. He's left-handed and can't write so he wants his report ready for Commodore Stirling by the time we make Canton. He needs you for dictation."

Madrid closes the wound with a final stitch, ties a surgeon's knot, and snips the catgut. He's about to leave but then asks.

"The Admiral permitted me to read your report, sir. The mission's had good luck. And if I may say so, a bit of blind luck when Wick lost his way and then found us by chance off Purba. And then you made your own good fortune at the East Glorious Gate. I mean, when you turned Lo Ting's avarice into a way to smuggle vedic soma inside the Forbidden City." Madrid sets down his kit. "But what's to come of the Admiral's endeavour? He chose us to take part in his quest. Me, de Clery, you, and Miss Jordain. I think it's because he believed we'd wouldn't give up." Madrid sits on my bunk. "Mister Harriet, between you and me, he won't live much longer. The fleet surgeon won't allow me to give the him vedic soma. Says he's never heard of it. The Admiral won't allow the man to cup him, so he bleeds him in his sleep. Which is most of the time. Before the fool bleeds the him dry, I believe he'd like to know we'll keep trying in some way."

"And you believe that way is for me to chronicle the Admiral's covert efforts."

"I do sir. People should be reminded of Parliament's tacit approval of the opium war. You could send your work to the Gazette."

"Hardly. The Gazette's not in the habit of publishing work submitted by a sailing master. But The Nautical Almanac . . . if I were to mention the Admiral's venture in the marginalia of my log, the Almanac might print it."

"But they can't do that until you write it, Mister Harriet. Are you well enough to try?"

"I am."

After deciding just where to begin, I set a sheet of parchment and a pot of ink on my desk, dress my quill and begin, beginning on the day I received orders to report to Dogs Island.

17. Apocrypha

We return to Canton on the first of March 1840, following in the wake of the mail packet arriving from Georgetown. The Eleanors are most keen for letters from home, and as the packet offloads its sacks of mail, they line the railing.

"Hope me bride writ me a letter," Cheeky Dravits calls out.

His best mate, Apple Swank, laughs. "Why? You don't read none."

Jode Hector boasts, "I read some,'cept I ain't got no wife."

"'cause yer too unbeautiful to be wed."

Hector shifts his quid and spits over the rail. "Still prettier than you, me darlin.'"

Light banter. Yet I know they miss their home waters. Even more so when there's mail. Same as me. For many years, my good wife Becca wrote to me most unflagging. Her last letter was postmarked just a week before she died. She'd always put a tassel of timothy grass in her letters because I said her scent was like a field of timothy. I can still smell her. I should have been the one who died first.

Seven bells in the forenoon watch. Thirty minutes until noon line. I've assigned Mister Zenith to take the sighting, and I'll join him on the maintop to supervise. On my way, I pass through the officers' mess, where Andrews and Dovecote discuss the newspapers just arrived from home. Among them are the Caledonian Morning Dispatch, and the Inverness Advertiser. The information is six months old, but new to us, although Andrews takes issue with a description of the Battle of Kowloon.

"I see in the Caledonian that hostilities began when the Chinese were first to fire on the fourteen-gun cutter, *Louisa.* That's when she was trying to relieve the cantonment at Hong Kong. But my cousin's a midshipman on *Louisa.* We had a chance to visit a while back, and he said *Louisa* fired first."

"Is that so." Dovecote replies.

"According to the Caledonian, three war junks closed on *Louisa*, causing great damage to the cutter. But that's not what my cousin claims. He told me *Louisa* was the first to fire. And when the junks responded, every one of their rounds threw high, leaving *Louisa* to answered with grapeshot. She swept the decks of a great many Chinese. I can't think why my cousin would lie, so I don't know why these papers are allowed to print such folderol." Andrews folds the broadsheet. "What do you think, Mister Harriet?"

"I have the right to silence, Lieutenant Andrews."

Dovecote enjoys my quip and then adds. "Unlike those called before the Star Chamber, Mister Harriet? Where at one time the accused were forced to choose between lying under oath or betraying their own selves? But beyond that, it would appear Her Majesty's subjects choose to look the other way, as long as they get their tea and silk. Well, at least the Advertiser bothered to include a statement from the Chief Superintendent of Trade at Canton. I'll read it verbatim. 'The men of the English nation desire nothing but peace; but they cannot submit to be poisoned and starved. The Imperial cruisers they have no to wish to molest or impede; but they must not prevent the people from selling. To deprive men of food is the act only of the unfriendly and hostile.'" Dovecote looks up. "So there you have it, gentleman. It seems most of the Queen's subjects simply don't care, while here in China we're left to do defend the Realm."

*

After recording the noon line, I ask Zenith how Gravy's getting along.

"Now that you ask, sir, not so good, at least not to my way of thinking. His mates inflate his own self-image when they say he's very stout for braving the horrors of the chain locker, and that he saved the ship when he spotted that sampan under the bowsprit. Father would ask me why a good self-image isn't so good, and that my conclusion is contrary to intuition. Even has a name for it. Calls it counterintuitive. But I doubt swabbing out the chain locker was an act of bravery. It was Gravy's punishment. And spotting that sampan was a matter of chance, although he did react quickly. And he's also learning Chinese. He said that before he left the mission at Tongqing Miss Pandya gave him a compendium of sorts. Chinese translated into English and such. Said she wrote it herself. He's become quite proficient, far as I know. I don't know how much good it will do him though, except father thinks if one wishes to command his own language, then he must also know a second language. When the time comes, I still might consider putting forth his name as a candidate for midshipman." Zenith sighs. "My apologies, sir. I've prattled on."

We're about to return to the deck when he spots a jolly boat departing *Cornwallis* and making direct for *Eleanor.* He trains his scope and follows the boat's progress.

"There's a lieutenant in that jolly boat, sir, clutching a canvas pouch."

The lieutenant's greeted at the entry port and led to de Clery's quarters. In not five minutes de Clery sends for his officers, and for me as well, and to bring my charts for Hainan Island.

"Gentlemen. I have orders from Commodore Stirling. We're to join *Redoubtable* and *Rook* in patrolling the Qiongzhou Strait, at Hainan. The island has a population of about one hundred thousand. Most of them are rice farmers, and on a good year the island yields three rice harvests, which contributes a substantial amount to the grain tribute. If the situation in Canton continues to worsen, the Royal Navy has been ordered to be in place to interrupt that supply of rice. Lieutenant Ramsey, how soon before we can get under way?"

"Tomorrow morning, sir, on the tide."

"Very well. Set the watch bill. Lieutenant Dovecote. What is the status of your guns?"

"All operational, sir. The shot racks are full. The powder magazine will be fully replenished by this evening."

"See that they are. Mister Harriet, inform us of Qiongzhou Strait."

I spread the chart on his table. "The straight runs east and west between Hainan Island, at nineteen degrees North, by one hundred nine degrees East. Hainan's a rather large island, sir, almost half the size of Ireland. And the strait's about twenty miles wide. Situated on the northern tip of Hainan, near the port of Haikou. The straight separates Hainan from the Leizhou Peninsula and connects the Gulf of Tonkin with the South China

Sea. It was sounded last December, with no bottom found in the middle passage. The Black Tide generates a current flowing west to east through the straight. Typhoons occasionally close the straight, which is heavily trafficked."

"Very well. You're all dismissed. Except you, Mister Harriet. Captain Montgomery will be in command of this operation, and he wants Negril and me to meet with him before we depart, and asks us to bring our sailing masters." de Clery checks the time. "We leave for *Redoubtable* in an hour."

As we approach *Redoubtable* I study her lines. A thirty-six-gun, Apollo Class frigate. She's been at sea for a year, on station in Canton for most of it, and beginning to show signs of a long deployment. Her brightwork's tarnished, her white gun stripe's in need of fresh paint. Her sails, although furled, look weathered and grey. But her Captain, Charles Montgomery, has kept his men most busy maintaining her trim. The brisk banter of the watch on deck and taught rigging humming in a brisk breeze as we pass under the gallery. But then, an ungodly screech comes from the great cabin. An inhuman shriek, although certain it's produced by some living thing.

"God Almighty!" de Clery exclaims. "What is that?"

I don't know. But before I can reply we've already tied on at the entry port, where we'er met by a midshipman.

"Captain, de Clery." He salutes and then looks at me. "And you're Master Harriet."

"I am."

"What was the abominable sound we just heard?" de Clery asks.

"Oh, that's the Captain's lyrebird, sir. Come, I'll bring you to his quarters."

"Is it dangerous in there?"

"Oh no, sir. L'rac's quite tame. And besides, he's just a bird."

He brings us to the great cabin, where Montgomery stands at an aviary taking up half of the cabin, hand feeding a bird that resembles some sort of grouse with long tail feathers.

He turns to us. "Ah, you're early. Be with you in a minute. Must finish with L'rac."

The bird tips up his bill, then cries out. But this time it sounds like the clank of a capstan.

"What kind of bird is that?" de Clary asks.

"It's a Supurb Lyrebird. From Australia. I've had L'rac for several years now. I used to keep a rather large assortment of birds. Kookburras. Bell Birds. They sound just like a bell, don't you see. A Peter Follanbee. A Willie Wagtail. I forget what others, but they all come from Australia. And a lively lot they were, calling out for hours on end. But an ornithologist friend told me a Supurb Lyrebird can mimic all those birds, as well a good number of other things. So now it's only L'rac."

Just then the bird makes a farting noise.

Montgomery tsks. "Please, L'rac, be civil."

A knock at the door. The marine sentry steps in. "Captain Negril here to see you, sir. And his sailing master."

Montgomery draws a drape to close off L'rac. "There now, time for your nap."

He begins with introductions all around, ending with his own Sailing Master, James Baily. A man renown among sailing masters for his most curious apocrypha.

Montgomery goes on. "Gentlemen, since the onset of this conflict the Royal Navy has had its way with Emperor's fleet. We patrol the South China Sea with impunity. Maintain a presence in his trade ports. And now this squadron is about to extend that presence. We will search any vessel we come across in Qiongzhou Straight and sink all Chinese war junks we find. This is an independent operation, and the Commodore has given me carte blanche. So I plan to divide the straight into three areas of operation. North, middle, and south. Negril, you patrol the north. de Clery you take the middle transit. I'll watch the south straight and on occasion sail *Redoubtable* into Haikou harbour and harass the city. The strait isn't all the wide so it shouldn't be difficult to stay in communication, especially if we all patrol along the same meridian, at approximately one hundred nine degrees east longitude. Questions?"

Negril clears his throat. "You plan to fire on Haikou?"

"Yes."

"What would provoke you?"

"No provocation necessary, Negril." Montgomery retrieves a set of dice from his desk drawer. "Every morning I shall roll these dice. If the sum turns up an even number, then I stand into Haikou and give them a broadside. An odd number results in no action on that day."

"The roll of the dice. That should keep them guessing."

"It will, de Clary. Even more so if I had someone who knows Chinese. That way I'd send the magistrate at Haikou a note telling him exactly what I intend to do." Montgomery laughs. "Except I won't even know myself, at least not until I roll the dice each morning. Do any of you know Chinese?"

No response.

"A pity. Nevertheless, we depart Canton tomorrow morning. Dismissed."

In the gig, I tell de Clery about Gravy.

"Do you think Walters knows enough Chinese to write a note for Montgomery?" de Clery asks.

"He might, if is was a simple note."

de Clery thinks it over, and by the time we reach *Eleanor*, he's made up his mind.

"Stay in the gig. I'm sending Gravy over to Montgomery immediately, and I want you to go with him."

"Yes, sir. Mister Zenith told me Gravy has a book for English and Chinese. He should bring that with him."

In not overlong, Gravy appears at the entry port holding his book and makes his way down the tumble home. After we fend off, I ask him if he understands what's expected of him.

"Will Captain Montgomery pay me for knowing Chinese?" he asks.

"No."

"Because Miss Jordain, she already paid me to learn. But if I don't know what he wants me to write, will I have to pay it back?"

"I don't think so."

Twenty strokes bring us closer to *Redoubtable*, and Gravy starts to fret.

"But if I can't write what he wants, will he send me to the chain locker?"

"No. He only wants to send the Emperor's magistrate a simple note. That his city will come under attack on any day the dice turns up even."

"I don't know how to write that."

"Just do your best, lad."

I count the strokes, groping for a way to ease to Gravy's disquiet, and an idea forms. Far-fetched, to be sure, but with Gravy, it may be worth a try.

"I know you recite poems in your dreams. I wonder, have you come across any Chinese poets in your book?"

A few more strokes while Gravy thinks.

"Li Po. He wrote poems on a leaf and threw them in the river."

And with that, my idea stands clear. The River Kennet. The Newbury Festival in full swing, acrobats tumbling across the greensward, posing as enumerations.

"The enumerations, Gravy. I wonder, if Li Po was an enumeration, which number do you think he'd be?"

Gravy grins. "Nine. Nine for sure."

As we close on *Redoubtable*, I suggest. "Then why don't you become nine? Just like Li Po. Write a poem like he'd write. Only not on a leaf, but on a slip of foolscap to be sent on to the magistrate. Just so he knows what the Captain has in store for him."

"But I don't know how to do that."

"Maybe not. But nine does."

For the last dozen strokes we sit quiet. As we hook on I ask Gravy.

"Do you know what a lyrebird is?"

"No, sir."

"Well you're about to find out."

*

The marine sentry posted at Montgomery's cabin tells me the Captain's not in but will return shortly. We wait, listening to the rasp of a saw, a hammer pounding a nail, followed by an ear-piercing shriek.

"That carpenter, he just hurt himself," Gravy says.

"That's Captain Montgomery's lyrebird."

L'arc carries on, this time mimicking a sailor taunting a marine. "Bloody fool marine! Bloody fool marine!"

The sentry roars back. "Shut up!"

"Kiss me arss! Kiss me arss!"

The sentry turns purple and about to burst, but just then James Baily, *Redoubtable*'s Sailing Master, comes by, and I catch his eye.

"You look familiar," he says to me. "Owen Harriet?"

"I am. And you're James Baily. I've read much of your apocrypha in the Almanac. I find your entries most intriguing."

"And I find your entries singular, as well. You and I met once at the Royal Observatory. You're from Newbury, as I recall."

"Yes."

"Then you must know Francis Baily. He was born in Newbury."

"Of course. An excellent astronomer. President of the Royal Astronomical Society for several years. Wasn't he the first to observe the red refraction of sunlight appearing on the rim of the corona during a total solar eclipse."

"He was. Baily's Beads."

"You're related to him?"

"A distant relative. But I'm no astronomer. I'm a sailing master, like you, and I was serving on *Invincible* when we passed through the Qiongzhou Straight on nine May of 1837."

"I've not seen your notes concerning the straight."

"They never made it into the Almanac. That's because it dealt with a personage not spoken of at Admiralty House. Shi Yang. Or I should say her pirate grandmother, Zheng Yi Sao. Fifty years ago the woman commanded a fleet of almost three hundred junks, and thousands of men. On several occasions the East India Company encountered Zheng Yi Sao in the Qiongzho Straight. They never fared well. Mostly because of Zheng Yi's flagship, *Wancheng*. And now her granddaughter Shi Yang's in the strait and commanding the very same junk. And with new French artillery.

Long guns designed to traverse one hundred eighty degrees. Operated by a sort of chain crank that works like a capstan. Very ingenious."

A chill runs on my spine with the return of a premonition long since departed, the familiar whisper heard by me alone.

Baily stares at me. "I say, Harriet, are you quite all right? You look like you've seen a revenant "

"It's nothing. How many guns on *Wancheng*?" I ask.

"Only two. But deadly accurate at long range."

"Does Captain Montgomery know about them?"

"I told him, but he won't believe it unless he actually sees it."

Baily finally notices Gravy, who's been sitting on the deck looking through his book.

"Who's the boy?

"Gravy Walters. Ship's boy on *Eleanor*."

"He's with you?"

"Actually, I'm with him. I've brought him to see Captain Montgomery. You recall that Montgomery asked if any of us knows Chinese. Well, for the last few months Gravy's been learning Chinese. He might be able to write what Montgomery wants."

"Commendable," Baily concedes, and then adds, "But how much Chinese could a ship's boy on a Royal Navy frigate know?"

The sentry comes to attention and slams the butt of his musket on the deck as Captain Montgomery approaches.

He looks at me. "I thought you left, Mister Harriet."

"I did, sir."

When I explain why I've returned, he can't help but laugh at the notion of an English lad knowing Chinese. Nonetheless, he invites Gravy and me into his quarters. The great cabin may be great, but on a frigate, not so grand. But just the same, Gravy stands at the door, dumbstruck by this new experience in his young life. L'arc calls out, sounding much like an empty cask rolling along the deck. Montgomery steps to the aviary to soothe the bird. "Now, now, L'arc." He gives him a grub worm, then draws the drape.

"What's your name, lad? "Montgomery asks.

"Gravy Walters, sir."

He sits behind his desk. "Come stand before me while I tell you what I want. It's not very much."

He writes it out, then asks Gravy if he can translate it.

"I think so, sir."

"Then go sit at the escritoire and begin."

"What's a eskitter, sir?

"That desk over there."

In not overlong Gravy puts down his pencil and hands Montgomery what he's scribed, written out first in English, then followed by the Chinese translation.

Montgomery scowls. "This is a poem, boy."

Gravy looks at me.

"If I may say, sir, I encouraged Gravy to write it the best way he knew how. And that happens to be the way an old Chines poet would have said it."

Montgomery regards us most queer, but then puts on his spectacles, clears his throat and reads out loud.

On the days when the dice roll
three, five, six, seven, nine or eleven
then I punish Haukou with my guns
on the days when the dice roll
two, four or eight
then Haukou is safe.

No telling how Montgomery will react, until he asks Gravy an unforeseen question. "I wonder why you've mixed in the even number six with the odd numbers?"

And his reply seems most reasonable, at least to Gravy and me. "Six belongs with the odd numbers, because he's not liked very much by the even ones."

Montgomery looks at me. "Is he mad?"

"No, sir. He thinks of numbers in a different way, that's all. Helps him to keep them straight in his head."

"Where did he come up with such tripe? From you? Never mind. Doesn't matter. The boy's got it just about right. I'll use it. Dismissed."

*

Three days out of Canton, bearing south by west in the South China Sea. Just as we're about to enter Qiongzhou Straight, de Clery summons us.

"Gentlemen, there's a five-masted war junk armed with advanced artillery operating in the straight. *Wancheng.* If this is the same junk that sank John Company ships in the passage, we've been under orders not to engage it."

A grumble of disapproval.

"But no longer. It's been reported that each gun requires ten men to traverse it, and it takes almost five minutes to swing it around to train on a target. And loading a thirty-two-pound shot takes almost as long. And here's the thing. Traversing and loading can't be done at the same time, don't you see. As a result the rate of fire on *Wancheng* is seven minutes for each gun. That's their Achilles heel. For a Royal Navy gun crew that's all lathered up the rate of fire is one round per minute. So if the opportunity should arise, we engage."

"Hear hear!"

de Clery goes on. "Mister Harriet's been reviewing the navigational charts with *Redoubtable*'s sailing master, and they've discovered something. Harriet, lay out your chart and show us what you've found."

I spread the chart on the table, secure each corner with a paper weight, and begin.

"It's been observed that *Wancheng* often calls at Haikou, and the only harbour entrance for a junk with her draft is here, off Baishamen Point. Then she can lie at anchor behind this small peninsula here, Guomao. The harbour entrance is about thirty feet deep at mid channel, but it's a narrow passage, only twenty yards across. I believe the Captain can use that to his advantage."

I sit down, and de Clery continues.

"Negril, Montgomery and I have agreed to coordinate our activities. Montgomery will proceed with his plan to harass

Haikou and relay a signal if he sees *Wancheng* entering port. I intend to capture a junk making through the straight, put its crew ashore and send our own men onboard. There'll be no prize money, though, because I intend to sink the junk in the harbour entrance. That way *Wancheng* can't leave."

Ramsey pounds his fist on the table. "Ha! And she'll be bottled up in port. A pity our guns can't fire over Guomao peninsula and sink the thing."

"Not so. We can sink the thing when Captain Negril brings his bomb ketch within range. He says his mortar's a very hungry beast."

*

A blue-and-white checkered flag flies from *Redoubtable*'s staff, signaling that *Wancheng* is closing on Haikou.

I stand with Ramsey as he shuts his telescope in disgust.

"We still don't have a junk to bloody sink in the harbour."

de Clery joins us on the quarterdeck. "There'll be more opportunities. This straight's heavily trafficked. As for now, signal *Redoubtable* that we're unable to comply."

Three days pass; eleven junks sighted. But they're all too small to sink at the entrance to Haikou harbour. But at first light on the following day a suitable vessel is spotted, and we soon overtake it. A decrepit junk making ponderous slow and paying little attention to us until we fire a warning shot across her bow. I count nine men rushing to haul her wind, and one man standing on the afterdeck. de Clery orders the barge put in the water and calls for Lieutenant Andrews.

"You will conduct this operation, Lieutenant. Select fifteen men to go with you and board that junk. Do you see the man standing at the stern?"

"I do, sir.

"That must be the captain. Make him know you intend to take command. I'll send the marines along to reinforce you. You are to sail the junk to Hainan. That's the small fishing village on the tip of Leizhou Peninsula. Put the captain and his crew ashore there. Then return with the junk and sail in my lee while we continue to patrol the straight. Questions?"

None.

de Clery calls for Sergeant Marley. "Take your marines and go with Lieutenant Andrews." He points to the junk. "Board that vessel and secure it. I'm sure no one on that junk speaks English, so it may be difficult to make them understand."

"By your leave, sir, marines have a way of helping people understand what we want."

"I'm sure you do, Sergeant."

The barge fends off, and soon we all watch as Andrews takes control of the junk and makes for Hainan. But in not overlong it's apparent Lieutenant Andrews has not understood what de Clery wants. He's sailed the junk to Hainan, but when the barge returns to *Eleanor*, the junk's not with it. de Clery's the first to meet Andrews at the entry port.

"Where is that junk, Lieutenant?"

"I sunk it, sir."

"What!"

"Those were my orders, sir. Sink the junk in the harbour entrance."

de Clery rocks and sways, hands clenched behind his back, breathing deep to vent his spleen. "Lieutenant Andrews, be so kind as to go to below and wait outside my quarters." de Clery turns my way. "Walk with me."

Everyone stays well to leeward when we reach the quarterdeck.

"I'm going to kill him."

"Yes, sir."

"He has no business serving in the Royal Navy."

"No, sir."

For a moment, de Clery observes the combers rolling on a copper sea. "It may defy logic, Harriet, but I'm of a mind to give Andrews a second chance. He wouldn't dare make another mistake."

*

That same afternoon the lookout hails the deck.

"Junk in sight! Bows on. Bearing east."

de Clery calls for Midshipman Moon. "Mister Moon, take your glass and go aloft. Try to determine if that junk's worth seizing."

Moon scurries up the ratlines like a daddy-long-legs. Soon he calls down.

"Four masted junk. Should serve."

de Clery orders the helmsmen to close on the junk, for Dovecote to run out the bow chaser and be ready to fire a warning shot, then sends a ship's boy to fetch Lieutenant Andrews.

When Andrews arrives, de Clery gives him the same orders as this morning, but this time he makes Andrews says them back.

He does.

"Now then, Lieutenant, I repeat. You will not sink that junk in the entrance of Hainan harbour. Do you understand?"

"Yes, sir."

"Then say it."

"I will not sink that junk in the entrance of Hainan harbour."

"Very well. Go you now."

de Clery's most pleased, for by the end of the first dog watch the junk sails in our lee. A handsome ship, with fresh green paint and red piping. Since I have more experience with how a junk takes the wind, de Clery puts me in charge, along with a dozen men to sail it. He also sends Gravy with me to interpret any Chinese paperwork we might find. .And indeed we find it.

"I never seen this kind of writing in Miss Pandya's book," Gravy admits, "but I think this ships's name is the *Humble Duck*, and its home port might be Canton. Captain de Clery, he says if I do good he might think of me for acting midshipman. Will he, Mister Harriet?"

Lieutenant Dovecote comes to report. He's placed a keg of black powder in *Humble Duck*'s hold. "I've made a shaped charge, sir. Set the powder keg at the bottom of the hold and stacked sacks of rice on top of it. That will cause the keg to explode downward and blow a big hole in the bottom. Twenty feet of slow fuse leading to the keg. That gives us about twenty minutes to abandon this junk and watch it blow. A splendid exhibition, I should think."

"It will," I agree. "But for now we can only wait."

It takes a week for the men to master the rigging and sail plan for *Humble Duck*. A week with nothing to eat but rice and salted fish, and everyone onboard is most pleased when on the horizon the blue-and-white checkered flag appears on *Redoubtable*'s signal halyard. de Clery brings *Eleanor* to within hailing distance of *Humble Duck*.

"*Wancheng*'s just anchored in the harbour. I'm sending the barge to you. I'll fire the signal gun when it's time for you break from us and make for the harbour."

Dovecote stands with me on *Humble Duck*. "Lieutenant, let's go over it one last time. When the barge arrives, I'll put everyone in it except you, me and a skeleton crew needed to sail *Humble Duck* to the entrance of the harbour. When we hear the signal gun we steer for the middle channel, haul our wind at the entrance and drop anchor. That's when you go below and light the fuse. Mind you, make sure it stays lit. Then we leave on the barge."

"Aye, Mister Harriet, and order the oarsmen to pull with alacrity."

And hope our venture goes as planned, said only to myself.

*

In not five minutes the signal gun sounds. We look to see *Wancheng*'s four masts rising above the low spine of Guomao Peninsula. And in ten minutes more we arrive at the entrance of Haukou harbour, where we stand into the wind and drop anchor. I nod for Dovecote to go below and light the fuse. However, the plan unravels instanter when Dovecote bounds up the companion way with a look of terror in his eyes.

"There's a cobra down there!" he gasps. "It's coiled on the fuse cord and when it saw me the thing raised its head and hissed." Dovecote's body shakes most violent. "I'm deathly afraid of snakes, Mister Harriet. I can't make myself go back down there."

Humble Duck's dead in the water, and in the middle of the harbour entrance. The fuse should be burning by now, with all of us in the barge and pulling away.

I reprove Dovecote. "Collect yourself, man. Order everyone into the barge and then join them if you must. I'll go below and light the fuse myself."

"Yes, sir."

Dovecote departs, slumped in shame. I stand at the companionway staring into the dim hold where an unlit fuse and a cobra wait for me. Was this the Sukiyama's warning? Is this how it ends? Like most men, I fear death. But it's the act of dying I fear more. To think that the last thing I'll ever know is to know what it's like to die from a cobra's venom. I recall my granddaughter's words. "Mummy, I don't want Grampa to go away."

I'm about to go below when Dovecote returns.

"Sir! There may be another way. I just remembered I brought along an extra powder keg, just in case we needed it. First let's get everyone in the barge and then I'll break open the keg, throw it down the companionway and toss the torch. That will catch the hold on fire and light the fuse all at once. It may start the fuse burning anywhere along its course, though. Maybe even right where it enters the powder keg I already have in place. I can't say. But I do say I'd rather do my duty rather than have you take my place. Please, sir."

I join the men waiting in the barge while Dovecote stands with a burning torch in his hand, looking down into the hold. Then he looks skyward, his lips moving as if in prayer. Again the signal gun from *Eleanor* rings out. de Clery's restive, knowing *Humble Duck* should now be at the bottom. Dovecote takes a deep breath, then flings the torch. Instanter the loose black powder ignites in a flash that blasts through the hatch and envelopes Dovecote in a plume of fire, followed by the detonation of the fused powder keg. *Humble Duck*'s sails burst into flames; her deck planks fly in the air. And along with them, pieces of Lieutenant Dovecote. One booted leg falls into the lap of an oarsman, who screams in horror as he heaves the bloody thing over. Dovecote's riddled torso lands in the water nearby, at first floating face up, then rolling under as his lifeless eyes watch on.

"Bowman!" I call out. "Use your gaff to retrieve Dovecote's body."

But the bowman freezes in terror.

"Give me the gaff, man."

No one helps me draw Dovecote to the barge and haul him over the gunnel. Finally someone takes off his own shirt and covers what's left of Dovecote. Only then do I see *Humble Duck* settling to the bottom with its top masts rising above the water. I turn to face the open sea. *Eleanor*'s making for us, closing fast.

*

I stand before de Clery finishing my report.

"*Humble Duck* is on the bottom at the entrance of the harbour, sir. No ship will enter or exit Haikou for a long time."

de Clery steeples his fingers under his chin. "You had a change of plans because of a cobra in the hold?"

"Yes, sir. Regrettably, that's what ultimately cost Lieutenant Dovecote his life."

Likely it would have cost my own life if Dovecote hadn't finally gathered himself. I won't mention it, though. He was a promising young officer and I'll not disrespect the man.

de Clery nods. "I shall write a letter to his parents letting them know their son died with honor. Is there anything you wish me to say on your behalf?"

Only that their son died for no good reason. That remaining here is anathema to anyone who has a sense of right and wrong.

"No, sir. Your words are sufficient."

"Very well. This evening I shall conduct a service and commit his body. After which, we go in search of *Rook*. We'll return with her to Haikou, where Captain Negril will proceed to sink *Wancheng* with his lovely mortar." de Clery peers out the stern gallery. "Ah, I see her masts rising above the peninsula, unaware of her fate."

18. Bodh

It takes three days of sailing full and by along the one hundred ninth degree of east longitude before we come upon *Rook*. Captain Negril reports that he's boarded seven junks, none of them worth sinking. A monotonous routine, he carps, although he's most pleased to join us, in hopes of soon bringing his mortar to bear on the enemy.

However, when we approach the island, we discover that *Redoubtable*'s no longer patrolling off the port of Haikou, and no longer do we see *Wancheng*'s masts rising above Guomao Peninsula.

Ramsey speculates. "Perhaps Captain Montgomery believes we've been delinquent in bringing Negrils' bomb ketch, so he's taken it upon himself to send his marines ashore, cross on foot over the peninsula, board *Wancheng* and scuttle her all on his own.

I remind him that Montgomery's in command of this squadron.

"Of course," Ramsey counters. "And take all the glory for it."

"Montgomery's eager for recognition," de Clery admits, "but he's not foolish. There are over twenty thousand inhabitants on Hainan. Many of them live in Haikou, or close by. No doubt they're unarmed. But they'd overwhelm the marines by their sheer numbers. No, something's happened. I think we'll find out shortly, but we won't like it." He turns to the flag midshipman. "Mister Abbot, a hoist to *Rook*. I wish Captain Negril to join me."

de Clery has asked Ramsey and me to join him as he discusses the situation with Negril.

"*Redoubtable*'s unaccounted for and *Wancheng*'s gone missing. A troubling turn of events. Negril, I want you to remain on station while I search for them. I'll return to Haikou within forty-eight hours. If *Redoubtable* returns before me, well, I can't think what you should tell him."

"If *Wancheng* shows up, de Clery, I'll engage her."

"Indeed you will."

*

Dovecote's grave misfortune leads to a dearth of officers, prompting de Clery to promote Gravy to acting midshipman. Now the lad stands his first watch on the quarterdeck as we patrol Qiongzhou Strait. At first light the lookout hails the deck.

"Deck there! A ship. Thousand yards off the starboard beam."

"*Redoubtable*?"

"Can't tell, Mister Harriet. It ain't got no bowsprit or foremast."

"Gravy. Fetch the Captain."

de Clery arrives just as the crippled ship shows her transom. We all train our scopes. Gravy's eyes are the youngest, the sharpest, and he's first to call out.

"That's *Redoubtable*."

We close on her most slow, wary of what we might find. Her gun ports are open and every gun run out. Foremast mast shot off at the fighting tops. Her rigging and sails trail in the sea. We watch for activity, any sign of life, but nothing stirs.

"Ghost ship," Gravy whispers.

Ramsey snaps at him. "Shut your mouth, boy.

"Bosun," de Clery orders, "put the cutter in the water. Ramsey, Harriet, take the loblolly and six steady hands and go find out what's happened."

A hundred strokes, and hundred more before we tie on at *Redoubtable*. No one hails us. No one pipes us aboard. A haunting disquiet pervades the air.

Ramsey turns to the bosun. "Brown, send a man up the main mast to keep a watch, then take the men forward and begin a search. Harriet and Madrid, come with me to Montgomery's quarters."

We proceed aft, heedful of the deck furrowed by cannon shot, and shards of splintered wood. Blood turning black in the scuppers. We press on until a shriek stops us cold. A shriek coming from the great cabin.

"Buggerin' marine! Kiss me arss! Kiss me arss!"

Ramsey reaches for his pistol. "Someone's in there."

"No, sir," I answer. "It's L'rac. Montgomery's bird."

The door stands wide and we step through. Montgomery! Blindfolded and gagged, his hands trussed behind him as he sits in a chair. Unconscious. Madrid steps forward and takes his pulse.

"He's alive."

"Remove the gag, take off his blindfold and untie him." Ramsey orders.

Montgomery slumps forward, still unconscious while Madrid holds him upright.

"Wake him."

Madrid gives him a nudge. "Captain Montgomery."

No response.

"Try brandy."

Gravy finds a small decanter. Madrid pours it in a snifter and swirls it under Montgomery's nose. The man stirs and opens his eyes.

"Montgomery. What's happened here?"

He blinks. "Who are you?"

"I'm Lieutenant Ramsey, First Officer onboard *Eleanor.* We found you unconscious."

"She put something on a rag and held it to my face."

"Who?"

"Shi Yang."

"Captain of *Wancheng*?"

A nod. "I held my breath long as I could, but when I finally inhaled, that's the last I remember."

"Could have been chloroform," Madrid explains, or maybe a new compound. Spirit of ether."

"Doesn't matter what it was," Ramsey insists. "I want to know why she did it."

"She managed to escape our trap at Haikou."

A scoff from Ramsey. "There was no escaping Haikou. The harbour's blocked."

"The main entrance was blocked until Shi Yang organized the peasants to dig through a dike and flood a back channel. She came out the back way."

"She told you this?"

"She did."

"Why?"

"Because I asked."

Ramsey calls for Brown and Shotwell, along with a hundred men to jury-rig the damage.

Brown's the first to report. "Two feet of water in the hold, sir, and takin' more on fast. Could swamp if we don't pump her out."

"Very well, send a detail below. Where's *Redoubtable*'s crew?"

"Didn't see none, sir."

"Where are you men?" Ramsey asks Montgomery.

He looks down. "Killed or taken prisoner." Then he holds his head high. "They fought well. But we were attacked at long range. She stood off at twelve hundred yards. Used those French guns to shoot away our bowsprit and foretop mast before we ever fired a shot. Then she approached from bows on so we couldn't fire on her and kept using those guns until she grabbled on. I don't know how many came aboard. Too many to repel."

"Why weren't you killed?"

"She left me to convey a message. She knows the Royal Navy's been ordered not to engage *Wancheng*. Called us cowards and dared any ship to try and sink her."

Shotwell comes to report. "I've taken down the bowsprit and foremast and cleared the deck, sir. We can get under sail."

A mate steps up. "Sir, the lookout's spotted *Wancheng* making for us."

Montgomery shifts in his chair. "Maybe Shi Yang's returning to finish me off."

Ramsey's quick to respond. "And de Clery can't see *Wancheng* because *Redoubtable*'s standing between. We'll return to *Eleanor* and report. I suggest you come with us, Captain."

Montgomery rises unsteady. "No. I stay and fight. *Redoubtable*'s guns are loaded and run out. When *Wancheng* draws near I'll go down the line and fire them all, one after another. That should distract Shi Yang long enough for you to explain the situation to de Clery."

"This time you'll be killed."

"I'm already dead, Ramsey. There will be a court's martial and I'll be found guilty. But I choose to die fighting. Be so kind as to take L'rac with you."

*

Ramsey leaves behind a skeleton crew as *Redoubtable* gets under way. While returning to *Eleanor*, L'rac sits in the barge hunched in his pen, screaming in some foreign tongue.

"*Ego sum episcopus! Ego sum episcopus*!"

"Good Christ," Ramsey exclaims, "the bloody thing knows Latin. It just said he's the bishop."

As we tie on, de Clery waits on the quarterdeck for Ramsey's report.

"Montgomery's the only one left on *Redoubtable*, sir."

"Good God. Where's his crew?"

"Killed or taken prisoner."

"But not Montgomery. Shi Yang spared him so he can relay a message. She says we're cowards for refusing to fight her. Now *Wancheng*'s been sighted on the horizon. She's making for *Redoubtable* but I don't think our lookouts on *Eleanor* have seen *Wancheng* yet."

de Clery knits his brow. "Means it can't see us, either. I'll use that to our advantage."

He steps to the chalk board and draws an arrow on the left edge of the slate, pointing toward the middle.

"Look here. The direction of the wind. Holding steady from the west."

Next, he draws a short horizontal line in the middle.

"This is *Redoubtable*. Dead in the water."

Then a vertical arrow drawn just above *Redoubtable*, pointed straight at it.

"This is *Eleanor*, making due south."

Another arrow, just under *Redoubtable*.

"This is *Wancheng*, making north. Both ships converging on *Redoubtable* from opposite directions."

He looks to Ramsey and me.

"Do you see it?"

We both nod, and he goes on.

"Right now we're about a thousand yards off *Redoubtable*'s starboard beam. *Wancheng* will see us soon unless we keep *Redoubtable* between us. But even when she does spot us we can still use *Redoubtable* as a shield. That way she won't be able to fire on us with those long-range guns of hers. But at a hundred yards, we'll sheer off and cut across *Redoubtable*'s bow."

He traces a slow, deliberate curve crossing her bow. "No." He rubs out the line. "We'll cross in *Redoubtable*'s wake. Just so."

He draws another curved line that cuts across her stern.

"By the time we clear *Redoubtable* we'll likely be within range of our long guns before *Wancheng* has time to react. And we shall sink her." He pats the chalk dust from his sleeve. "Do you see it, Ramsey?"

"Aye, sir. We use *Redoubtable* as a screen then at the last moment cut cross in her wake and open fire on *Wancheng*."

"There you have it. Now then, Ramsey. I'll assume your duties on the quarterdeck because I want you as my gunnery officer. Load the odd numbered guns with round shot and the even numbers with canister. Tell the gun captains to concentrate their fire on the guns mounted fore and aft on *Wancheng*. Those two guns must be reduced."

"Aye, sir."

"Very well, gentlemen. Beat to quarters."

*

Within the hour *Eleanor* cuts across *Redoubtable*'s wake. When Shi Yang's slow to train her guns, de Clery relishes the moment.

"It's true then. It takes a long time to traverse her guns and bring them to bear."

But despite her slow response, *Wancheng*'s the first to fire, and punches a hole through our spanker, not ten feet above our heads.

"Outstanding," de Clery crows. "It'll take them five minutes to re-load and traverse. Time enough to bring our own guns to bear."

I train my glass on *Redoubtable* and watch the skeleton crew rush to get under way while Montgomery starts firing his starboard guns, one gun at a time down the starboard battery. Every gun throws wide and high, but still they serve to distract *Wancheng*. The diversion gives us more time for our port guns to open fire with every gun aimed at *Wancheng*'s bow gun. None of our round shot finds its mark. But the canisters filled with grapeshot sweep the bow, leaving three of *Wancheng*'s gun crew lying dead. As we pass, her stern gun fires, hitting our spanker gaff and sending it crashing to the deck. *Eleanor* falls off the wind, which at the same time brings our starboard guns to within point-blank range of *Wancheng*'s stern. The gun crews crouch eager, anxious for the order to fire. But no order comes, for the spanker's crashed on de Clery, who lies unconscious on the quarterdeck.

Word that de Clery's down reaches Ramsey, who's quick to take command and orders the starboard battery to fire. The salvo knocks *Wancheng*'s stern gun off its carriage. A ragged cheer arises as I kneel at de Clery's side. Unconscious and bleeding from a head injury.

"Gravy, fetch the loblolly."

By the time Madrid arrives de Clery's eyes are open, but he stares unfocused. Madrid examines his split skull. de Clery tries to stand, but when he can't, Madrid tells us to take him below.

The crew tries to bring *Eleanor* before the wind, but with no spanker she's slow to react, and although we've managed to reduce *Wancheng*'s guns, the wind brings her down to us, with a boarding party amassing at her bow.

Half of *Eleanor*'s port battery fires round shot into *Wancheng*'s hull, and the junk shudders from bow to stern under the broadside. The other guns fire canister into the boarding party. Every boarder goes down but are replaced by more men spewing forth from the hold like ants from a hill. Another round of canister, followed by the next gout of men erupting from the hold. *Wancheng* drifts closer. A man stands on her bow with a grappling hook. Sergeant Marley fires his musket from the maintop and hits the man full in the chest, only to be replaced by another man who starts swinging the grapple line. I think of what Montgomery told us, that he didn't know how many of *Wancheng*'s men boarded *Redoubtable*. Too many to count. Certain there's more men here than I can count, all most eager to board us. Until a hail from the lookout.

"Deck there! I see *Rook*!" He points beyond *Wancheng*. "Guns run out and closing fast on the junk."

Wancheng stands between us and *Rook*, who soon comes within range with her long guns. *Rook* fires a tight salvo, and one round hits *Wancheng*'s main mast and brings down her sail and disrupting the men primed to board *Eleanor*. It gives us time to fire our carronades. I count how many stand on *Wancheng*'s deck. Thirty-seven. But after the latest round of canister I count only twelve, with not so many coming to replace them. Instead, it's Shi Yang who replaces them when she climbs over a heap of bodies and begins firing her pistols at us, even as two more broadsides discharge from *Rook*'s port battery. Sergeant Marley levels his musket at Shi Yang and takes careful aim, just waiting for *Eleanor* to rise on the swell. But before he takes his shot one of Shi Yang's crew comes from behind, covers her with a burlap sack and carries her away, whereupon another mate takes her place, waving a white flag.

*

de Clery lies senseless in his bunk. The right side of his scull is split open. Even from five feet away I see his brain showing through. Madrid waits for *Eleanor* to top the next swell. Then, with measured strokes he shaves the hair from around de Clery's wound. Then, with a gentle touch, he dabs it dry with gauze.

"Wipe my face," Madrid tells me, "then stand close with the lantern."

Next, he uncorks a squat, wide-mouthed crock and coats the wound with an ointment. He studies his work, then steps back. Only then do I see the label on the crock. Vedic Soma. A knock, and the marine sentry steps in.

"Mister Harriet, Lieutenant Ramsey wants you topside."

On the quarterdeck Ramsey interrogates Shi Yang, who stands with her hands tied behind her back. Ramsey tells Gravy to translate.

"Ask her what's she done with *Redoubtable*'s men."

Gravy translates, then gives her reply. "She says they're on Haikou."

"I want them returned at once," Ramsey demands.

"She says they're to be executed."

"Is that so? Then tell her what's good for the goose is good for the gander."

"I don't know how to say that, sir."

"Never mind. Just tell her I have over three hundred of her crew under guard in *Wancheng*'s hold. If *Redoubtable*'s crew isn't returned immediately her men will suffer the same fate."

A long exchange. "She wants a … a prisoner swap. I think that's what she said."

"I'll consider it. But as for her, tell her she's going to Canton and stand trial."

Shi Yang shrieks like some banshee until Ramsey slaps her face.

"Shut your mouth. You chose to climb over your dead, so now you pay the butcher's bill." He turns to Sergeant Marley. "Frog march her to the chain locker." Then to Lieutenant Andrews. "Prepare to get underway."

Ramsey sends Shotwell and a hundred men to jury-rig *Redoubtable*'s foremast and bowsprit, and all his marines to *Wancheng* to stand guard over her crew. Captain Negril sends a dozen men from *Rook* to sail *Wancheng*. And after a half day of fevered effort the squadron sets a course for Haikou. Under reduced sail *Redoubtable* leads first in line, with Captain Montgomery fully recovered and in command. *Wancheng*'s next in line, followed by *Eleanor* and *Rook*. In not overlong our signal midshipman calls out.

Captains and sailing masters report to flagship. And a final hoist, as if an afterthought. Bring L'rac.

While on our way to *Redoubtable* Ramsey tells me Qianfen, the man who surrendered the junk, says we should set to sail for Sanya. "Where is that, Harriet?"

"It's a small port on the south coast of Haikou, sir. About half a day. If this wind holds."

"I see. Qianfen says there's a pier at Sanya that can serve as the transfer point for a prisoner exchange."

Once onboard *Redoubtable*, I'm most pleased to see her sailing master, James Baily, waiting outside the great cabin.

"Mister Baily! I thought you'd been taken prisoner and sent to Haikou."

"A bit of luck there. I was in Canton when *Redoubtable* was attacked. I've just returned. Oh, I have a letter or you." He hands me a thick envelope. "A Chinese man gave it to me when I was about to board the mail packet. I don't know how he knew to give it to me."

The envelope's addressed to me in a cursive I know. It's from Cyd Jordain. The return address is the mission at Tongqing, and instanter I recall her last words to me.

"I don't know what will come of it," she said, "but two nights ago, at Langfang, this wild mare was in oestrus."

I look to find the translucent sliver of moon hanging in the afternoon sky, and recall what I told Cyd, that the sea is a wild mare ruled by the moon. I tuck her letter away. I'll read it later, for just now L'rac harps from the cabin.

"Yangguizi! Yangguizi."

"Good gawd!" Baily declares. "Is that Chinese? The bloody thing already speaks Cockney, Spanish and Latin, And now Chinese. Can you believe it?"

"No doubt Montgomery believes every word of it." I respond.

"Maybe so. But he doubts Qianfen. The man claims that one hundred ninety-four of *Redoubtable*'s crew are held captive. Montgomery thinks that number's about right, but he suspects Qianfen intends to lead us into a trap at Sanya. The Captain insists that any exchange takes place somewhere else."

"Where?"

Baily's eyes brighten as he brings out the coastal chart he's brought with him. He turns to the marine sentry. "Private, I want to make use of your back to spread this chart. On you hands and knees then."

"I'm not a piece of furniture," the man grumbles, yet he complies.

"If Montgomery's right about this being a trap, then Sanya's a likely place to spring it. But look here. Just fifteen miles west of Sanya there's a small fishing port. Yacheng. Baily taps on a peninsula. "Not so good either, except for this sandbar just off the coast."

And instanter I recall the Mesurado River, where forty years past I partook in an uncertain exchange conducted on another sandbar.

"I can't recommend it."

"Of course not, Harriet. I've read your account of a sandbar swarming with fleas. A stalemate of sorts. I mean between the Dutch captain and your own commander."

"And unbeknown to anyone on that sandbar," I add, "at that very moment the Treaty of Amiens was being drawn up."

"Well wouldn't you know. There's rumor of a treaty to end the hostilities here in China. Seems our cumulative efforts are taking effect. Interrupting the Emperor's flow of money. Occupying Chinese cities and disrupting major river systems. Not quite a treaty, though. More like a truce after the Emperor's losses at Amoy and Canton. Now I hear there's four regiments of foot soon to deploy at Hong Kong with marching orders to fight their way inland to Chapoo. And what's worse for the Emperor, the overbearing presence of the Royal Navy's forcing him to open the trade ports of Nanking and Shanghai." Baily taps on the chart once more. "And I believe this sandbar has a feature that will strengthen our position."

But before I ask how, the door opens and we step into the great cabin.

*

Montgomery asks Ramsey straight away. "How is Captain de Clery?"

"The loblolly says he hasn't regained consciousness. He remains unaware of any prisoner exchange."

"Good Christ" Montgomery reacts most adamant. "I abhor the very notion of a prisoner exchange. Tantamount to defeat. My own defeat."

"But you weren't defeated, sir," Ramsey's quick to amend. "You never lost command of *Redoubtable*. And later you fired your guns to draw off *Wancheng*. Your actions gave us time to close within range with our long guns. I agree it's unfortunate, but it would appear that a prisoner exchange is our best option now."

Montgomery curls his upper lip. "Or the least intolerable one. But I don't want the transaction conducted at Sanya. I suspect a ruse. Another location's highly desirable. Suggestions?"

Baily steps forward. "Sir, there may be a better location. You're familiar with Saint Michael's Mount?"

Montgomery squints in thought. "The archaic tin port in Cornwall. Also known for its tidal island, as I recall."

"Correct, sir. May I lay out this chart for the south coast of Hainan?"

A nod.

Baily spreads the chart. "This is Sanya. But fifteen miles west there's a small fishing village. Yancheng."

Montgomery studies the chart. "Nothing but a pier and a godown."

"Even so, I think you should consider an exchange taking place at Yancheng because just offshore there's a small tidal island. A sandbar, actually. But at high tide it's cut off from the mainland. Something akin to Saint Michael's Mount, don't you see, though on a much smaller scale. But here's the thing, in order to get to the sandbar during high tide one must use a boat, since the tide creates a channel sixty feet wide, six feet deep, with a strong current."

Montgomery begins to pace, stopping at the stern windows to regard the sea, then returns to the chart.

"We're about three days out from Yancheng. So tell me, Mister Baily, in three days' time . . . that would be twenty-one September, when is high tide at Yancheng?"

Bailey refers to his log. "First high tide at approximately eight in the morning. Ebb tide at about two that afternoon."

"Then we shall make use of it." Once more Montgomery begins to pace, but soon he stops abrupt. "Here we have it. First, we must pass bypass Sanya, and instead just send … I forget, what's that first officer's name?"

"Qianfen," Ramsey replies.

"So I'll tell Qianfen I've changed my mind, but as an act of good will release him and send him ashore at Sanya with a message for the Emperor's magistrate. If the magistrate wants *Wancheng*'s crew returned, then the prisoner exchange must take place at Yancheng. On the tidal island. And if he says no, then for sure Shi Yang will be executed. But if he agrees to my request then I promise that Shi Yang will be given a fair trial at Canton and likely set free. She spared my life, so now I spare hers."

"Quid pro quo," Ramsey suggests.

"I think not. More like tit for tat. But either way, we then proceed to Yancheng and arrive before first light to deposit our prisoners on the sandbar. Questions?"

None.

"Then go make preparations."

Once at Sanya, Qianfen's rowed ashore under a white flag to deliver Montgomery's ultimatum. When *Redoubtable*'s longboat returns, the squadron continues onto Yangheng. But as the watch changes, we hear ragged musketry coming from *Wancheng* and look to see thick smoke billowing from her hold. When I train my glass, I see a man squeeze his way through the grating and attack a marine. Sergeant Marley shoots the man and then directs his squad to fire directly into the hold. By now the fire's licking through the grating, creating an inferno below decks. Most odd that we hear no screams, just some ungodly chant.

"God's balls!" Montgomery growls. "It's a mass immolation. They intend to the incinerate the ship along with themselves." He turns to the deck officer. "Send our boats to take off our sailors and marines."

I count one hundred and three sailors and twelve marines climb down into the waiting boats. Sergeant Marley's the last to leave, his tunic smoking as flames leap from the deck.

In not one hour I join a council of war gathered on *Redoubtable*'s quarterdeck. Montgomery waits for Ramsey and Negril to have their say, then states his intentions.

"A pity, I suppose, so many lives lost on *Wancheng* and all that. And we all regret loosing the prize money, of course. But I dare say this loss presents a more favourable prospect for us. We may not have … I wonder, Harriet, just how many prisoners did you say were on *Wancheng*?"

"Three hundred and twelve, sir. And one hundred ninety-four of our men are held on Haikou."

"We can only hope they'll be at Yangcheng," Negril adds.

"There's one way to assure that. We no longer have three hundred twelve prisoners to exchange. Just one," Montgomery grins, "but she's the only one who counts."

*

When I return to *Eleanor* the sight of my berth reminds me of how long it's been since I've slept. Twenty-seven hours. But when I remove my waistcoat, Cyd's letter falls out. In spite of my deep yawn I light a glim and begin to read.

> 20 September 1840
>
> Owen,
>
> Last time we spoke I told you I was in estrous on the night we slept on the floor at Langfang. I must tell you now that I've quickened. Doctor Pandya says I'm well, but what can a man know about giving birth? I rely on Satara. She's midwife to many of the women who give birth here at the mission. I chose you to be the father of my child despite knowing we may not meet again. I will name the child Owen, if he's a boy, Rowena, if a girl, and vow to raise this child with love, watching for the moments when he, or she, reminds me of you. Not for your courage, although you have it, but for the way you are with children. You see in them the child who you once were. They sense it and love you without knowing why. It's why Gravy loves you.
>
> Last week I took a canal junk to Zaozhuang and met with Xi. I asked him to send along this letter. Of all my agents, he knows how to get it to you. Xi informed me that Lo Ting is still keeper of the East Glorious Gate, and he wants to buy information about a certain shipment of opium that's not arrived at the Forbidden City. Xi knew you and I had business with Lo Ting and wondered if I have something to say about the missing shipment. I said

yes, but only if he had something for me. Following our custom, Xi went first. Based on his own informants, he thinks he knows what will take place within the year. There's talk of a British regiment preparing to land at Hong Kong and then proceed up the Pearl River to Canton. But any foreign occupation of Canton would give rise to efforts to end this proxy war. However, no one believes any attempt could ever be accepted by Daoguang. The British will surely insist that he increase the number of treaty ports. They'll remind him that all English subjects residing in the cantonments must remain accountable only to English law. Any treaty would also stipulate that the Emperor cede the territory of Hong Kong to Great Britain. Xi says it would be an untenable situation for Daoguang. Even if he signed it wouldn't last long.

Xi also told me that Lo Ting's sent notice to the Viceroy in every province to have us arrested. I think you're safe enough at sea, but if you go ashore, be mindful. I'm grateful for Xi's warning but do not wish to be indebted to him, so please inform me if you know what happened to that vedic soma, even though Lo Ting, fool that he is, still thinks its opium. Send a letter with Hop and he'll stop at Tongqing.

Coming from another source, I heard that in September of last year a French missionary, Father Jean-Gabriel Perboyre, was taken prisoner in Hubei Province. The local militia tortured him for a year. And on eleven September of this year, by way imperial edict, the viceroy at Wuchang had him executed. Tied to a cross and garroted. No one knows how many Christian missions are in China. The mandarins generally treat them with indifference, but the execution of Jean-Gabriel may foretell the start of a purge. Doctor Pandya believes we're safe in Tongqing because we're the only Baha'i mission in China and not associated with either the catechists or the colonial powers. But even if the Chinese turn against Tongqing, Doctor Pandya and Satara vow they will never leave. Will live and die here. It is their life's work. Now it's mine. bodh

*

My beloved Becca told me once that if she should die before me, she'd hope for me to chose another wife. Even have more children. I've never considered such notions. But what now? Now that Cyd Jordain, who's named herself bodh and spells it with a lower case, tells me she's chosen me, instead of me choosing her, to be the father of her child. Dear Becca would smile and remind me that's usually how it goes, although the man doesn't know it. After all, she would add, it was she who chose me, and without me knowing it. I do feel honoured, even if somewhat put upon, and will tell Cyd as much. But not just yet. First, I must respond to her request and tell her what's happened with the shipment of vedic soma that Lo Ting's expecting. That, in fact, there will be no shipment. Admiral Wynyard's grand experiment has failed. His botanist, Mister Chowdry must start over since his graft is a hybrid that failed to produce seed. I know Cyd will pass this on to Xi. Hopefully, he'll concoct some story for Lo Ting and charge him exorbitant for the lie. A lie that may sail close to the wind, though untrue.

I dress a new quill while considering what I'll say to Cyd in a second letter. A missive penned only after I think of how to tell her that by staying at Tongqing she's not only putting her own life at risk, but the life of an as yet unborn child. My child.

*

Four bells in the morning watch. The light monsoon rain falls steady, yet I smell land and open my eyes to sunlight pouring through the companionway. I look at my desk. A stoppered inkwell and a dressed quill remain just as I left them last night. Alongside is the letter I've folded to make an envelope with my seal affixed and addressed to Cyd Jordain. This letter holds the information she wants. But a single folio of parchment remains, with its salutation not to Cyd, but to the woman who now calls herself bodh. I'll send this second letter along with the first, but I want to post them separate, for they address different matters. I gather my thoughts, asking myself how to begin, when Jesus Madrid appears at my door.

"Where's the wind, Madrid?"

"I don't know, sir. But please come and help me turn Captain de Clery on his side. I'm afraid I might have missed something."

We make our way aft, and when we roll de Clery I gasp at the festering splinter wound imbedded in the small of his back.

"Oh, Mother of God I missed this," Madrid grieves. "No wonder the man's burning up."

I send word for Ramsey, who remains as captain while de Clery's unfit.

"Will he live?" Ramsey asks.

"I can't dare say, sir. A major infection."

"He won't die in the next few minutes, will he?"

"I don't think so, sir."

"Then step out for moment, if you will. I have matters to discuss with Harriet."

Madrid's most reluctant to leave his patient, but he complies.

Ramsey turns to me. "Normally, when the First Officer in one of Her Majesty's ships must assume command, it's the second lieutenant who steps up. But between you and me, I don't believe Andrews is up to the task. You and I have our differences when it comes to the duties of a sailing master, and I have no doubt that in the future the first officer will assume the duties of a sailing master. Even so, onboard *Eleanor* the situation is the reverse. So as of now you're my first lieutenant. You and I shall share the duties of sailing master. I'll shoot the noon line and log in the co-ordinates while you're attend to the responsibilities of First Officer."

Eleanor shudders as an errant wave takes her bows on. We both stand broad afoot to ride it out, then Ramsey goes on.

"The squadron will be approaching Yangcheng shortly. Your first duty will be to go ashore and supervise the prisoner exchange. After the proceedings Captain Montgomery believes our orders will be fulfilled and the squadron will return to Canton. Our orders were to secure Qiongzhou Strait and sink or capture *Wancheng*, and we've done it."

*

Monsoon rain. The midday ebb raises the sandbar connecting the tidal island with the peninsula. Midshipman Walters, who I've brought with me to translate, stands at my side, along with Madrid, who must check the prisoners for contagion before allowing them back onboard *Redoubtable.* I signal for Sergeant Marley to march Shi Yang from *Redoubtable*'s hold, still barefoot, but with her hands no longer bound. She wears Gravy's extra set of slops, for the clothes she wore in the chain locker are filthy, and Gravy's slop fit her. The Viceroy of Haikou, a mandarin named Li Qiang, sits in his sedan chair looking from the near shore through a small, silver telescope. After the man confirms that it's Shi Yang, he nods at his minion, who then signals for the prisoners to come forth and stand on the beach. I walk with Gravy along the sandbar, then stop and wait for the Viceroy's acolyte to meet us halfway. The fellow treads light on the wet sand, trying not to get his embroidered slippers wet. While we wait, I watch the magistrate sitting in his sedan chair. Even from a hundred feet I see the brick-red birthmark covering the lower part of his face. He's the one they call Sangshu.

When his minion joins us, Gravy asks in Chinese, "How many prisoners?"

The man ignores Gravy but instead speaks to me.

"He wants to know how old I am."

"Tell him you grew up fast."

"I told him. But he says he still won't talk to a boy."

"If he wants to talk to me then he must talk to you."

The man turns and walks away. After a lengthy conversation, it's the Viceroy himself who finally joins us, looking most splendid in his sable lined silk robe. As he approaches, his lackey follows three steps behind. Once more I think this is Sangshu and dare to break protocol by speaking first.

"Ask the Viceroy if he's Bai Guang, the one who's called Sangshu."

His minion steps forward and shakes his fist at Gravy for his impertinence, but the Viceroy quiets him with the wave a hand, flicking the long nail of his little finger as he replies.

"He says he is."

"Ask him how many of *Redoubtable*'s men he holds prisoner."

"One hundred and eighty-nine."

"There's supposed to be one hundred ninety-four."

"Five died of their wounds."

"Were they given a Christian burial?"

A light shrug. "Their mates buried them. Several more can't walk."

I call for stretchers.

"Now explain to him how we'll proceed. Start with the watch bill."

"Mister Harriet, he has a … "

"Belay that, Midshipman. Don't say my name."

"Aye, sir. The Sailing Master, he calls out their names. When they hear it, they come forward and wait for Madrid to inspect, then walk to the far end of the sandbar and get on the boats. After about half are taken off the sandbar a sergeant, he'll escort Shi Yang and join us here, halfway. That's when we wait for the rest of *Redoubtable*'s crew to be released."

Sangshu nods. "Start now. The tide turns at three."

By noon I've checked off one hundred and two names, and call for Sergeant Marley to bring Shi Yang.

"Shi Yang," the Viceroy asks, "have they mistreated you?"

First, she spits in the sand, then spits out her words. "They put me in a filthy chain locker."

Sangshu scowls at me. "You would mock her honoured ancestor, Zheng Yi Sao, by treating her granddaughter this way?"

"No insult intended, sir. She's a young harridan. Locking her away was necessary to keep ship's order."

Shi Yang stands with Sangshu as the last of *Redoubtable*'s crew returns to their ship, soon joined by Madrid, then the marines. I send Gravy with them, for in the channel the tide's staring to run. The Viceroy and I are silent, each taking one last measure. Finally, I bow to Sangshu. That's when he nods to his man, who withdraws a small pistol from his sleeve and points it at my heart.

19. Money Island

I'm given a cob to ride and led in the rain for fifteen miles along the coastal road to Sanya, where I'm locked in a cell. The place is pitch black. A hard packed dirt floor, three paces from one wall across to the other. I've not eaten. Am I to starve to death? A slight stirring from beyond one wall, followed by the door opening. A hand pushes through a ball of sticky rice, about the size of a six-pound lead shot, and a cup of water. I've never liked rice, but this rice, I savour. The water's brackish, same as the water stored for overlong in a cask. I just wipe my teeth to clear the slime. Small fare, but enough to suspect they don't intend to starve me to death. But who are they? Bai Guang, no doubt, the one called Sangshu. Which leads me to think Cyd's warning proves to be more than a caution.

The island province of Hainan is a thousand miles from the Forbidden City. But even so, the hue and cry for my arrest may have reached Bai Guang. Not a good thing for Gravy to have said my name. Of a sudden someone shoots the bolt and the door swings wide. Two guards step in, march me down a hall and up a narrow flight of stairs. Another guard stands at the wide entrance to a long, narrow chamber. At the far end, Bai Guang sits on a dais. On a red-lacquered milk stool rests a ball of opium. He flicks his long fingernail before he speaks, and I'm most surprised to hear him speak the King's English.

"Where is your little finger?" he asks.

"Her Majesty, may God bless Her, ordered it removed. She was offended by the length of my fingernail."

I can't say why I'd tell such a lie, since my finger was shot off by the Onion some forty years ago while on the Mekong River. But the less of the truth Bai Guang knows about me, the better.

"Is your queen a reasonable woman?" he asks.

"I don't know."

He points at a small vase on the stool. "Then perhaps you know about the opium in this vase. It was sent to me by the Keeper of the East Glorious Gate."

Does Bai Guang know what he has before him? That the shade of this mould's not the same charcoal grey as that of a pure mould of opium, but the pearl-grey tint of opium mixed with soma? I don't know how to reply, so remain silent, waiting for him to go on.

"It was found in the chest you tried to deliver to the Forbidden City, concealed under a gift of porcelain intended for the Emperor. You are charged with trying to smuggle opium into the Forbidden City."

"I was not smuggling opium. What I mean to say is that what you have, it's not just opium, Bai Guang. May I call you Sangshu?"

"You may."

"I'm familiar with your efforts, Sangshu, and honour you for trying to rid China of opium. A good measure of the Queen's subjects honour your enterprise as well, for they believe that those who trade opium desecrate the empires of China and Great Britain alike. But the ingredients in this mould are a cure for the addiction. Yes, there's opium in it, but only a small amount. But it also a contains a substance which helps overcome the addiction. An herb called soma."

Sangshu frowns. "Do you mean Xiangma? The animist texts speak of this herb. But few Chinese are aware of it. Lost in antiquity."

"But still found in the Vedic hyms of India. Lost or not, Sangshu, my orders were to introduce soma to the Emperor's court. A gift to the Chinese to relieve their mortal craving. Before you pass judgment, I ask that you try it."

His brick-red birthmark darkens. "I have fought the dragon and defeated it. With my own will, not through your Xiangma."

"I praise you. But the struggle must have made you aware that most men lack the courage to confront the dragon."

Sangshu sits quiet but then picks up the mould. "I will offer this to my ancient. My own father, lost in his opium dream. If in twenty-one days I begin to see improvement, I will reconsider your fate."

"How will you know he's improved?"

"By his desire to live."

He sets the mould aside, pulls a velvet cord, and a tiny bell rings to summon the guards.

"As for now, I place you under house arrest. You have a few tael in your purse. Use them to buy food and water."

*

The guards walk me past the cell where I've been held captive, and certain I'm most grateful of not being stuffed back inside. Instanter, I start taking stock, for it's also most certain it's my duty to attempt an escape. I note the fish market awash with the day's catch. Could the mayhem on the market be of any use in an escape? Or the sampan village swarming with vendors. Maybe the step-mast dogger with a crew of only two, an over large man and a small boy, just now standing into Yancheng bay. I watch as they tie on to a sampan. Only two planks, just wide enough for two. It's been moored at their buoy, and I watch as they scull their way to shore. I see where they keep it. When the guards shove me along, I count off one hundred seven paces as we walk. A wide lane with a great many hutongs lining the way. A treelined street that ends at the entrance to a gated hutong. I assume this must be the Viceroy's residence, since there's a five-foot wall. We approach and enter a stone courtyard with a well, and laundry laid out to dry on the pavers. Six wooden dwellings, living quarters, I suspect, all with separate doors and windowpanes made of rice paper. At the far end of the courtyard, a bigger lodging with a tall, green door. I count a footman and two scullery maids enter, and two more leave before the guards walk me to a dark recess with its own door. They push me through and bolt it from outside. A room with bare walls. One high window that lets in light, but too small to use as an escape. A low sleeping pallet and a pitcher of water. Splendid accommodations for a monk, or someone under house arrest. A sea breeze carries the smell of the ocean. I stand on the pallet to look through the window. The South China Sea lies not far beyond the tiled rooftops of the surrounding hutongs. If the gate to the Viceroy's residences is always unguarded, could I just walk out?

At noon line, or thereabouts, I mark each day. And for the next twenty-one days I eat sticky rice. But the water's fresh, likely drawn from the well. At first light I'm allowed to walk in the courtyard for an hour. It's always deserted when I'm there, with only my guard watching me. Like most soldiers, he's learned not to stand when he can sit, not to sit when he can lie down, and not to stay awake when he can sleep. But this soldier's learned the skill of sleeping on his feet. For three weeks he's been practicing his talent, until the morning he's ordered to bring me before the Viceroy.

Sangshu wastes no time. "Your captain demands your release. I told him you're under arrest and awaiting trial. Is he as reasonable as your monarch?"

"He's unpredictable. But only to his enemies."

Sangshu grins "As am I. My father is dead."

"I'm sorry."

"He did not die from opium. It was your soma. It was restoring him. He was regaining his strength. Desired to walk in the moonlight, as was his habit. But last night he fell, struck his head and died. You might say the soma set him free, but only by killing him."

"I regret how it ended for him. Nonetheless, I wish for my own self to be set free."

Sangshu removes a scroll tucked in his sleeve and reads it aloud.

> Honourable Superintendent of Trade at Canton,
>
> I am Sailing Master Owen Harriet, serving on HMS *Eleanor*, deployed at Canton. I am currently being held prisoner at Sanya, in Hainan Province. I am charged with trying to smuggle opium into the Forbidden City. The Viceroy of Hainan Province has graciously allowed me to write this letter as an act of good faith in transactions to secure my release to British authorities. He requests you deposit one hundred Spanish reales into his account at Jordain Bank, in Macao. Upon deposit he will release me. Please respond with proof of retainer, and arrangements for my deliverance. If you do not, he will proceed with my trail.
>
> I Remain Your Most Humble & Obedient Servant,
>
> Owen Harriet, Sailing Master

Sangshu gives me the scroll. "Sign it."

"I will. But you've overestimated my value. On the way to Canton a shipmate and I discussed how much we might be worth if held for ransom. Not over much. Not a hundred reales, to be sure."

"A pity. If the ransom is not paid you will stand trial and be found guilty. And I will execute you." He nods to his clerk, who gives me a pad of foolscap and a few pencils. "I believe the English have a curious custom of writing what's called a last will and testament. Use the time you have left to write yours."

I forego the will but keep the foolscap.

*

The ransom note written by Sangshu must go by sea. But even with a favourable wind it will take a junk four days to reach Canton. No matter when it arrives though, most certain it will be dismissed, for as I told Sangshu, no sailing master's worth a hundred reales. I start to calculate how much time before my trial.

At least four days for the note to arrive in Canton, where it won't be seen by the Superintendent. Some clerk won't wish to trouble His Eminence and decide on his own to reject the very idea of a ransom. Add four more days for the earliest response. Eight days in all, though Sangshu might wait a few more. But I think it can be no more than three weeks before I'm brought to trial, and on that day, perhaps even before lunch, I shall be found guilty. Of a sudden I have no appetite for the next ball of sticky rice.

Escape or die. Yet a glimmer of hope arises, for I'll make use of what I know best. The sea. Haikou's an island. If I'm to escape it must be by boat. Certain the fishing boats moored in the bay all require a small crew, but not so the dogger. Her name is *Regina D.* I make note that her buoy's midway between the headland and the dock light. Every day I've watched a man and a boy sail it and know I can sail it on my own. Yet hope starts to fade, for I might die of starvation at sea. Not quite. It's the rice balls. I'll save out a portion every day and tuck them under the sleeping pallet, then take them along to keep me from dying of hunger. Water? It's rained in the afternoon for eighteen days and will likely continue for another month. And best hope of all, my guard sleeps on duty. Yet I don't trust any of it. A plan tends to come undone at the first chance. Even so, with a following wind I'll make it to Qiongzhou Strait and be come upon by a British ship. Or doomed, if first seen by a Chinese junk. Either way, my preparations must begin and start with my scribing the next mark on the wall.

Five new marks etched on the wall. And after ten more there will be a new moon, along with monsoon rain. Aside from my dozing guard, the courtyard's deserted at first light. Even so, there's always laundry set out to dry on the pavers before the rains. Shirts, trousers and such. Always a few burlap sacks which will serve most splendid to tote my sticky rice. On the morning of my escape I'll take a peasant's shirt and trousers and one sack and be sure to leave a few tael for payment. A peasant has only one set of clothes.

On day eleven, two bells ring out and I awake with the night air still breathing at the window. Certain there's no ships bell here to wake me, just my habit of hearing them in my sleep, and on this occasion providing an early start for my escape. It's five in the morning when my guard slips the bolt. He opens the door and I visit the leiting hezi. Gravy told me once that leiting hezi means thunder box. Some things are never lost in translation. But on this day, I've already lost my chance to take French leave, for my guard's been replaced by a new one, one not likely to sleep on his feet. But the plan's not undone yet, since I've allowed several more days for my next try.

Day twelve starts most promising, for my dozing guard has returned. I walk in the courtyard for half an hour, always passing close by to check if his eyes are open. On the third pass his eyes begin to droop. On the fourth pass they're closed and remain closed for the next few. I fetch a gunny sack, return to my cell and stuff it with twenty balls of sticky rice. I return to the courtyard, check my guard's repose, put on a shirt and trousers left at the well, leave a few tael for some peasant. I stroll through the gate. I'm no taller than a Chinese, and for that reason alone I'll likely go unnoticed. But certain I still have sea legs and try to walk steady as some footman toting a burlap sack. It's not far to the sampan, about a mile. As I approach the waterfront the denizens of Sanya begin to stir. But they pay no heed to a man with his face smothered in a ragged scarf, eyes cast down, walking bent over while bearing a heavy load, too poor to have a choggi pole to balance the load on his shoulder. I cast an eye in search of the sampan and stop abrupt, for it's not onshore. Instead, it's tied at the dogger's buoy, and *Regina D* is gone. Most unexpected, and I waste no time in returning to the courtyard. Where my guard still sleeps on his feet. I set the shirt and trousers just where I found them and take back the tael I'd left in their place. But the sack I take with me to my cell and hide it under the pallet, ready for my next attempt. Soon my guard comes to find me, looking most refreshed after sleeping through my hour of exercise.

The next morning Sangshu conducts a ceremony in the courtyard. A gathering of swells sitting in their sedan chairs and wearing silk robes. Every guard stands at attention with eyes wide open. No chance for me to walk out the gate. I can only hope tomorrow begins better.

It does, and I'm most pleased to see *Regina D* still tied at its buoy. I don't wish to steal it, but the few tael I have would hardly be enough to buy the thing. So in the mind of Sangshu, I've now become a thief as well as a trafficker in the opium trade.

*

The monsoon rain arrives early. All the better, for there's no one to see me depart the bay, and with only one tack I clear the headland and stand into the South China Sea. I intend to bear east along Hainan's coastline, then north for a hundred miles to enter Qiongzhou Strait at Jiao Point. But a dark squall line builds in the north, carried on a strong wind. When spindrift starts to run on the sea I lock down the tiller, work my way forward and take in the jib. But the dogger falls off steep when a big sea takes her on the beam. I'm knocked to the deck and almost washed overboard. I struggle to the mast, take down the lug sail and wait for the storm to run its course. But instead of blowing itself out, the storm builds to a gale, testing the dogger's worth. *Regina D*'s a stout one, though, with the lines of a north sea boat made for heavy seas. Mahogany hull. A teak deck cabin. A small coracle lashed to the foredeck. Two hatches, fore and aft, leading to the small hold. Probably built on Hainan by some ships carpenter who the navy paid off in Canton, then took himself a China bride, built a boat and named her *Regina D*. I see a name carved in the transom. Cross Woodall - by my hand. Was it him I watched handling *Regina D* the first time I saw her?

The wind takes me out to sea. If I had a crew, I'd send them below to wait it out, because there's no good reason to stay on deck. The nearest landfall is Luzon, a thousand miles east, with nothing in between. No need for me to remain on watch. For now nothing more can be done, except not to be pitched into the sea. I lash down the tiller, make sure the hatches are secure, and for the first time I step into the deck cabin. Two bunks, port and starboard, a narrow mess bench set between, a small galley against the forward bulkhead. I move to the galley. A water butt full of rainwater. A small sack of dried peas. Useless, since there's no firewood. But there is a wicker basket with salted fish. And best of all, I find what's been missing ever since the guards at Sanya took mine away. A knife. Of a sudden I'm most tired and take a bunk.

*

In my sleep I once more hear two bells and know it must be five in the morning. I go to the tiller, unlash it from the stern rail. The wind is calm, with gentle rollers on a small sea. The sun's just rising, casting its copper sheen across the water. I begin my day by bringing the water butt on deck. Open both hatches and go below to inspect the hold. A small landing net, a fish line and several hooks. Most useful. And also find what I'm looking for. Sailcloth. With my new-found knife I cut a strip to divert rainwater into the butt. Once in place I stand at the tiller and eat a portion of rice ball and a morsel of salted fish. How long must I make these rations last? Judging from the sunrise, my position is approximately twenty degrees of north latitude. But as for how far east the storm took me, I can only guess what my longitude might be. Best if I still had a pocket watch. But I left my prized chronometer behind, on *Eleanor*, and my guard took the one I was carrying when I was captured. I must wait for the sun to reach its zenith before taking a reading. I find what's needed to fashion a backstaff, then wait to shoot the noon line. A makeshift devise yielding little information. At times, a little knowledge is worse than none at all.

The next day the rains arrive early. The sun remains hidden behind heavy cover. It might be noon, or maybe not. I must wait until tomorrow to shoot the noon line. So I put myself to good use by setting the jib and lugsail and wait on the wind. Then fashion a chip log to determine my speed. To serve as a drogue I remove a two-foot plank of teak from the deck cabin. Teak wood is most dense. Too heavy even to float. But a short plank of teak will fill float well enough to serve as a chip log. Next, a coil of jute. Unbraid its fibers to make a fifty-foot strand of twine, then tie a knot at one-foot intervals. It takes not overlong for me to set the chip log afloat. It's most alarming, though, to watch the thing just sitting there alongside the *Regina D's* hull. There's no following sea or any stretch of line to account for. We're adrift, going nowhere.

At the sun's zenith on the following day I shoot the noon line. But my approximate measure of longitude is most troubling. I've not made easterly; therefore Luzon is still a thousand miles. I'm faced with a choice. My rice balls won't last overlong. So do I starve, or start fishing? But I'm no fisherman and can't know if any fish will rise to the bait of salted fish. And what then if I did catch a fish? Eat it raw? Cyd once told me to burn that bridge before you cross it. A breakdown in logic, to be sure, but even so, I untangle the fish line and tie on a treble hook. However, as I'm about to put in the line, a thought befalls me. The Paracel Islands. It seems a long time ago, but it was just this January when I told Jesus Madrid the Paracels might be a good destination for an escape. I recall their coordinates. Sixteen degrees north by one hundred twelve degrees east. It seems they're as close, if not closer, than Luzon. And one of those islands, Money Island, is a refuge for fishing fleets that frequent the archipelago. Yet I'll never make Money Island or Luzon if there's no wind.

That night the wind is still down. The sails hang limp as I lie on the roof of the deck cabin observing the constellations. Pegasus and Draco direct overhead Andromeda and The Princesses to the north. I've not caught a fish. They don't like me overmuch, I don't think. It might be best to write my son a letter in hopes that someday it might find him. I've never told Albert about the bank account I keep at Barclays. Prize money. Two hundred pounds to start, and over the years it's accrued most smart. I used a hundred pounds of it to help Albert start his wheelwright shop. The rest will go to him someday. I can only hope that day isn't here yet. No, not quite yet, for the sails begin to fill with a slight breeze from the north. I free the tiller and bring the dogger about. Her rigging starts to sing and the sea pearls beneath her bow. I'm underway, bearing south by west, most grateful that now there's no need to write Albert that letter.

The wind holds steady for the next three days. On the third night the smell of land awakens me. Faint, but unmistakable, and at dawn I sight an atoll. Most likely it's Tree Island, the northern most islet in the Paracels. Not more than seventy miles east of Money Island, which I hope to raise by nautical twilight. The wind shifts, though, and I'm forced to tack on an overlong reach. But even so, during the night I arrive off Money Island and work my way through the coral reef on its eastern shore. I stand into a lagoon with a dark tree line. Except for the waves washing ashore, I hear nothing. See no fishing fleet anchored in the small bay. Smell no cooking fires. Only a few bamboo huts with thatched roofs and open doorways. The camp is deserted. I lower the lugsail and jib, then anchor in the middle of the lagoon. The shoreline consists of sand and shale, shrub brush clinging to a small berm that gives way to a stretch of stunted trees. I could take the coracle and go ashore but think it best to wait until full light. So for now I put my senses to good use. Remain sharp for what there is to hear, to smell, what might be watching from shore. And even though the night's calm, I hear a distant warning from within. A premonition? The Sukyama? I don't know but can only feel someone watching me. But no matter what I sense, I'm hungry, and suspect there's some sort of field kitchen on shore. A cauldron, a fire pit, driftwood. My stomach grumbles at the thought of boiling up a pot of pease porridge. Yet I wait for sunrise to lower the coracle, put the sack of peas in it, and row myself ashore. If someone's watching, so be it. Perhaps he'll reveal himself when he smells food.

When the coracle grounds on the beach I take my peas and trudge toward the nearest hut but stop in my tracks when I see two words spelled out with several small blacks stones. Oslo Sypes. I read the words aloud, and instanter a man steps from the brush.

"Oslo Sypes. That's me."

He's a scrawny one. About forty. Five feet ten. Brown shaggy hair touching his bare shoulders. Watery blue eyes, flat cheekbones and a bent over nose.

"Who are you, mate?" he asks.

"Owen Harriet. Sailing Master on Her Majesty's Ship, *Eleanor*."

"A load of nonsense. I don't see a ship. Just a dogger." A nasal whine with an English accent.

"Believe what you want. But I'm hungry and plan to boil up these peas. Looks like you could eat, too."

Sypes beams a toothless grin. "Right you are, mate. I'll fetch driftwood."

In a sparse cook shack I find a ladle, porcelain spoons and wooden bowls. Sypes tends the fire while I stir the porridge.

"Let's eat," he says.

"Not yet."

But in not one minute, he asks. "Now?"

"No."

A few minutes more. "Now?"

"Now."

We sit eying each other as we gorge on the porridge. When my stomach's full I set down my bowl and ask.

"How did you get here? I don't see a boat."

"My boat was the *Marimba.* Lovely little sloop with a bright yellow hull. I was sailing her on my own when a storm snapped my mast. I started taking on water and just managed to get off in the dinghy. Next day a fishing junk pulled me out and left me here."

"When was that?"

"About two months." Sypes scrapes his bowl and sets it down. "What are you doing on the South China Sea?"

"Heading for Luzon when a storm blew me off course." A half-truth, but enough.

Sypes squints doubtful, suspecting there's more to tell, but leaves it. "You're not a very good cook, mate, but you've just cooked the best meal ever." He belches overloud.

"What were you doing in the South China Sea?" I ask."

"Looking for stardust."

"What?"

"Tektos. That's Greek. It looks like sand or gravel so it's easy to overlook. But it's actually the sublunary detritus caused when a meteor impacts the earth. Tiny things. None larger than a small marble. But always shiny black with random shapes. I used some of them to spell out my name on the sand."

"And you look for tektos?"

"Look for it and collect it."

"Why?"

"Because my father searched the world looking for stardust. And I follow his quest. When he married mother, they lived on Mariposa and went searching for heavy deposits of tektos."

"Sounds like he was just looking for large grains of sand."

"How many grains of sand does the earth hold? In all the deserts? All the beaches? In the crop of every sparrow? Vast amounts. But not an number. Some consider that finite number is the key to the universe."

"Like endless enumerations on the greensward."

"I'm not sure what you mean. But there's an obscure society in London that would be curious."

"You're from London?"

"That's where father was born. But I was born at sea. On *Marimba*. Mother was from Norway and she gave me a Norwegian name no one could pronounce. Not even her. So everyone calls me Oslo." Oslo cocks an eye. "If it's true you're in the Royal Navy then you know there's money in the opium trade. Are you a smuggling it?"

"No. Are you?"

"Certainly not. *Marimba*'s hold was half full of tektos. That's why I was heading for Hainan. There's more stardust on Hainan than anywhere in the world."

He looks at me curious. "Are you a priest?"

"No."

"Doesn't matter. Will you hear my confession?"

"Didn't I just hear it?"

"And now I shall hear yours. Isn't that why we're on this island? To confess?"

*

The night I row back to *Regina D* and lie on the deck. Oslo stays on the beach tending a small fire. His shadow leaps about as if dancing a frantic jig. Deep in the night I see a shooting star. Some stellar fragment that's journeyed for a million years only to vanish in the blink of an eye. Stardust, delivered from the sins of its origin. Remindful of what Oslo said.

Isn't that why we're on this island? To confess?

Rubbish.

Olso might think I'm complicit in the opium trade, but he knows nothing of Admiral Wynyard's covert mission. I've nothing to declare. Well, maybe stealing *Regina D*. Little chance for me to return it, though, unless I get off this island. I fall asleep trying to think of a way.

In the morning, more pease porridge. Another grateful belch from Oslo, followed by more questions.

"Does anyone know you're here?" he asks.

"Not for certain. A while back I told a shipmate that if either of us was captured and managed to escape, then maybe try for the Paracels. If Jesus Madrid remembers that conversation, he'll be sure to tell our captain."

"And your captain would come looking for you?"

"No. *Eleanor*'s not on an independent action. She's attached to the fleet in Canton. Captain de Clery, even if he's recovered from his injuries, wouldn't be allowed to sail on his own. But I hope Admiral Wynyard would send him."

"Why would an admiral bother with you?"

"Because it was the Admiral who chose me to go on a mission that eventually brought me here."

"What mission?"

I just stare at him.

"Well, I doubt an admiral would bother with a sailing master."

"I can only hope so. Hope and wait.

"How long do you plan to wait?"

"Not over long. Money Island's probably visited by the fishing fleet at Hainan. I'm sure they've been told to watch for the dogger I stole at Sanya. If there's a reward they might try to take it back."

"Probably would. So where will you go from here?"

"Not back to Hainan. Where would you go?"

"Hainan. For the tektos. But you should try for Haiphong. That's the closest port."

Of a sudden the ground rolls under us and the lagoon stirs like water trembling in glass.

"My God! What's happening?"

20. Tsunami

Oslo replies with his voice unsteady as the ground we stand on. "It's a … I think it's an earthquake. Yes, I'm sure of it. I was in a small one once."

"How long do they last?"

"Not long. There, you see? Already stopped. Sometimes there's another one, though. If we were in a building we'd need to get out. But we're standing in the open so we don't do anything. Couldn't anyway. Just wait it out and hope it won't cause a tsunami." He searches the horizon. "Even a small tsunami would break over this island and carry us out to sea."

"Then we should stand out to sea before we're swept away." I study the wind. "This wind will take us straight out of the lagoon and bear us westerly. But we need to leave instanter, so if you have anything you want to bring with you then go fetch it."

"What if there's no tsunami? What then?"

"Then we'll be on our way to Haiphong. I've enough provisions to last us a week. Tsunami or not, best not wait here and find out."

Oslo's a good hand. Most efficient in hauling in *Regina D*'s anchor and setting the jib and lugger sail. In not over long Money Island sinks below the horizon. After I set our course, south by west, Oslo holds forth about the tsunami.

"Euclid said tsunami are caused by underwater earthquakes. No wait, it was Thucydides who said that. The Japanese call it a harbour wave. But I don't know why. Tsunami waves are nothing like a normal wave. Much longer. More like a fast-rising tide. One tide after the next. Sometimes they're over thirty feet."

I'm busy at the tiller and have no time to reply. Oslo stops talking and just trims the jib.

After the evolution he picks up where he left off. "A hundred years ago the Lisbon earthquake caused a tsunami. Thousands of people drowned. Most of them pulled out to sea in the undertow."

He stops short, though, when we feel the thing well before we see it. Still low on the horizon, off the starboard bow and approaching from the west. A tsunami. I steer *Regina D* to quarter it.

"How long before it gets here?" I ask.

"Don't know."

"Then that gives us enough time to strike the mast."

"Are you mad? We need a sheer hulk to take down the mast."

"We would if the mast was keel-stepped. But it's deck-stepped so we can do it ourselves if we're strong enough.

"Have you ever unstepped a mast?"

"No. You take down the jib and I'll handle the lugsail. Then we lift the boom off the mast and secure it along the gunnel."

While Oslo secures the boom I lock down the tiller, rig a block and tackle to the stern post, feed the line through the sheave and release the backstay. When I'm done, I call to him.

"Now we unstep the mast. With our mast down it won't break if we pitchpole. I'll unpin the mast plate and release the collar while you loosen the shrouds. Tie them to the mast, then go to the forestay and cut it. Hold tight, though, just feed it out slow as I lower the mast with the backstay. When it's down we lash it to the deck. We'll re-step it when the worst is passed. Go you now."

The first tsunami wave comes on unabated and in disquieting silence, with a ten-foot swell passing beneath us. We're in deep water though, and it's not breaking on any shoal, so it causes no damage. Oslo and I share a look. Relief mixed with dread. Both waiting for the next wave, which rises to fifteen feet. Another eerie silence as we meet this wave, but not as well met, though, and its impact drives the stern under. But *Regina D*'s the plucky one, and sheds the water, seeming indifferent to her circumstance.

Oslo comes aft and calls out. "Third wave's get bigger."

"Then go to the deck cabin and close the hatch behind you. I'll stay on deck and tie myself to the stern post to keep from washing over."

The third wave comes on thunderous loud, a thirty-foot wall with sea foam and debris cresting on the swell. As it approaches, I study the debris and realize it's the flotsam from some ship caught in the maelstrom. Broken masts, shredded sails, and a most frightful sight, a drowned sailor ensnared in a mesh of rigging. I manage to bring us about in time to quarter the wave as it breaks savage over *Regina D.* It drives her under and I lose my grip on the tiller. But I'm still tied to the stern post and holding my breath, hoping *Regina D* will right herself. But she's taking overlong, and for the first time since I learned to swim in the River Kennet, I take in water and expect to become drowned. Has the Sukiyama deserted me? Found some other soul to inhabit? Some say when you're about to die, your life passes before you.

Rot.

I have no time to dwell on the past. Instead, I will for *Regina D* to regain the surface. And as if with a will of her own, she rises, with Oslo rolling me face down over a cask to press the water from my lungs.

I'm still coughing as he props me against the transom. "Took in a lot of water, mate. Hope I got it all out. Sort of like rolling out dough."

I try to stand but fall to my knees and start coughing. My chest's most painful. I can't breathe over good.

Oslo pats my back. "You need to rest a bit."

"No. There's a ship out there that's lost a mast and might be sinking. We need to look for it."

"Not much we can do even if we find it."

"Better try and fail than not try at all. We need to re-step our mast."

The mast is quicker to re-step than to let down, and soon we get underway. Oslo takes the tiller. I climb on the shrouds to watch for a ship. I see nothing, but soon Oslo calls out.

"Look to starboard. There's a dismasted ship. About a thousand yards. I'll steer for it."

I struggle farther up the shrouds for a better look. At five hundred yards I call down. "I see a white gun stripe. Might be a frigate. Every mast is gone." I look hard as we approach, and at two hundred yards I cry out. "Bloody hell! That's *Eleanor*!"

*

Eleanor's deck swarms frantic with her crew as they cut away the broken yards and masts. No one notices us approaching until I hail them.

"I'm Harriet. Permission to come aboard."

Gravy Walters steps to the rails. "Mister Harriet? I'm sorry for when I said your name on the sandbar. It caused you to be arrested. Are you okay, sir? I mean 'cause you don't look okay. You look very hencha."

"What?"

"Chinese, sir. You look very bad."

"Never mind the Chinese or how I look. Where's Captain Ramsey?"

"Gone overboard in the tsunami. Lieutenant Andrews, he went too."

"Good God. Who's in command then?"

"Mister Zenith."

"Midshipman Zenith? Why's he in charge?"

"I'll take you to him, sir. He'll explain."

Gravy leads me through the havoc to where Peter Zenith stands listening to the bosun. Once he sees me, he looks most confused of my presence.

"Mister Harriet? How can you be here? When did you come aboard?"

"I arrived just now on that dogger lying alongside. You're in command?"

"It's awful, Mister Harriet. Captain Ramsey and Lieutenant Andrews, I'm afraid they've both drowned."

"Where's Lieutenant Oliver? He's next in the chain of command."

"I'm sorry, sir, but Lark broke down. Said he couldn't work the problem and started to weep. He had to be relieved, sir. As senior midshipmen I stepped up. Did I act out of turn?"

"I'm sure you did right, Zenith. But now I relieve you. Go find out how many men we've lost. Write down their names. Keep a list." I turn to the bosun. "Brown, we need to jury-rig a mast. I see the foremast top yard's undamaged. Secure it to the stump of the main mast. Use the spanker gaff for a yard. Where's Cheddar?"

The sailmaker steps forward.

"Bill, shape a sail for the jury-rig. Where's Bunny?"

"Here, sir."

"How much water in the hold?"

"Eleven inches. Not taking on no more though."

"Hold off pumping it out. If there's another tsunami wave the extra ballast might kept *Eleanor* from capsizing. What else?"

"The rudder, sir. Won't respond. It's jammed. That's how we got dismasted. Couldn't steer proper and the tsunami caught us broadside. Snapped off every mast."

"The rudder's jammed, you say?"

"Aye, sir. Haven't found the problem yet."

"Let's have a look."

On the way below I stop at the entry port and call down to Oslo. "Tie on and come aboard. Find Cookie and help in the galley."

The carpenter and I weave ponderous slow through *Eleanor*'s crew as they clear the wreckage. All hands working steady to make their ship seaworthy. On our way to the rudder I think of the first time *Eleanor*'s rudder was a problem. May 1798. On our initial voyage we ran afoul of a ghost trawler with a heavy cable trailing after it. We crossed that cable and it snagged our rudder. When *Eleanor*'s carpenter replaced the pintles and gudgeons he thought he'd fixed it. But the rudder's failed several times over the years, always needing a refit.

"Bunny, do you have extra pintles and gudgeons for the rudder?"

"I do, sir."

"You may need them."

Within the hour Shotwell wields his spike mall to drive the last pintle into its gudgeon. As he puts away his tools he remarks about the rudder.

"Ain't many Lively class frigates in the fleet no more, Mister Harriet. She's old. Must 'a had her rudder replaced plenty much, but I ain't never seen no rudder made this way."

"That's because *Eleanor*'s had problems with her rudder. The third time she was in dry dock they built her a rudder that's easier to repair at sea."

A ship's boy finds me. "Beg pardon, Mister Harriet. Mister Zenith says to tell you we can get underway."

"Tell him to proceed."

I join Zenith on the quarterdeck to hear his report. "Two officers missing, sir. Captain Ramsey and Lieutenant Andrews. Cyrus Trice, Purser's Mate. Two ratings. Bott Billiard, Able Seaman. Apple Swank, Ordinary Seaman. Ship's Boy, Jake X, last name unknown. Seven ratings unable to stand their watch. Broken bones and such. Mister Madrid's tending them in the officer's mess."

I find Madrid in the officer's mess. The captain of the main mast comes to tell me he can use the top gallant yard of the main mast for a second mast. The chief gunner says he's checked every gun to make sure they're all secure. Cookie says he's re-stoked the stove and can start feeding the men hot rations. When Madrid finally has a moment, he tells me to lie down.

"Later."

"Now. You're off colour and rasping for air." He takes my pulse and feels my forehead. "Weak heart and clammy to the touch. Chest pains?"

"No. Well, yes."

"I was told you just showed up in a boat and took command. I don't know what's happened to you, but you're exhausted. Lie down."

"No. I need to be on the quarterdeck. The men must see someone's in command."

Gravy comes looking for me, but Madrid stands in his way.

"Gravy, Mister Harriet won't say it, but I think he almost drowned."

"Drowned, sir?"

"Almost drowned, Gravy," I reply. "But I survived. Madrid's right, though. I need to rest. Fetch Mister Zenith."

When Zenith arrives, I transfer command, then fall to my knees. Madrid helps me to stand and tells Gravy to take me to my own quarters.

*

Gravy talks away as I fall into my berth.

"I'm learning to become a midshipman, sir."

"Show me your manual."

He pulls it from his waistcoat.

"You've made notes. How much have you committed to memory?"

"Almost all of it, sir."

"Then I'll pose you a problem that won't be found in the manual. As a junior midshipman what would you do if an officer ordered you to send Dunoon up the mast to serve as a lookout?"

"But Milt's blind as a bat, sir."

"He is. But maybe the officer doesn't know that. So what do you do?"

"I don't know, sir. What should I do?"

"First, you make sure Dunoon doesn't serve as lookout. Then it's your duty to inform the officer of the situation."

"But he'd yell and tell me to mind my own business."

"Likely he would. But that's how it is for a midshipman. Even when you've done your duty."

"Yes, sir."

"Now tell me what happened after I was taken prisoner."

"I'm sorry I said your name, sir."

"You already apologized. Now go on."

"We watched you get marched off the sandbar. And the next morning, when you were still gone, the Captain, he sent Lieutenant Andrews to ask why. They told him you were arrested for smuggling opium and would stand trial in the Forbidden City. That afternoon the Captain threatened to lay siege to Sanya if the Viceroy didn't return you. He said you're an English subject and must be tried in an English court of law. But the Viceroy said you'd already been sent away. Did he send you, sir?"

"I escaped before he had the chance."

"Oh! Good on you, sir. But how did you ever get here? I mean back to *Eleanor*?"

"I stole a dogger. *Regina D*. That's her tied alongside" I relate the account, then ask Gravy. "How did you come to be in the South China Sea?"

“We were on our way to Georgetown for dry dock, sir. That’s when Mister Madrid, he asked the Captain if he’d stop and look in at the Paracel Islands. It’s not far off course, and Madrid remembered you saying the Paracels might be a place to run. But the Captain said he couldn’t take the time, and he didn’t need a sailing master. That’s when the tsunami almost sunk us, Mister Harriet. Captain Ramsey and Lieutenant Andrews, they were on the quarterdeck when they got washed over. And Lark, I mean Lieutenant Oliver, he … well, Mister Zenith did his best. But it was too much all at once.”

We hold tight as *Eleanor* rolls heavy on the swell, still struggling to get under way.

“I should like to ask you something, sir. It’s Miss Cyd. I still need to pay her for when she bought me from slavery. But I don’t know how to find her. She might think I’ve forgotten.”

“Be sure she’s not forgotten, Gravy. And if you don’t find her, then certain she’ll find you.”

“Oh that’s good, sir. Because if I had a mum, I hope it was her. Will I see wo mama again, Mister Harriet? Ever?”

At some point I’ll tell Gravy just how it is with Cyd. Her choice to stay at Tongqing. Choosing me to father her child. Some day. But not this day.

“Shouldn’t you rest now, sir?”

*

I awake with Madrid taking my pulse. “You’re doing better.”

“What’s the status of Lieutenant Oliver?”

“He’s in a stupor, sir. Acute reaction to stress. Midshipman Zenith was forced to relieve him of duty.”

“Do you support what Zenith did?”

“Yes, sir.”

A silent moment before Madrid asks. “You’ve been isolated in the Parcels, so you don’t know the latest events in Canton.”

“Tell me.”

“I don’t know where to begin. Certainly not at the beginning. But when we returned to Canton after patrolling the strait, the Ninety-Eighth Regiment was mustering for an assault on Canton. The Chinese army’s never been a match for the Ninety-Eighth, and now they're threatening to pillage the Pearl River estuary until the Emperor agrees to meet with Sir Charles Elliot. He's the Crown's Plenipotentiary to Imperial China. It's inevitable there'll be a treaty signed at Nanking. Soon, maybe. That's the gist of it, sir. Do you still have a headache?"

When I nod, he reaches for his kit, brings out a small bottle and shakes two pills into his hand.

"Ground magnesium. I cut it with some caster sugar."

"I need your opinion, Madrid. I'm a sailing master, not an officer. Or at least not in the chain of command. Do the men have faith in my ability to lead them?"

"They do, sir. You know their names and always speak forthright to them. You know more about *Eleanor* than any captain ever would. It was you who knew how to fix the rudder, sir, or we'd still be adrift. Or gone down."

"Do the men believe I tried to smuggle opium into China?"

"The talk below decks doesn't sound that way. I wanted to tell them about the Admiral's mission but …" He hands me a glass of water. "Take the pills."

I knock them back, then state with resolve, "We're not going to Georgetown."

"Sir?"

"At least not yet. First, we're calling at Sanya."

"To put paid to the Viceroy? I've never known you to be vindictive, sir."

"No. Rather to vindicate my own self. That dogger at the entry port. I stole it to escape from Sanya. Now I wish to return *Regina D* to her owner. Cross Woodall. Now send for Sypes."

Oslo knocks on my door.

"Did Cookie feed you?"

"After I chopped about a thousand potatoes. Cheap old turnip."

"It's because the pursuer lists you as super cargo, therefore not allotted ship's rations. But that's about to change. Now you must make a choice. Either sign on as Ordinary Seaman and work your way to Georgetown. Or assist me in returning *Regina D* to Sanya. At that point you can either take the risk of going ashore. Or you can return to *Eleanor* and I'll put you in for Able Seaman. But you must decide now."

"I'd not go far in the Royal Navy. Besides, I'd be a fool to come all this way and not search for tektos on Hainan. But if you let me take to coracle to go ashore, then I'd be pleased to help you bring *Regina D* back to Sanya."

*

I find the unopened letter tucked in a cubby hole on my chart table. Dated Fifteen October 1839. Written by my son, Albert. It must have arrived when *Eleanor* was in Canton and I was held prisoner. The purser probably left it for me, but he never told me because he went missing in the tsunami. I never saw the letter until now.

> Father,
>
> I hope this letter finds you before you return home. Last month we got a letter from you dated three years ago. A message in a bottle would have made it sooner!
>
> We are all healthy and doing good. Rachael is with child. Expected in March of next year. If it's a boy we will name him after you. And then call him Owee, like you brother Albert called you.
>
> I'm very busy making wheels. But I found the time to build another room on the back of the house. Rachel started a book business. Buying and selling rare books. Mostly postal service. Now that I've built the addition, she wants to open a bookstore in the front room.
>
> Sami misses you. Sometimes at night she comes to wake her mummy. She asks where you are. Says you were just with her feeding the goldfish. She cries when we tell her it was a dream. Then she asks when you will come home. It's just a dream, but she has it quite often. We all want you to come home.
>
> Your son, Albert

Eleanor finally gets underway. But with two jury-rigged masts and *Regina D* towed in our wake, we barely make four knots. It takes us five days to reach Hainan. We approach Sanya at nautical twilight but stand out to sea and wait to close under the cover of darkness. While we wait, I call for the bosun.

"Brown, do you have any blue paint? Same blue as *Regina D*?"

"Yes, sir."

"Good. I want you to paint her transom. Paint over her name."

The paint dries. The moon is down. A following breeze, and at four bells in the middle watch, two in the morning, I order the barge into the water and have Brown step the mast. Oslo and I bring it around to *Regina D* and tie on at her stern, for I shall use the barge to depart Sanya once we secure *Regina D* at her old buoy. Number twenty-seven. We soon enter Sanya's inner roads.

"Watch for when we intersect the line between the headland and that lantern on the dock," I tell Oslo. "It's about a hundred yards off that dock's where *Regina D* was moored when I sailed her off. Twenty-seven. We'll tie her back in place."

"Then you sail off in the barge?"

"Not just yet. First, I'll leave something for the man who built *Regina D*."

"Money, eh?"

"Not quite." I peer through the dark. In the inner roads every boat snubs its buoy. All but one. "There, that's hers. We leave her there."

Oslo stands in the bow and ties *Regina D*'s painter to her buoy, then joins me at the tiller.

"You know, Harriet, revisiting the very place you were taken prisoner takes a great deal of pluck. Either that, or you're a fool, though I doubt you're a fool. But just the same, you know the risk of entering Sanya and being captured again. This time there might be no chance for ransom."

When I say nothing, he goes on.

"War never ends, mate, it just pipes a different tune. This war's no different. They say there's a treaty in the works, but no one believes it. Do you?"

"You best go ashore now and look for more star dust."

"That I will. Don't stay here too long."

"I won't."

Oslo nods, and without a sound he rows into the night. I sit alone in the stern, just listening. A muffled thump. A wet cough. Sanya's a fishing village, and at three in the morning the waterfront's already stirring. Soon I see the first cook fire. It's time to leave. But not before I take my knife and carve a new name on *Regina D*'s transom … SAMI.

Glossary of Nautical Terms

ballistics - the science of projectiles and firearms

banded jacky - a brand of plug tobacco popular in 1798

beam end - a ship listing more than 45 degrees

beam reach - to sail at a right angle to the wind

beat to quarters - to clear for action

belay - to stop

belaying pin - a short wooden stick stowed in the pin rail and used to secure a line

bicorne - a two-cornered hat worn by naval officers

binnacle - the stand on which the ship's compass is mounted

blue jacket - the term for a sailor trained to fight at close quarters

bosun - slang for boatswain, a sailor in charge of deck operations

brig - a square-rigged, two-masted sailing ship, a ship's gaol (jail)

brigantine - a ship smaller than a brig

broad reach - to sail with the wind coming from behind but at an angle

Brown Bess - the standard musket for British armed services during the Napoleonic era

bulkhead - an upright wall within the hull of a ship

bunt line - a type of knot

canister - lead balls packed in a can and fired from an artillery piece at short range

capstan - a winch used to raise the anchor

carronade - an artillery piece intended to be fired at a short range

cathead - a beam extending from the port and starboard bow used to secure the anchor

cabin boy - usually about twelve years old, duties include serving the captain of the ship

carlin - a wooden spacer secured between the beams of a ship chains - a series of deadeyes used to secure shrouds at the mast tops

chandler - a merchant selling maritime supplies

chip log - a piece of wood used to determine a ship's speed

cleat - a stationary metal or wooden device used to tie down a rope

close-hauled - to sail close to the wind, sailing with as little angle as possible

come about - to change course

companionway - the stairs or steps in a ship

corsair - a privateer

coxsun or coxswain - a steersman man serving as boat handler, a captain's steward

crosstrees - a wooden support used to secure the shrouds at the top gallant mastheads

crossjack - the square yard used to spread the foot of a topsail where no course sail is set

davits - a crane used to bring objects on board (usually used in tandem to handle boats)

deadeye - a wooden block with holes

Dispatches, London Gazette - periodicals used to report on military engagements

dogger - a commercial fishing vessel

downhaul - the running rigging used to lower a yard

dragon - a firearm, usually a sawed off blunderbuss fired as a pistol

fathom - a measure of six feet

fid - a sailmaker's tool used to stretch grommets before inserting reinforcement

fife, fife rail - a small flute usually played at the rail around the mainmast (fife rail)

fifth rate - a frigate with armed with 24 to 40 or 50 guns

fighting top - the platform resting on the top of any section of a mast (topmast, mast top)

first rate - a ship armed with 98 guns or more

flog - to whip, usually with a cat-o-nine tale

full and by - to be close hauled with sails filling

futtock shrouds - the shrouds gathered below the mast tops and crosstrees

gallery - a small walkway aft of the great cabin

galley - a ship's kitchen

glim - slang for a lantern

grape shot - ammunition similar to canister shot, used for anti-personnel

great cabin - the captain's quarters located aft on the gun deck

grog - a drink, usually about one part rum to four parts water served twice daily

gudgeon - the female part of a fitting used as a hinge (see pintle)

gunnel (gunwale) - the upper edge of the side of a ship

hand - to furl a sail (hand and reeve)

halyard - a rope used to raise a sail, see running rigging

hawser - a large rope used for mooring or towing a vessel

holystone - a block of sandstone used to scour the deck

HMS - His (Her) Majesty's Ship

hornpipe - a lively dance

hull down - a ship seen with the hull still below the curvature of the earth

Indiaman - a merchant ship serving in the East India Company (see John Company)

in irons - when a ship's bow is headed directly into the wind

in ordinary - a naval vessel out of service for repair or maintenance

jeer - a block and tackle used to handle sails

John Company - East India Company

jury-rig - a temporary repair

king post - the spoke on the wheel indicating when the rudder is steering straight ahead

lambda - a ship's longitudinal position

langrage - the debris fired from an artillery piece to cut through rigging leadsman - a man assigned to measure water depth with a long rope weighted with lead

lighter - a small harbor vessel

loblolly - a surgeon's assistant, apothecary

long gun - a long range artillery piece

lubber - a landsman, the lowest rating on a ship, a land lover, a green crew member

lubber's hole - the opening used by a lubber to gain access to a mast top

mast top - the platform resting on the top of any section of a mast

marlin spike - a hand tool used to reeve or unknot a rope (see spike)

midshipman - the lowest rank for an officer in the Royal Navy (ensign)

monkey rail - a light railing surrounding a mast

neap tide - a minimal tide occurring just after the first or third phase of the moon

Nore - the mutiny occurring in the Thames Estuary in 1797

oakum - old rope fibers used for caulk

orlop - the deck covering the hold of a ship

outlier - a ship detached from the fleet serving as a lookout

pintle - the male part of fitting used as a hinge (see gudgeon)

pitchpole - to sink a boat bow first

point of sail - the relationship between direction of wind and direction of ship

quarterdeck - the last quarter of a ship's top deck, now called the bridge

queue - a braid of hair popular among sailors

ratlines - the horizontal ropes tied between shrouds used as the rungs of a ladder

reeve - to prepare or mend a rope (hand and reeve)

roads - (inner roads, outer roads) the open expanses in a harbour where ship's anchor

rope walk - a long shed in a chandler's shop used to store and measure out rope running rigging - the ropes employed to raise and lower yards

running - to sail with, or nearly with the wind

sailing master - the chief navigational officer, also responsible for the best use of sails

salt - an experienced sailor

sea - a sea refers to heavy weather, the sea refers to a body of water

scupper - a hole in the ship's side to ship water overboard from the deck

sheave - a hole or a space for a rope to run through

sheet bend - a type of knot

sheer hulk - the hull a decommissioned ship used to transfer heavy loads to another ship

ship's bells - the bell rung every half hour to measure the time elapsed in the each watch

shroud - the standing rigging employed to keep masts standing upright, port and starboard

sheet - a rope used to trim a sail

skeg - the trailing edge of the keel where the rudder attaches

slops - the clothes worn on a daily basis while at sea

slow match - a slow burning fuse

smasher - slang for a carronade

spanker - a boom sail rigged fore and aft at the lower mizzenmast

Spithead - the mutiny occurring at Portsmouth in 1797

spike - see marlin spike, or to ruin an artillery piece by ramming a spike in its touch hole

standing rigging - the shrouds and stays that stand in place to support the masts

stay - the standing rigging secured to keep masts standing upright, fore and aft

stepping the mast - to erect and secure the mast to its vertical position

strake - the overlapping boards making the hull of a boat

studding sails - the additional sails extended beyond the yard ends

tack - the course of a ship

tacking - the zig-zag pattern of sailing into the wind

taffrail - the railing on transom

tar - a sailor

topmast - the platform resting on the top of any section of a mast (fighting top, mast top)

transom - the aft wall of the stern

tumblehome - the curvature of a ship's hull from waterline to gunnel

waist - of a ship, midway between the bow and the stern

watch - the blocks of time served on duty (first watch, morning watch, etc.)

wear ship - to tack away from the wind

windlass - see capstan

xebec - a small sailing ship common in the Mediterranean

www.ingramcontent.com/pod-product-compliance
Lightning Source LLC
LaVergne TN
LVHW100525110826
845146LV00002B/774